Walk Proud, Stand Tall

Walk Proud, Stand Tall

A Western Story

Johnny D. Boggs

Five Star • Waterville, Maine

First Edition
Second Printing: June 2006

Published in conjunction with
Golden West Literary Agency.

Set in 11 pt. Plantin.

Printed in the United States on permanent paper.

Library of Congress Cataloging-in-Publication Data

Boggs, Johnny D.
    Walk proud, stand tall : a western story /
by Johnny D. Boggs.—1st ed.
        p. cm.
    ISBN 1-59414-348-X (hc : alk. paper)
    I. Title.
PS3552.O4375W35 2006
    813′.54—dc22

                                              2006003024

For Minta Sue Jack

Chapter One

Well, Lin Garrett, you've come a long way. Stealing a horseless carriage to take some dude up to Mars Hill so you can buy crackers and a cup of coffee for supper.

A simple fact stopped him. Lin Garrett had no idea how to start the Chevrolet touring sedan parked at the depot—didn't even know it was a Chevrolet till the dude told him—let alone keep it going or stop it. He had hoped to find a jerky or mud wagon. Horses or mules, those he knew, but this black box with gold trim, decorated with red, white, and blue bunting and American flags—well, that was as foreign to him as the heavy-accented scientist and all his speechifying about the canals on Mars, spectrographs, and Percival Lowell.

"That's a fine-looking automobile," the dude said. "Bet it's a lot more comfortable on your backside than a saddle, too, eh, old-timer? How long have you had it? Can't be long, being a Classic Six. High-priced, too, for a taxicab. And all decked out for Lincoln's birthday. Or Washington's, maybe. That your idea, or the taxicab company's? No top, though, and cold as it is tonight . . . you won't be charging me full fare for that inconvenience, I take it."

Lin Garrett grunted, about all this guy would let him get in. The man talked more than his pal Randolph Corbett, and Ol' Corb could fill volumes of absolutely nothing. Or maybe it was just Lin Garrett, never much for words. In fact, Holly Grant—no, she was Holly *Mossman,* now, had been for decades—had once told him: "Having a conversation with you, Lin, is like pulling teeth."

Impatient from the bite of the winter night, the dude gave Garrett an odd stare. *Waiting for me to throw his luggage in the back,* Garrett thought. Garrett glanced at the grip parked beside the man's Cordovan Congress shoes, the fanciest, blackest shoes he had ever seen, almost made Garrett ashamed of his fourteen-year-old, mud-stained boots.

His empty stomach knotted, making up his mind for him, and Garrett reached for the door, but hesitated. *Stealing.* He had hanged horse thieves himself. Of course, that had been in a different century. He wondered what sentence Arizona jurists pronounced on automobile thieves in this day and age. Not a rope, for sure, not with civilization's encroachment. Jail time, or the penitentiary. Prison, of course, had a few things in its favor. Three squares, a cot to sleep on, and not in that hell-hole down in Yuma, either, but the new pen they had opened a couple of years back in Florence. In prison, he might relive old days with pals, and enemies, men like Ollie Sinclair and Jude Kincaid, if they were still breathing. Only . . . well . . . it was still stealing. Garrett had never stolen anything in his life, excepting a few cows when he was sowing his oats, and in those days lots of honest men threw a wide loop, and a piece of peppermint candy back in Missouri when he was just a boy. His pa had left welts on his buttocks with a razor strop for that misdemeanor.

"Old man," the scientist said, no longer courteous. "It's twenty degrees out here. I'd like to get to the observatory before daylight. It's a perfect night for viewing, and Mister Lowell is expecting me."

Garrett swore underneath his breath, and jerked the bag. Pain shot up from deep in his back, his legs cramping, and he staggered, grimacing, steadying himself by grabbing the freezing metal of the Chevrolet's front door. The luggage wasn't heavy, especially for a man who had often carried forty-pound saddles without breaking a sweat, yet lifting it had hurt like blazes.

The dude just stared, and Garrett threw the suitcase into the back seat. It bounced off the leather and onto the floor, and the dude muttered more than a few complaints. Another mistake, throwing the grip like that. That had hurt even more, and he bent over, trying to catch his breath. He hated being old, hurting in places he never knew existed as a young man. When he looked up, the dude was staring toward the depot, probably hoping to find another hack to haul him over to Mars Hill.

Should have stayed on that train, Garrett thought.

Fact was, he wouldn't have jumped out of the boxcar had he known this was Flagstaff, would have kept riding west to California, but the other hobos didn't look friendly, and he figured it best not to push his luck with those tramps or some nightstick-wielding railroad dick.

He had leaped out when the locomotive had slowed, and a few minutes later had stumbled into the path of one Mr. Slipher, an Easterner who had come to study the planets using Mr. Lowell's observatory. Slipher didn't cotton to everything Professor Lowell espoused. For one, he didn't believe those alleged canals on Mars proved there had once been life on the red planet, wasn't even sure those canals existed, having never seen them himself, although he had savored Lowell's books and respected the man as a scientist and an astronomer, and certainly believed, as did Lowell, in Spencerian evolution. No, Mr. Slipher was more interested in the entire solar system, not just Mars, and using the Brashear spectrograph to observe spiral nebulae. Not only that, but Lowell's fascination with the theory of Planet X, a ninth planet, well, that intrigued Mr. Slipher, too.

It took Garrett all of about two minutes to decide that Mr. Slipher probably came from Mars, odd as that bird was.

Years ago, Garrett had met Percival Lowell, the Boston scientist who had built an observatory in Flagstaff back in 1894, to search for intelligent life on Mars using a twenty-four-inch Clark Telescope, whatever in blazes that was. Flagstaff had sure changed. So had Arizona. Criminy, so had the entire West. Folks piled off trains these days to see Grand Cañon National Monument. Forty years ago, even thirty, a body would have been hard pressed to find anything in this country other than Indians and sheepherders, and a journey to the massive hole in the ground carved by the Colorado River was one risky enterprise. Garrett wondered what the folks who had run that flag up a pine tree back in 1876 would think about this town—no, this city—now. There hadn't been a town on that 4th of July, hadn't been anything except some Bostonians from the Arizona Colonization Company, Lin Garrett, Randolph Corbett, and Ollie Sinclair. The nearest town had been Prescott, and most of the Arizona Colonization Company quickly had given up on settling underneath the San Francisco Peaks and turned south for Prescott or went back East, defeated. *Look at her now, though,* Garrett thought. A railroad, new-fangled taxicabs, brick buildings, hotels, lumber companies, and sprawling ranches barely spitting distance from the city limits, an observatory where scientists could spy on Mars, and omnibuses hauling tourists.

Flagstaff, Arizona Territory—no, a state, had been a

state for almost a year now.

Then the slicker named Slipher had asked: "Did Percival Lowell send you?"

Garrett had shaken his head.

"Well, you drive a hack, correct? Of course, what else would you be doing at the depot after midnight? Didn't see you on the train. I mean, you can take me to Mars Hill. What's the charge? This is all the luggage I have. A dollar? Two?"

"Three dollars," Garrett had said, scarcely believing his lie.

"Three! What are you, some mercenary?"

"Tourists," Garrett had answered. "Driving the price of everything up in these parts."

"Three dollars! My word. Well, all right, my good man. I trust your hack is comfortable."

Comfortable? The metal door bit into Garrett's palm, but the cushioned leather seat did look pleasant enough, although he didn't like the smell, preferring leather and horseflesh over metal and oil. If he could just figure out how one got a Chevrolet to belch smoke and sputter to life. He had seen automobiles before, and recalled a fellow once turning a crank on the contraption. Not a Chevrolet Classic Six, though, but a Ford Model N. Garrett caught his breath and walked to the front of the sedan. Sure enough, a handle poked out of the metal between two circular headlamps. But did you just turn this thing—and, if so, which way—or did you first have to fiddle with the wheel, stick, and pedals up front?

Liars, his father had warned, always tripped up somewhere. Best thing for him to do would be tell Mr. Slipher that this was all some misunderstanding, a joke, and he most likely would find someone inside the depot to telephone a hack to cart him up to Mars Hill. Besides, newspaper ink-spillers would be overjoyed if they got wind of the story: Lin Garrett, former Coconino County sheriff, former Flagstaff and Prescott town marshal, legendary lawman, the man who captured Ollie Sinclair, the man who had killed the Yavapai Kid, arrested for stealing a horseless carriage.

If anyone remembered who Lin Garrett was.

He was seventy years old—seventy!—although he told most folks he had just turned sixty, and never had expected to reach fifty. He had lost about two inches in height and thirty pounds in weight, part of growing old. Only things to his name were the clothes and gear he wore, and a few cents in change, part of outliving one's time. The sleeves and collar of his coat were badly frayed, his underwear held together by a few threads and dirt, and his hat battered beyond recognition. His boots were well ventilated, too. He didn't even own a saddle. And he stank of boxcar straw and filth. It was a wonder the dude hadn't run away from him. Three bucks slicked off Mr. Slipher would mean a fortune. Food in his stomach. A new pair of socks. Then he'd hop another train, eastbound or west, Los Angeles or Kansas City, it did not matter to him. Not any more.

He put his hand on the crank.

I can't.

The dude was still staring toward the depot, dimly lit by gas lamps, when Garrett pulled himself to his feet. "I ain't spitting on my life," he announced, but Mr. Slipher didn't move, didn't even blink.

At that moment, he heard them, saw the dude's face registering fear, and Garrett spun. Three men, about as pleasant-looking as the tramps in that boxcar, one holding a razor, another a broken piece of two-by-four. The third kept both hands in the pockets of his coat. All bearded, with eyes reflecting whiskey, violence, their breath frosty. For a brief moment, Garrett thought this trio might be protecting the Chevrolet, maybe one of them even owned it, but that had been a stupid notion. These ruffians, bundled up like old buffaloes, had about as much business in a Classic Six as did Lin Garrett.

Flagstaff hadn't changed that much after all, Garrett reconsidered. It had always been a bit woolly, attracting as many ne'er-do-wells as tourists and astronomers. People could get killed as easily in 1913 as they had back in 1883, for nothing more than a little hard money, a woman, or some senseless argument.

"What's in the suitcase, *amigo?*" the stick carrier said with a black-toothed grin.

"You and grandpa shouldn't be out this time of night." The smallest man let his razor flash. "Don't soil yourself, boy."

The third man said nothing.

Garrett stepped in front of Mr. Slipher.

"Grandpa," the first man said, "you gonna play the hero? It'll just get you hurt, or kilt."

"You call the tune," Garrett said, and pushed back his coat.

The shell belt and holster had been made for him by a saddle maker named Ghormley up in southwestern Colorado. Both belt and holster were older than any of the three thugs. Worn, comfortable, with a nice patina to the leather after all the years, the belt even had a money pouch, although Garrett hadn't carried enough cash or coin worth hiding in months, years. He had paid Ghormley a month's wages for the rig—Ol' Corb had accused Garrett of squandering—but he sure had gotten his money's worth. The revolver was even older, an Army Colt he had carried during the rebellion—"Your six-shooter is antiquated," a newspaper editor up in Cheyenne had informed him once, and that had been back in 1885—although he had made the concession of converting the cap-and-ball .44 to chamber brass cartridges. Garrett's right hand rested on the walnut grip, his thumb on the hammer.

"Look, Riggs," the razor man said with a snicker, "this codger thinks he's that Bronco Billy Anderson gyp from them flickers. Feature that."

Garrett knew of Bronco Billy Anderson, although he had never dropped a nickel to see one of those moving-picture shows. A few years back, he had gotten a letter from something called the Selig Polyscope Company about making a moving picture based on Garrett's life. Bronco Billy himself would play Marshal Lincoln Garrett, the toughest *hombre* in Arizona Territory. Garrett had tossed the letter away, unanswered.

He kept his eyes trained on the man with his hands hidden. This one was the one to watch. The other two were blow-hards, cowards.

"Uh . . . gentlemen . . . there's no need . . . ," Mr. Slipher began.

"Shut up," Garrett snapped. He had been wanting to tell the dude that for a spell.

The wind picked up, colder now, or maybe it was just Garrett's imagination. The three hardcases lost their smiles. The one with the two-by-four shuffled his feet. Razor glanced at Hidden Hands. Too cold for a Mexican stand-off, Garrett decided.

Patience had passed him by. Garrett spoke evenly: "I'm filling my hand, and, once I do, I'll be killing. Skedaddle, or commence to fighting."

He didn't wait, either, palming the Colt, thumbing back

14

the hammer, never taking his eyes off the man he assumed was Riggs, the tallest of the three. Riggs was stepping back—jerking a tiny Smith & Wesson from the right pocket—while his comrades turned tail and fled into the darkness. A horn blasted—so loud, it startled both Riggs and Garrett—had to be the dude, laying on that automobile's horn.

Annoying . . . deafening.

Garrett leveled the Colt, squeezed the trigger, would have hit Riggs dead-center, but something smashed the back of his head—a fourth man? Maybe the Chevrolet's legitimate owner, or even Mr. Slipher?—and Garrett felt himself tumbling into the void. He heard one gunshot above the blaring, let his Colt slip from his fingers, and glimpsed the depot's warped pine planks rushing up to greet him.

Chapter Two

That pip-squeak burned his arm with his blasted cathode ray tube contraption, burned Garrett so badly he jumped out of the hard metal chair, startling the doctor, who screamed at Garrett to be careful, that the X-ray device he almost knocked over was the only one between Albuquerque and San Bernardino.

Garrett asked the freckle-faced kid if he wanted to get shot, would have been tempted to shoot him, too, if he still had his Colt, and stormed out of the dark room.

Rounding the corner, Garrett pushed another man aside and stepped outside, onto the porch, rubbing his arm. *Idiot. My arm ain't even hurting . . . wasn't hurting, that is, till now.* He had told the young doctor as much, but the sawbones acted like a boy with a new toy, kept bragging about the strange-looking box and spouting out nonsensical words such as platinum, wavelengths, electrodes, and someone named Roentgen. Fool talked as much as Mr. Slipher.

Things had changed too much for a fellow born in a one-room cabin in Cass County, Missouri, Garrett told himself as he calmed down. Cathode ray tubes, spectrographs, telescopes that could detect canals on Mars, automobiles. The X-ray device had bothered him the most, though, with its glowing green screen—"florescent", the doc had called it—and seeing his own bones in his arm. The kid said he would print out an image, but that's when Garrett felt the burning sensation in his arm, and his temper boiled over. His mother, hardshell Baptist that she was, would have called the X-ray tube the work of the devil. Might have been right, too.

The screen door creaked, and Garrett turned to see Doc Steinberg, the mustached gent who had bandaged Garrett's head when he had come to early that morning.

"How do you feel, Mister Garrett?"

"When I come here, only my head hurt!" He rubbed his arm again, even though the pain had subsided, to make his point. That's why he didn't like going to doctors. They found stuff wrong with you. Stay away from them sawbones, Ol' Corb had often said, and a body might live forever.

Steinberg fished a pipe from his coat pocket. "I think more than your head hurt, Mister Garrett. Let's go inside and talk in my office. I'll speak to Doctor Meredith, too. He gets a tad carried away with our Muller X-ray tube. Come, sir."

It didn't sound like much of an invitation, more like an order, and Garrett sighed, staring uneasily at the painted sign nailed to the tofa-stone building above the door.

COCONINO COUNTY HOSPITAL
FOR THE INDIGENT

Yeah, Lin Garrett, you've come a long way.

The first face he had seen, when he had finally regained consciousness after being clubbed at the depot, had been Doc Steinberg's. Well, Werner Steinberg wasn't that old, compared to Lin Garrett, but he didn't look like he had just

17

finished *McGuffey's Readers*, which was more than he could say about Eli Meredith. Steinberg wasn't a doctor, either, just the hospital superintendent, although he had set a few bones and stitched a few wounds in his time.

"What happened?" Garrett had asked.

"That's still under investigation," Steinberg had answered, and introduced himself while finishing wrapping Garrett's head and saying how the county could send over a physician in the morning.

Garrett had just stared, and Steinberg had filled him in.

A detective with the Atchison, Topeka & Santa Fe Railroad had been walking around the depot when he had observed three men approach Garrett and Slipher, had seen Garrett draw a revolver and Slipher push the horn on Lewis Fox's Chevrolet, the automobile the mayor parked in front of the depot to impress passers-by and tourists, let them know Flagstaff was civilized, had more to offer than just a way station on the trail to Grand Cañon National Monument. The railroad man had then grabbed his billy club and gone to work.

"So this yard boss cracked open my skull?" Garrett had spit in contempt. "Why not that rascal trying to rob us?"

"Well, according to the detective, you pulled your gun first."

That had galled him. Swearing, pushing himself to a seated position, blocking out the dizziness and his pounding head, he had argued: "That cut-throat had his hand on his pistol, finger on the trigger, the whole time. Ain't my fault he was just stupid and pulled it out of his pocket, instead of shooting me through his coat."

Exhausted, he had dropped back on the examination table.

"The young astronomer said as much, and you managed to hit the other fellow in the shoulder," Steinberg had allowed. "Riggs, Joe Riggs, a bad customer. I doubt if you have much to fear, sir, pending the police department investigation."

"Where's my revolver?"

"The police have it, for now, Mister . . . ?"

"Garrett. Lin Garrett." He had stared, waiting, maybe even hoping for a flicker of recognition, but Doc Steinberg had merely nodded.

"You are welcome to stay here, Mister Garrett, for as long as necessary . . . providing the police don't arrest you. Doctor Meredith should be here this afternoon."

So, here he was. This was Garrett's home, where he could live out his days. County home for the indigent, better known in Flagstaff as the poor farm. Steinberg lived there with his wife. Luckily young Doctor Meredith hung his shingle in Williams, and just popped in on occasion to torture patients with that cathode ray contraption. Other doctors, also paid a small stipend by Coconino County, shared duties treating the sick and old. A nurse, cook, and some flunky also worked at the hospital, and then there were the patients—opium addicts, transients with assorted ailments, a woman upstairs who had gone insane, drunks sleeping off benders, one stove-up cowboy, and Lin Garrett.

Garrett walked past the lobby, where the flunky stood feeding the wood stove, then stepped inside Doc Steinberg's office. Meredith was there, too, sitting in the corner chair, pouting. Steinberg pointed his pipe stem at a vacant chair, and Garrett sat down to hear them pronounce their verdict.

19

★ ★ ★ ★ ★

Two days later, they moved Garrett downstairs into the permanent quarters, gave him a room to himself, away from the insane woman and the opium addict who screamed half the night and tossed slop buckets against barred windows. At least, it was quieter downstairs.

Garrett had known this as the old Livermore Ranch, but the Livermores were all dead and buried, and Flagstaff had needed a second hospital. Made of consolidated volcanic ash called tofa, the hospital had been built in 1908, and still looked new. It was two stories, with a thirty by fifty-foot addition with a cellar, and a barn where the county stabled horses and other livestock. All of this on 200 acres, including a quarter-section for crops, potatoes mostly, and some hay, and Garrett was told he was more than welcome to help out in the fields, if he felt up to it. He had laughed. He never begrudged manual labor, as long as it could be done from horseback. He had cowboyed too long, before pinning on a star, to become a sodbuster now.

He sat in his room, staring at the depressingly gray walls. The hospital had running water and electricity, sinks in every room, a telephone, and the cook wasn't some bellycheater, either, but knew how to make strong coffee and sourdough biscuits, although a man got sick of eating potatoes at every meal. There were worse places to be. He just couldn't think of one right now.

Sighing, he sat on his cot and pulled off his boots. That Italian boot maker would have thrown a conniption fit if he could see them now, the right toe almost separated from the sole, threads coming loose, holes in both feet, permanently stained from mud and miles, counter leather almost worn through by spurs. He had bought the boots, handmade, in San Antonio in 1898, before meeting Teddy Roosevelt at the Menger Hotel, trying his best to convince Teddy that Lin Garrett wasn't too old to fight the Spaniards, that he could still ride and shoot, but the *colonel* had turned him down. They had sent a bunch of boys to fight down in Cuba, college boys and football players, some Western men, sure, but they had left Lin Garrett behind.

"By thunder, Lincoln, you are sixty years old," Teddy had told him.

"That ain't true," Garrett had said, and it wasn't. He was only fifty-six, although he told Teddy he was fifty-one.

Teddy wouldn't budge, though. He seldom did, much like Lin Garrett. "I admire your desire, sir, your courage, but war is for the young," Teddy had said, trying to placate Garrett. "You had your war, Lincoln, suppressing the rebellion. It's time for others to see the elephant, to reap glory. No, Lincoln, I cannot let you volunteer. Besides, Arizona needs you, sir."

Only Arizona didn't need him, either. Not any more. Three years after Roosevelt dismissed him, Garrett had appealed to Governor Oakes Murphy for a commission with the new Arizona Rangers, but Murphy had ignored him, too, wouldn't reply to Garrett's letters or even grant him an interview in the Capitol in Phoenix. Well, Garrett had showed both Teddy Roosevelt and Oakes Murphy, had refused to vote for Teddy—not that that had hurt the two-term president—and had grinned smugly when Murphy was replaced after charges of malfeasance. Now even the Arizona Rangers were gone, disbanded in 1909, stopped by politicians, not outlaws. Everybody was gone. Everything was gone.

Garrett stared at the boots, wondering if that Italian cobbler was still around, making boots for the Army and anyone who appreciated Old World craftsmanship. What was his name? Lucchese? Something like that.

He looked at his new socks, courtesy of the Coconino County Hospital for the Indigent, and felt sick. Like he was living on tick, riding the grubline.

A man cleared his throat, and Garrett looked up to see a tall, well-dressed young man standing in the hallway. The face looked familiar, clean-shaven, brilliant blue eyes, gray derby hat held at his side.

"Mister Garrett?"

"Yes?" Quickly he pulled on the boots, feeling undressed, embarrassed, and would have reached for his hat, except he knew it wouldn't fit over that cumbersome bandage. His head itched.

"I am Daric Mossman with the Flagstaff City Police Department." Mossman, in his twenties, pulled back his coat to reveal a badge pinned to the vest lapel, or maybe he was showing the Colt stuck in his waistband. Lin Garrett's revolver.

"Come to arrest me?" He liked the lawman's grin, but then the name struck him. "Daric *Mossman?*"

"Yes, sir. Holly Mossman is my mother."

Yep, Daric Mossman had his mother's eyes, same hair color, too, sandy brown and unruly, but he was built like his father, wiry yet broad-shouldered and pigeon-toed.

Slapping his thigh, Garrett smiled for the first time in ages. "By jacks, son, I haven't seen you since you were this high." He had tried to stop in midsentence, but the words just kept flying off his tongue, even though he knew it might embarrass the young police officer as much as it embarrassed Lin Garrett. Fifty, sixty years ago, Garrett had always hated it when some old codger had told him the same thing. Only now, Lin Garrett was the old codger.

Mossman took no offense. "It has been a while, sir."

"How's your ma?"

"She's fine. Still up on the Kaibab by Red Mountain."

"And your pa?"

Mossman's gaze fell. "Pop died five years ago."

Pop? He didn't care much for the words today's youth used. "Pop" sounded disrespectful, but maybe Garrett was just too set in his ways. No, there was no *maybe* to it.

"I'm sorry."

"Don't be. A horse kicked him in the head three years before. He had been in bed, couldn't talk or feed himself, all that time. Death was a blessing for Mama, Pop, for all of us."

Garrett was standing, had started to extend his hand, but stopped after learning of Ben Mossman's passing. Didn't seem proper, shaking hands after learning bad news, not that Garrett ever cared that much for Ben Mossman. Yet he did care for Holly, wondered how she was holding up. A few years earlier, she had lost her daughter and son-in-law. Now her husband. Well, knowing Holly, she would be fine. Anyway, he'd shake hands later. Besides, he didn't think Policeman Mossman came here to catch up on old times. Instead, Garrett pointed to a chair in the corner, and Mossman stepped inside and sat down. Garrett dropped back onto the cot.

"You're here about that shooting, I warrant," Garrett said.

"Yes, sir."

"Well, it's like I told the doc. Three hard rocks come at us. I shot one in defense of my life, and the life of Mister Slipher."

Mossman nodded. "No one doubts that, sir. Chief Bell hauled Riggs out of the other hospital, threw him on the stage to Prescott, and told him not to show his face in Flagstaff again, and we are trying to round up the other two undesirables and send them packing. But . . . well . . . there is the matter of Mayor Fox's car. What did you plan on doing with it? Slipher said he thought you were driving a hack, said you told him as much."

"Was gonna borrow it, if I could figure out how to get it to go."

"Borrow?"

"To take Mister Slipher to the observatory. I'm sixty years old, son." He thought about saying more, but decided against it. Sounded like he was begging, saying he was an old man or, rather, an old fool.

"Chief Bell has warned Mayor Fox against parking his automobile at the depot, but he won't listen. Anyway, the mayor doesn't want to press charges, and the editor of the *Sun* was satisfied with the official police report that a railroad detective stopped an attempted robbery."

"Railroad detective! All that fool did was give me a headache!"

"Be that as it may, sir, that is the story, and both Mayor Fox and Chief Bell like it better than dragging your name, sir, through the mud."

"I was just gonna borrow that carriage."

"It's called *stealing*, Mister Garrett."

"No, it . . . ."

"Would you rather see your name in the *Sun*, sir, as a railroad tramp, maybe even a confidence man, trying to swindle a Boston astronomer and steal the mayor's Chevrolet?" Before Garrett could interrupt, Mossman fired off another volley. "According to Slipher, you told the three robbers that you were going to draw your gun, and, when you did, you would start killing. That doesn't sound so much like self-defense, with all due respect. And you were

charging Slipher three dollars for the ride from the depot to Mars Hill. You could be jailed, sir, but no one desires that."

Daric Mossman had sand. He'd give the boy that much. Just like his mother. Garrett didn't want to look like he was sulking, but he couldn't force a grin. Instead, he sat on his hands and waited. The boy was dead right, had Garrett down to a T.

Mossman rose, put on his hat, and drew the Colt, handing it butt forward toward Garrett. "It's unloaded," Mossman announced.

"Didn't plan on shooting you." Garrett took the revolver.

The young policeman smiled. "It's good to see you, Mister Garrett. Mama says to tell you hello."

Suddenly Garrett trembled. "She . . . does she . . . know where . . . I'm . . . ?"

Mossman shook his head. "I telephoned her the other day, told her you were in the hospital, didn't tell her which one, but that would be fine. She says when you're feeling up to it, maybe you can pay her a visit. Mama doesn't get away from the trading post often these days. If you'd like, we could ride up there together sometime."

"We'll see," Garrett said. They shook hands.

After Mossman left, Garrett tossed the Colt on the bed beside him, then pulled off his boots again. He felt tired again.

Chapter Three

At first, he thought he was dreaming. Garrett opened his eyes, and swung his legs over the cot. He felt fatigued again, his joints aching, a little short of breath, although not as bad as this morning. The aroma of coffee and bacon pleased him, and he automatically reached for his hat and started to slap it on his head, only to remember that annoying bandage.

Voices sounded from the parlor again, and he realized he hadn't been dreaming. *Laughter.* That old lady named Mrs. Aikin kept cackling like a bantam hen chased by a pesky rooster, but it wasn't just her. Seemed as if everyone at the Coconino County Hospital for the Indigent had gone mad. "A-learnin' to be half-wits," Ol' Corb would have said. After dressing, Garrett opened the door, catching a Missouri drawl followed by more chortles. Even Doc Steinberg guffawed.

The drawl started up again. "It's like my pappy always tol' me. 'A broke feller'll order oyster stew just a-hopin' he'll find hisself a pearl so he can pay the bill.' "

Mrs. Aikin shrieked again, and Garrett allowed himself to grin.

"I know that rooster," he said to himself, walking quickly down the hall.

"Doctor Steinberg," the youngest of the opium addicts

26

was saying when Garrett reached the lobby, "told us that you were one of the first white men ever to settle here. Is that true?"

"Not one of the first. I was the firstest in Coconino County."

Garrett studied the old man sitting in rocking chair like it was his throne, surrounded by hospital staff and patients. He was built like a telegraph pole—tall, bronzed, his hair thinning everywhere except for that thick mustache that hid most of his mouth. The mustache, like the rest of his hair, was white, except the tips permanently stained brown from tobacco juice. His pale blue eyes twinkled as the opium addict and crazy woman laughed, and he recrossed his legs. He wore scuffed brown boots and spurs, patched duck trousers held up by dirty canvas suspenders, a red and black checked flannel shirt, and soiled bandanna. Ancient Mackinaw, gloves, and a high-crowned adobe-colored hat were piled on his lap, and he gripped a cup of coffee in his left hand, the arm of the rocker in his right. A pair of chaps lay beside him, along with a bedroll and a small-caliber Winchester rifle, the barrel sawed off to a carbine's length.

"And not just the first white man, neither. No-sirree-bob, I come here 'fore the Navajos and the Hopi. See this here finger." He held out his right hand, showing off a stub of an index finger. "I lost this from a-pointin' out all the sites of northern Arizona. And truth be tol', t'weren't no sites afore I come along. Shucks, I dug that cañon up the road that ever'body marvels at."

"What did you do with the dirt?" Garrett shot out.

Seeing him, the old man stopped rocking. They stared, the newcomer leaning forward, squinting a bit, then falling back in his chair and started rocking again. His mustache twitched, revealing a warm smile.

"Shucks, son, ain't you ever heard of the San Francisco Peaks? That's where the dirt went."

Amid the laughter, Randolph Corbett rose from the rocker, finished his coffee, and announced that he would step outside for a minute for his morning chaw, not wanting to offend the ladies present. The cook started the applause, and others joined in while Doc Steinberg told Ol' Corb that his room would be ready and hoped he would stay longer than he did last time.

"Sounds temptin', Doc," Corbett replied, shooting Garrett a glance, "providin' Marshal Garrett don't snore like he used to."

"*Marshal* Garrett?" one of the patients asked. "You mean . . . Pat Garrett, slayer of Billy the Kid?"

"No, the other one." Corbett pulled on his coat. "The mean, no-account one, Lin Garrett."

On the porch, Corbett worked his tobacco while Garrett sipped coffee he had poured before following his old friend outside. Frost covered the ground, and the pines swayed in a chilly breeze. Above the snorts of frisky horses from the barn rose the sounds of 1913: puttering horseless carriages, a telephone's ring, and whining saws from the lumberyards.

"So you were the first man in Coconino County," Garrett said at last. "Seems me and Ollie came with you, along with I don't recall how many settlers with the Arizona Colonization Company. Seems to me there wasn't even a Coconino County till 'Ninety-One. And come to think of it, Bill Williams, the old mountain man, beat us here by a good spell."

"Could be." Corbett spit off the porch. "It's like my pappy used to say . . . 'Age weakens teeth and memories.' "

"Hasn't weakened your gift for gab."

"Like you'd know, Lin. You never said more'n two dozen words the first ten years we knowed each other."

"Well, I always liked hearing how Ollie Sinclair, Jude Kincaid, even Cole Younger or Sitting Bull shot off your finger. Sounds better than just pointing."

"Only the folks inside don't know who them folks was. Don't remember Lin Garrett or Randolph Corbett, neither. Surprised that one gent knew of Billy the Kid. Besides, they liked my stories. Even thought I saw you a-grinnin'."

"You were squinting."

Chuckling, Corbett held out his hand at last. "Been a long time, Lin. I give you up for dead."

He had a strong grip. That much hadn't changed.

"They haven't buried me," Garrett said. "Yet."

"Me, neither. Tried to, but the ground just keeps a-spittin' me back out. What happened to your noggin?"

Garrett kept the story short, and waited for his friend to crack some joke, but Corbett merely nodded, his jaws working the tobacco. Garrett tried to think of something else to say, but couldn't. The silence only lasted a moment, however, for words never failed Randolph Corbett.

"This be your first time a-stayin' in them fine accommodations?" Corbett hooked his thumb at the hospital.

He nodded. "Take it you've been here before."

"It's a place to hang my hat. Used to just sleep off a drunk now and then, but lately I'm a-comin' when I find myself betwixt jobs. Got hired on with the Aztec Cattle Company 'bout six weeks ago, but they let me go."

"How come?"

"Didn't like me sleepin' off my drunks there."

"Well, you never were much of a cowhand, Corb. Surprised you'd even try that line of work again. Seems to me you told me, once we became lawmen, that you . . . ."

"That was thirty years ago, Lin. No, thirty-five. Man's gotta eat."

Garrett knew that feeling, and didn't want to see his friend turn sullen. "Speaking of grub, let's get some breakfast, Corb."

After four scrambled eggs, ten slices of bacon, five biscuits, a mound of hash browns, and several cups of coffee—Garrett couldn't see how a man, especially one as old as Ol' Corb, could hold that much grub in his stomach—Randolph Corbett was himself again, happy-go-lucky, telling anyone who would listen about anything he could think up.

"How did you really lose your finger?" asked a young hobo on crutches, his right leg in a hard cast.

Corbett's mind remained sharp, remembering the patient had asked about Billy the Kid and Pat Garrett before breakfast. "Billy the Kid shot it off durin' the Lincoln County War," he said.

"You're fooling?"

"No, I ain't. Ask Marshal Garrett there. He was with me."

Garrett was glad when the tramp just looked at him, didn't ask. He had never been much for lies, even stretching the truth, and didn't want to learn. Well, maybe he was learning, he reconsidered, remembering Mr. Slipher and the mayor's Chevrolet. Besides, it always amazed Garrett how Ol' Corb could keep a big windy going, stretching it for hours at a time, making up things as he went along, and never once tripping. The man had a gift.

"Then what happened?" The hobo sounded intrigued.

"I shot at the Kid. Didn't hit him, mind you, but I blame' sure tried."

"But how could you? I mean, with your finger shot off."

Corbett reached inside his coat pocket, and pulled out a Smith & Wesson .38, a short-barreled, double-action model with nickel plating, although both the metal finish and ivory grips showed much wear.

"I'm from Missouri," Corbett said. "Grew up durin' the Border Wars with Quantrill and Bloody Bill and them sorts. You heard tell of them?"

"You mean, like, the Lawrence raid."

"That's right. Lawrence, Kansas. I was there, just a-butcherin' and a-slaughterin' a mess of citizens. None too proud of it, but that was war. Anyway, you take anybody who growed up in Missouri durin' them times, and they shot guns differently. Missouri boys would use our pointer finger to sight with, but pull the trigger with this one." He laid the nub of his index finger against the cylinder while slipping the middle finger inside the trigger guard.

"Ain't that right, Marshal Garrett?"

"It's the best way," Garrett said. "Natural. That's how we were all taught."

"That's right." Corbett twirled the revolver, and offered it, butt forward, to the hobo.

He took it eagerly, and tried to copy Corbett's instructions.

When the patient said—"It doesn't feel right."—Corbett snatched the Smith & Wesson out of his hand, and shoved it back inside his coat.

"Then you ain't no Missourian," Corbett told him.

"No, I'm from Illinois."

"Well, that's how we shot back in those times, and how we still shoot. That's how I managed to keep a-pluggin' away at the Kid."

"And you were at Lawrence, too?"

"I was, but I ain't a-talkin' 'bout that."

Was Ol' Corb pulling their legs? Corbett hailed from Missouri, but from Clay County while Garrett had grown up farther south in Cass County, and Garrett knew Corbett had worn the gray during the rebellion while Garrett had fought to preserve the Union. But had Corbett ridden with Quantrill? Had he taken part in the Lawrence raid? Likely Garrett would never know. He certainly wouldn't get a straight answer out of his pard.

Most Missourians pulled triggers with their middle fingers—Corbett did; so did Garrett—but Billy the Kid hadn't shot off Corbett's index finger. Fact was, they had never crossed paths with William Bonney or whatever his real name was, had never fought in the Lincoln County War. During those times, Garrett and Corbett had been peace officers in Prescott. The closest either had gotten to Billy the Kid had been when Garrett met the Kid's slayer long after the war, down in El Paso. Not that Pat Garrett would have remembered, drunk as he had been. As far as Garrett knew, Randolph Corbett had never set foot in Lincoln County.

Nobody had shot off Ol' Corb's finger. A lariat had mangled it while Corbett had been hitching a dally around his saddle horn after roping a calf. The ranch cook had liquored Corbett up later that afternoon, and Ollie Sinclair had chopped it off with his Bowie knife. That had been on the Picketwire River in southeastern Colorado back in '74, long before Garrett had even considered becoming lawman or dreamed of moving to Arizona Territory.

For another half hour, Garrett marveled at Corbett's lies before venturing outside again, leaving Corbett and his avid listener somewhere in the Dakotas hunting bears with Teddy Roosevelt. Part of that story was grounded in the truth, although an historian would have to shovel off mounds and mounds of lies before finding it.

The sun had reappeared, and Garrett took pleasure in walking toward the barn. Inside, county laborers mucked stalls, none giving Garrett much attention. He liked the aroma of horses, always had. Hailing from Cass County, he knew all the attributes of manure. Horse apples—he had never found anything displeasing about the smell. A man could even grow accustomed to cow pies. Hog manure, now, that reeked, and chicken dung—nothing could turn a body's stomach quicker.

Lord have mercy, I am an old fool, he thought, *reminiscing about crap.*

A horse snorted, and he moved closer to the stall, holding out his hand, whispering gently.

It was a blood bay gelding with a thick winter's coat, broad-chested, short-backed, maybe a bit of a star gazer, but a pretty good horse, nonetheless. It sniffed Garrett's palm, blew its nose, and urinated, as if telling Garrett what he thought about his empty hand.

"I'll bring a carrot next time," Garrett said, and tried to rub the gelding's neck, but it shied away.

Good. He doesn't trust me . . . yet. Always admired that in a horse.

A big one, too, looked like a Tennessee Walking Horse, the way he carried that tail high, almost sixteen hands, with a star on his forehead. Garrett wanted to look in the horse's mouth, see how old it was, but he would have to go inside the stall for that, and didn't want to. Wasn't his horse, but Coconino County's, and, well, a couple of the workers eyed him with suspicion now, as if he might be a horse thief or some crazy old loon wanting to flee the poor farm.

At last, he noticed the saddle on the top rail in the

corner, and inspected it while the Walker nosed the ground for remnants of hay and grain. The rig didn't impress him much, not with all the dust on it. Rats had chewed up the latigo, too, and one stirrup was missing. "A man who don't care for his saddle ain't worth spit," Ol' Corb often said, and Garrett agreed. So would any good cowhand, any man who had crossed the West before the railroads came, before automobiles stank up the streets. The saddle was double-rigged, with a wide, flat horn, hand-tooled, probably cost $40 or better when it had been made twenty-five, thirty years ago. In its current condition, though, it wasn't worth a nickel. A wonder somebody hadn't thrown it out with the rest of the garbage. Garrett felt the stamp in the corner and, curious, tried to brush off the filth and dust with his fingers. He quickly gave up, fetched a handkerchief from his trousers pocket, and spit and scrubbed, scrubbed and spit.

Only now he had to read it, and dark as it was inside the barn—he leaned forward anyway, squinting. Garrett could see far as well as he had when he was twenty, but reading something close, be it a newspaper or a saddle maker's stamp, well, that could be a challenge.

His heart beat faster. He looked again. *Couldn't be . . . could it?*

W. G. G. Ghormley
—Maker
Durango, Colorado

"I'll be . . . ." Garrett shook his head. Wesley "Gone to Glory" Ghormley, the same fellow who had made Garrett's belt and holster all those years ago, probably around the same time he had been stretching leather to build this saddle.

Garrett grabbed the horn and jerked. His legs hurt again, the pain sharp, jolting, but he wouldn't let that stop him. And he didn't care what any of the men inside the barn thought. He swung the saddle over his shoulder, grunting, breathing harder, and made a beeline out of the barn. None of the workers said a thing to him. They probably thought him loco, taking that relic, caking his clothes with dirt.

A Wes Ghormley saddle deserved a better fate than to rot in a county barn, and Garrett planned on taking it to his room, working on it, repairing it, bringing it back to life. If Doc Steinberg or that flunky put up an argument, they'd rue the day. At least he'd have something to do, something with purpose, and, for once, he'd have a story to tell Ol' Corb.

Chapter Four

"I ain't hung nothin' up, sonny," Corbett answered one of his admirers the morning after Abraham Lincoln's birthday celebration. "I'm still a special sheriff's deputy for Coconino County." He reached into a shirt pocket, behind the tobacco pouch, and brought out a six-point star, tarnished, thumbed the pin on the back, and clipped the badge beneath the pocket's missing button. "That's how come they let me ride with 'em in that Model T yesterday durin' the parade. And why I'll be a-wavin' my hand and a-grinnin' like an idiot tomorrow durin' all the speechifyin' and paradin' and celebratin' us being a by-grab *state* now for a whole year."

Even from his seat in the corner, Garrett could smell whiskey on Ol' Corb's breath. The superintendent's wife pretended not to notice.

"What is it a special deputy does?" the flunky asked.

"Iffen they need me, they'll come fetch me," Corbett said. "Right now, I'm a-keepin' the peace in this nefarious establishment."

A few chuckled lightly, and Corbett's eyes flashed brightly at the reaction.

"Where all did you marshal?" an opium addict inquired.

That made Ol' Corb sit a little straighter, his eyes twinkle brighter.

"Well, I was here, two, three times, mostly with the marshal yonder." He tilted his head in Garrett's direction. Garrett didn't acknowledge the attention, merely made another saddle stitch on the latigo, pulling the sinew tight, careful not to prick his fingers with the needle. He had forgotten just how hard it was to work leather, but he liked doing it. It reminded him of winters on the Picketwire, mending saddles, chaps, and bridles, or just darning socks, inside bunkhouses while the walls creaked from wind, sleet, and snow.

"We was always restless in them days," Corbett went on, rubbing the badge with the frayed cuff of his shirt sleeve. "Like my pappy said . . . 'We'd rather leave our hides on a fence than stay put in no corral.' First job me and Lin got was as deputies down in Prescott. Wasn't no Flagstaff back then, and Prescott was the territorial capital." He pronounced it *Preskit,* the way most Arizonans did, and always corrected some new patient from out of state who didn't know better.

"We sheriffed there, marshaled there, then worked a spell in a hell-on-wheels east of here durin' the buildin' of the railroad. Come back to the Flag, which had just sprouted up its ownself, and Lin yonder got hisself made marshal, appointed me deputy. Mighty kind of him, don't you think? Got restless again and moseyed up to the Dakotas to be what them big cattle barons called 'stock detectives'. Did that a couple of years till the bad winter of 'Eighty-Six and 'Eighty-Seven froze most of them boys out, and we didn't have nothin' to protect. Went down to Cheyenne, Wyoming, for a month or two, then come back to Arizona. Lin Garrett got hisself made a deputy United States marshal, and me, too. Our footloose ways took hol' again, though. I went down to Tucson, Lin drifted over to Texas and all over. Last I heard tell, Lin Garrett was dealing faro in San Diego, and I went back to a-punchin' cattle. Times changed." He looked at the badge, satisfied, and smiled. "But I'm still a lawman. And you folks got nothin' to fear, not with Lin Garrett and Ol' Corb here to protect you from varmints like Eli Meredith, that crazy mean pill-roller."

"I wish you would arrest Doctor Meredith," Mrs. Steinberg said, and Garrett almost smiled at the ovation she received.

The tramp with the broken leg then asked about Jude Kincaid, and Garrett looked up. Kincaid's obituary had appeared in the Coconino *Sun* a week earlier, just a few lines in the back of the newspaper, hidden under weather reports, cattle prices, and the latest guests at the Weatherford Hotel, and the ink-spillers had spelled both of his names wrong.

NOTORIOUS GUNMAN DEAD

From the Lovington *Leader* in New Mexico comes news of the suicide of Judd Kincaide, an outlaw of infamous notoriety who was released from Arizona Territorial Prison in Yuma in 1906 after serving twenty years for manslaughter. According to the *Leader*, Kincaide had been suffering from the grippe. He was found at his sister's home on the evening of Jan. 29th, dead from a self-inflicted revolver shot to the head. Would to God he had killed himself forty years earlier. Both Arizona and New Mexico would have been better off.

Garrett hadn't even known Kincaid had been released from prison. Hard to believe twenty years had passed since Deputy U.S. Marshal Tom Nott had captured Kincaid in

38

the Mustang Mountains and hauled him up to Tucson, where he was tried, convicted, and shipped off to Yuma. Garrett and Corbett had been in Dakota Territory at the time, didn't even learn of Kincaid's capture until two or three years later after returning to Arizona. Oddly enough, he didn't agree with the *Sun*'s assessment. Kincaid's death saddened him, shocked him, and he had never cared one whit for that hard rock.

"First of all, sonny, his name was Jude, not Judd," Corbett said. "Paper got it wrong. Ought to rename that thing the Coconino *Misprint*. But to answer your question, Jude Kincaid wasn't worth a barrel of shucks, as my pappy would have put it. Ol' Texas boy the Rangers run off, come to Arizona to kill and rob. Orneriest louse that ever drew a breath, especially in his cups, and a pure-dee demon with a six-shooter. Should have strung that boy up, but the onliest thing they could convict him on was manslaughter. Yeah, I knowed Jude Kincaid. I was there the one time that *hombre* showed yeller. 'Course, they was all yeller, them killers. Deep down, they was. Except Ollie Sinclair, though his brother, Troy, ain't no better than Jude Kincaid."

Corbett stared at Garrett, neither of them smiling.

"When was that?" the hobo asked.

"Cañon Diablo," Corbett said. "At the White House Saloon. Eighteen and Eighty-One."

"Cañon Diablo?" The superintendent's wife turned pale. "That's a horrible place. Why, that deputy sheriff, Paine I think his name is, why, that's where almost eight years ago . . . oh, it's just too terrible to mention."

"I heard about what Paine done," Corbett said, "but he was nothin' compared to Jude Kincaid."

"Tell us about it." Even the flunky sounded curious.

39

"You ought to tell 'em, Lin," Corbett said, "it bein' your story."

Garrett drew sinew through the leather with the needle. "Always liked how you told it better, Corb," he said, refusing to look up. He wondered about this Deputy Sheriff Paine, and what had happened at Cañon Diablo in 1905. That Cañon Diablo still existed, or had existed eight years ago, surprised him.

Corbett didn't hesitate. Garrett never once thought he would, knew his old friend would get right to the story.

"The railroad had reached the cañon in November of that year, but stopped on account of they needed a mess of lumber to build the bridge over that chasm. So a hell-on-wheels sprung up, a rowdy, mean little town that would make Gomorrah look like Eden. The railroad and some decent citizens pleaded with the governor, and he appointed Lin and me special marshals to clean up matters. There was killin's practically every day. Nasty town. Always been nasty mean. Didn't have no jail when we got there, so we just started a-buffaloin' drunks and tinhorns, persuaded the blacksmith to put leg irons on them we didn't run out of town, and turned the corral into a hoosegow.

"Well, things tamed down a mite, but Jude Kincaid rode to town, just a-itchin' for trouble. Killed hisself a gambler, then waited at this bucket of blood for someone to try to do somethin' 'bout it. Problem we had was, by all accounts, the gambler had been a-cheatin', had even pulled his pistol first. Solicitor might have gotten an indictment, but no jury would have convicted him, not today and certainly not back then. Still, we knowed we had to run him out of town. That's when Lin stared him down.

"I ain't foolin' y'all none. The marshal there just walked into the White House Saloon, and Kincaid was just

40

a-leanin' again' the bar . . . bar wasn't nothin' but some planks nailed atop some empty kegs. Lin didn't say nothin', just hooked his thumbs in his belt, and stared. Well, Kincaid finished his whiskey and turned, put his hand on his pistol butt. Folks made a beeline for safer climes, I mean to tell you. Fled the center of the saloon and stuck to the walls like bugs, thems that didn't just skedaddle out of the saloon. Don't know how many minutes passed, but Kincaid's Adam's apple started a-fidgetin' and he broke into a sweat, cold as it was in December. And, finally, he just walked right out of the White House, mounted his horse, and loped out of town. We never saw him again, after that. That's the gospel, folks. Marshal Lin Garrett stared Jude Kincaid down at the White House Saloon on December Tenth, Eighteen Eighty-One."

It had happened that way, too. More or less. Of course, Garrett had been scared to death, had pushed through the saloon doors with a speech in mind, some tripe that would have sounded good in a Beadle's dime novel, but he had been too paralyzed to say anything once Kincaid had faced him. So he had stared. More than thirty years later, he could still picture it all so clearly: Jude Kincaid, wearing tall boots, embroidered *vaquero* britches, deerskin shirt, old Army coat, and a black Stetson, Remington revolver shoved near his belly in a red sash, the wind howling outside, moaning through the saloon's adobe walls. Finally Kincaid fished a coin out of his vest pocket, tossed it on the floor, and walked past Garrett. Even then, Garrett hadn't moved, hadn't even turned around until he heard the horse's hoofs over the wind. That's when the men inside the White House left the corner walls, cheering, screaming, a few firing pistols inside. His legend had been born that afternoon. *Marshal Lin Garrett staring down Jude Kincaid at the*

41

White House Saloon at Cañon Diablo in 1881.

Of course, no one, not even Jude Kincaid, ever mentioned that Randolph Corbett and Ollie Sinclair had been standing outside by the saloon's two glass windows, Ol' Corb holding an English-made W. & C. Scott double-barrel shotgun, Sinclair brandishing a monster of a weapon, a Colt five-shot revolving shotgun, a relic that likely would have blown up in his hands had he pulled the trigger. Maybe no one had seen them, except Kincaid. By jacks, Garrett hadn't known about their presence until Sinclair had told him two weeks later.

Garrett had finished the saddle. Pretty good job, too, out of practice as he was. Even Doc Meredith complimented the work when the young sawbones showed up the following Saturday with his Muller X-ray tube and began examining new patients and a few old ones, not to mention the flunky, cook, and another doctor from Flagstaff who enjoyed seeing their bones in that unholy device.

The doctor kept his examination of Garrett brief, and didn't bother asking if Garrett would submit to an X-ray. Likewise, Garrett kept his answers short, and didn't bother to thank Meredith for his time. *Don't need the bandage on my head any more, that's why I'm wearing this hat. . . . No, head don't hurt. . . . Feel as good as anyone sixty years old and stuck in a hospital for the indigent. . . . More cramps? A little, but not that much discomfort. . . . Ain't nobody's business how many times I peed, or how long it took, and don't bother asking about bowel movements. . . . The bandages on my fingers came from a needle . . . you try punching leather without an awl.* He left the examination room, holding the door open for Mrs. Aikin, walked back to his room, grabbed a coat, and headed to the barn.

★ ★ ★ ★ ★

The blood bay gelding's name, Garrett had learned, was Scarlet Knight, seventeen years old but still thought he was a four-year-old stallion. Garrett went to the stall and pulled a carrot from his coat pocket. He liked the cook well enough but wondered at the man's sense now and then, putting raw carrots on plates when most patients had only gums. Garrett had most of his teeth, but had never cared for carrots. Maybe the cook was just trying to give folks a repast from potatoes, or maybe he knew Garrett would collect the vegetables to feed Scarlet Knight.

He rubbed the gelding's neck—Scarlet trusted him now—and found another carrot. Sometimes, he dreamed of throwing that Wes Ghormley saddle on Scarlet's back, taking the horse, and leaving the Coconino County Hospital for the Indigent behind him. Horse theft, yeah, but a man who would try to steal a Chevrolet Classic Six certainly wouldn't hesitate to borrow a horse. Not that the county would miss Scarlet, or the hospital would miss Lin Garrett. He probably would have run by now if Ol' Corb hadn't shown up.

Then there was Policeman Daric Mossman, who came every Sunday morning, asking Garrett if he'd care to ride up to Red Mountain to visit his mother. Every week, Garrett made up some excuse, later regretting it when Ol' Corb would ride him so. Mostly, though, the regrets came late at night when he dreamed of Holly Grant Mossman. Not that his dreams made much sense, but he would wake up, smelling lilacs, seeing Holly as a seventeen-year-old beauty with plenty of sass and more backbone than most of the men from the Arizona Colonization Company that came with her from Boston. He could hear Ol' Corb again, quoting his pappy—"When a petticoat like that Holly Grant gal starts a-draggin' a loop, there's always a feller more'n willin' to step in and get hisself hog-tied."—and then, years later, telling Garrett: "You should have stepped in her loop, Lin. You should have stepped in her loop."

After tossing the rest of the carrots on the ground, Garrett went back inside. The stove-up cowboy stopped him, surprised him, as he praised Garrett's work restoring the saddle. The old cowhand had never said two words in the weeks Garrett had been in the hospital, but he nodded with approval at Garrett, and they shook hands.

There were times when living out one's days at the county hospital wasn't so bad.

George Washington's birthday came, and Flagstaff held another parade. The broken-legged hobo cheered and waved his hat as the procession puttered past the hospital. Of course, they only started the parade this far out of town so those Aztec cowboys could empty their bottles out of sight from the Temperance ladies in Flagstaff, and show some charity to the residents of the poor farm. That galled Garrett, but then so did the parades. Three holidays and parades in one month. Ol' Corb would be downright tuckered out when he came back, although he'd probably have a dozen stories to tell.

After the sheriff's cars and wagons had rolled past, Garrett headed back inside, tired of the noise and smoke, the stink of automobiles. All of these holidays! Didn't folks work these days? By jacks, there hadn't been an official holiday for Honest Abe till 1892, and Congress hadn't recognized Washington's birthday as a national holiday until 1870. Arizona was a one-year-old state, but there hadn't even been an Arizona *Territory* when Lincoln Garrett had been born.

He pulled off his hat and ran fingers through his thinning gray hair, then stroked his mustache. It needed trimming. He needed a shave, too. His sinuses ached from the exhaust, the fireworks, the cheering of the hospital patients who had nothing better to do. The old cowboy sat in the rocker—Ol' Corb had relinquished the throne for a seat in the Coconino County Sheriff's Department's Ford—and stared at the wood stove.

"Not one for parades, eh?" Garrett said, and pulled on his hat, expecting Mrs. Steinberg to appear as she usually did, and scold him, tell him—one more time—how rude it was to wear hats indoors, that he must have a head cold, or have been raised by wolves. "No, ma'am," he often answered. "By Missouri Baptists." In his time, cowhands rarely took off their hats, except, maybe, to impress some town lady, take a bath, or go to sleep. But come dawn, the first things they reached for were their hats. The last thing they took off, too, if they even took it off. And you never put a hat on a bed. That was bad luck.

When the old cowboy didn't acknowledge him, Garrett frowned, never much good at striking up conversation. The old man had only spoken to Garrett that one time, lauding his saddle work, so Garrett started down the hallway, turned, and looked at the cowboy again.

Sighing, Garrett swept off his hat, letting out a muffled curse as he walked back to the rocking chair and knelt.

"Bet you were one to ride the river with in your time," he said, trying, but failing, to remember the old man's name. He didn't think anyone in the hospital had ever mentioned his name.

Slowly Garrett reached up and closed the cowboy's eyes. He shivered as he rose, wondering where he would find Doc Steinberg, staring at the dead man, only not seeing a worn-out, stoved-up cowhand but himself.

Chapter Five

The cowboy's death bothered him, but not as much as the article in the Coconino *Sun* the following week. Garrett had never cared much for newspaper editors. Few cowboys, even fewer lawmen, from his generation did. Oh, sure, some elected county sheriffs and appointed federal marshals played politics quite well. Wyatt Earp would talk for hours to a reporter, providing he wrote for a newspaper with Republican sentiments, and even Tom Nott knew how to make those ink-spillers work for him. Nott, God rest his soul, had never passed on that talent to Lin Garrett. In all his life, Garrett had probably never read more than a dozen newspapers until taking up residence at the Coconino County Hospital for the Indigent.

That front page editorial angered him so much, he grabbed his coat, even buckled on his gun belt, held the crumpled newspaper in his fist as he stormed out the front door, raced down the stairs, and almost tripped and slid down the hill to the road, catching a ride on a Studebaker wagon hauling lumber. His face reddened as the words in the *Sun* fueled his anger.

NO JUSTICE
DESPERADO RELEASED FROM PRISON

Ollie Sinclair Freed
After Twenty-Five Years
Tales of His Wretchedness
Rapine, Murder, and Other Misdeeds

For the past twenty-five years, Coconino County and all of Northern Arizona have been blessed with a quiet peace. The Apaches have been removed, the Navajos quiet in their hogans, and with the exception of a few outlaws—the saloon robbery in Winslow and the gory, callous extermination of John Shaw in 1905 prominently coming to mind—our country has put the violence and lawlessness of the frontier days behind us.

Now comes word of the release of Ollie Sinclair, the brutal killer, after completion of a twenty-five-year sentence in the Yuma and Florence penitentiaries. The law even shortened his sentence by a few months for good behavior. Good behavior? Sinclair wreaked havoc in our fair state, indeed across much of the West, before finally being brought to justice. Alas, our territorial jurists elected not to give him the rope but let him rot in prison for all too brief a spell.

Now, he is freed.

Those Easterners—those same fools who bemoaned the removal of the Apaches, those sanctimonious scoundrels who cry injustice

from the comforts of their fancy homes surrounded by whitewashed gates, protected by
abundant police forces, and no closer to a rampaging Apache or murderous renegade like
Ollie Sinclair than nickelodeons or dime
novels—may say give Mr. Sinclair a chance.
They remind us that he has paid his debt to society.

Forgive us, please. Oliver Sinclair has com-
mitted rapine; he has plundered and killed. You
will find the grave of the son of a territorial senator underneath the San Francisco Peaks. Ollie
Sinclair shot down Jed Dunlap in 1883. The
noted desperado, however, pled to manslaughter and a few other crimes and thus
eluded the hangman's noose. How blind is Justice! Ollie Sinclair was at Mountain Meadows,
murdering scores of Arkansas settlers in Utah.
He is a Mormon fiend, a raider with Porter
Rockwell's Danites. He is the scourge of Arizona, a villain who, along with his brother,
Troy, and a nefarious operator named Handsome Harry Prudhomme, should have been
hanged many times over.

Statehood has come to our bloodstained territory at last, statehood and peace. Flagstaff,
Williams, Winslow, etc. know peace at last, and
prosperity.

Ollie Sinclair may be free, but he is not welcome in Coconino County. Go back where you
belong, Mr. Sinclair, which is Hades, where the
Devil spawned you and your evilness. Leave us
alone.

★ ★ ★ ★ ★

Ol' Corb hadn't minded the story so much. In fact, he had chuckled when he read it while Garrett had buckled on his gun belt.

"You mad because they didn't mention you in the paper, Lin?" Corbett had asked. "After all, you was the one who brung him in."

"Ollie didn't do half the things they say he did," Garrett had fired out in defense. "You know that as well as I do."

"Yeah." Ol' Corb had spit, missing the spittoon in the corner of Garrett's room and splattering the wall. Likely on purpose. "And Ollie made up for all them things with things we don't know he done. Relax, Lin, I bet Ollie would smile just a-knowin' he's still remembered in these parts . . . which is more'n either of us can say."

Garrett had snatched the *Sun* out of Corbett's hand as he stormed away, hearing his friend call out behind him: "Don't be a-shootin' the editor, Lin. Citizens frown on such behavior today."

Flagstaff had changed more than he had realized, he noticed when the wagon stopped at the depot. Garrett jumped down, thanked the driver, and crossed the street. The mayor's Classic Six was parked out front again, still decorated in patriotic colors, still no top despite cloudy skies. A monstrous 4-6-2 Baldwin locomotive belched steam, and a Ford sputtered down the road, causing a burro to bray and kick.

People crowded around the stone depot, built in 1889. Garrett remembered when the depot was only one boxcar, then two. Hell, the AT&SF hadn't even bothered to put up a real building till '88, and it burned down the following year.

Over the years, fires had taken a toll on Flagstaff. Old Town had been wiped out back in '85 when a strumpet kicked over a lantern at a dance hall. The Valentine's Day Fire the following year destroyed much of New Town, and several people packed up, figuring that was the end of Flagstaff. But the town recovered, surviving other blazes in '88, '92, and '97, and the merchants had grown smarter. Wood façades had become rare. Now, brick buildings lined most of Front Street. Where Doc C.F. Manning's buildings had stood, Garrett found a strange, iron structure called the Coconino Chop House. A line of men in derby hats and women bundled up in coats stretched out the door, and the smell of food pinched his stomach even though Garrett detested Chinese cooking.

He wandered the streets, pitching the newspaper somewhere, lost among the streets he had once patrolled. About the only thing Garrett recognized was the Babbitt Brothers store, a red sandstone building that had once looked out of place in Flagstaff. Finished in 1888, the store—run by brothers David, William, George, Charles, and Edward—called itself the largest general mercantile in all of Arizona. It had even housed the Coconino County offices from '91 through '94, but now the county had its own courthouse. He stared through the window, envious at those shopping for new clothes, keenly aware of his own ragged appearance.

Finally, disgusted with himself, Garrett went inside the Weatherford Hotel and asked a clerk for directions. The lobby bustled, too, with men sipping coffee or noon brandies, smoking pipes and cigars, talking about the stock market, new President Woodrow Wilson and the Balkan War, none of which interested Lin Garrett. Some folks had considered John Weatherford mad when he built the hotel, but business boomed here as well as at the Majestic Opera House, which Weatherford had opened a couple of years ago to show moving pictures. The last time Garrett had been inside the hotel, he had played faro with Wyatt Earp. He would never step inside the Majestic, however, as long as it played those flickers.

A grumpy clerk gave him directions to the newspaper office, and Garrett finally found it with no problem. He pushed open the door, spotted a young but balding man wearing sleeve garters, the only one inside, and shoved him against the desk, spilling lead type to the floor. The clerk's eyes widened, and he let out a shriek that sounded like something from a mouse.

"I don't like what you said about Ollie Sinclair!" Garrett bellowed. "You ain't nothing but a pup, anyways. Doubt if you was even born before I took Ollie to Yuma."

"I . . . I . . . ," the man stuttered.

"I know Ollie, rode with him, fought him, brought him in. He never done nothing to no woman, and Jed Dunlap got what he deserved. Porter Rockwell and Danites, I never heard such lies. And Mountain Meadows. Use your sense, boy, that massacre took place back in Eighteen and Fifty-Seven. Ollie would have been no more than eight or nine at that time. Mormon, sure, but that don't make him no killer. I've known many a fine Mormon, and plenty of Methodists, Catholics, and freethinkers that ain't worth spit. The fact of the matter is, boy, you ain't earned the right to say nothing about Ollie Sinclair. I have."

He released his grip, and let the kid fall back on the desk. He had to, out of breath, sharp pain shooting up his spine, knuckles aching.

"I . . . I . . . I . . . I . . . ." The kid had to catch his breath, too.

"Go ahead." Garrett couldn't remember half of what he had just said, could hardly believe he had even made such a speech. Suddenly he felt mighty foolish, which turned to downright embarrassment when the newspaperman spoke.

"I'm just a tramp printer, sir. I don't write a thing, except what Mister Burnside puts before me. You should . . . uh . . . register any complaint with him."

Momentarily Garrett stared, not even blinking, not knowing whether he should laugh, curse, or cry. Finally he just shook his head and turned to leave, disgusted with himself once again, but a tall man in a black Prince Albert and handsome mustache blocked his path. A deputy sheriff's badge shined from the coat's lapel. His black hair smelled of Rowland's Macassar Oil.

"This man pestering you, Jarvis?" the deputy asked from the doorway.

"No, Mister Paine," came the typesetter's squeaky reply. "I'm all right, sir. He was just . . . well . . . upset at Mister Burnside's article."

The lawman sniggered, reaching inside his coat, allowing Garrett to glimpse the left shoulder holster and a nickel-plated automatic pistol on his right hip. He pulled out a newspaper clipping with his left fingers, and flicked it across the room.

"That's why I dropped by," the deputy said. "That tripe about turned my stomach."

"What tripe is that, Mister Paine?" the printer said, then realized the stupidity of his question.

"The tripe in that story about Ollie Sinclair!"

Garrett wet his lips. "You know Sinclair?" he asked. The deputy didn't look that much older than the printer.

"No." Paine stepped inside, slamming the door shut behind him with such force the windows rattled. "The part about 'the gory, callous extermination of John Shaw' galls me. John Shaw got what he deserved, and I was proud to do it back at Cañon Diablo. You tell Burnside that he'd best watch what he writes, Jarvis. I know what he's aiming on doing, and I won't stand for it. You tell him that Evan Paine aims to be the next sheriff of Coconino County, the first to be elected since statehood. You tell him."

"He's likely eating at the Bright Angel," the printer said.

"I done et." Evan Paine turned his attention on Garrett. "Old-timer, there's a law against carrying firearms in Flagstaff."

"I know," Garrett said. "I made it the law thirty years ago."

Paine measured him with his eyes, tugging on one end of his handlebar mustache. "Then you'd be Randolph Garrett, I presume."

He could imagine Ol' Corb getting a good laugh over that one, several laughs, in fact, all at Garrett's expense.

"Lin Garrett," he corrected. "Randolph Corbett was my deputy, most times anyway."

With a smile, the deputy stepped back and opened the door. "I reckon the county can make an exception for you, Lin. Care to join me? I have a hankering to wander over to David Tate's liquor store and partake of some Cedar Brook Whiskey."

Garrett just shook his head, walked out the door, and made a beeline for the poor farm. Exhausted, he didn't eat supper that night, and spent much of the next day in his room.

City Policeman Daric Mossman came by Saturday evening, asking, as Garrett knew he would, if he felt like riding up to Red Mountain with him in the morning to visit Mossman's mother. Usually the boy came early Sunday morning. Must have figured some advance notice would change the old man's mind.

Polishing the saddle while sitting on the edge of his cot, Garrett simply shook his head.

"Mama's making venison stew," he offered.

He looked up, almost asking how in blazes he knew that, but remembered—the telephone. "Reckon not," he said instead.

Daric Mossman stood there, hat in hand, defeated again. A few minutes passed in silence, and Garrett expected the boy to turn and leave, but instead he brought up the *Sun* article about Ollie Sinclair's release from prison.

"I read about it," Garrett said abruptly. Actually he had expected Mossman, or some other peace officer, to visit him earlier in the week, on official business, after the printer filed an assault charge.

"Mama said it was outrageous, what the paper printed."

"Lies, mostly."

"She doesn't talk about him much. Just you, and Pop."

Garrett knew he needed to change the subject. "What are your impressions of Deputy Sheriff Evan Paine?"

The stare was inquisitive, skeptical, and lengthy, for such a short reply. "He's county. I'm city."

"That wasn't what I asked."

Mossman nodded. "I wouldn't invite him to dinner with Mama and me."

"I wouldn't share a bottle of Cedar Brook Whiskey with him," Garrett quipped, which brought about another wondering look from Holly's son. "What happened at Cañon Diablo back in Aught-Five?"

Mossman kept the story short, kept saying it was all hearsay since he was down in Tucson at the time. But,

Mossman said, most of the story rang of truth, and there were photographs in Winslow to prove it.

John Shaw and a Mexican friend rode into Winslow, and went straight to a saloon. Shaw was one of the last of the Arizona hardcases, had done everything from cattle rustling to murder, a squat assassin. The two men ordered a drink of whiskey, then eyed the poker game going on.

Before they even touched their drinks, the two men pulled their guns, robbed the gamblers, and bolted outside, mounting horses, firing pistols in the air, and loping out of town toward Flagstaff. A harebrained scheme, Mossman said, probably didn't even occur to them until they spotted the pile of greenbacks and coin on the table. They made off with better than $1,200—no small change for a poker game in Winslow.

The town marshal telephoned Flagstaff, and the sheriff sent a posse toward Cañon Diablo. Deputy Evan Paine led the posse. Sure enough, Shaw and his *compadre* rode into Cañon Diablo a couple hours later, where Paine and his men waited.

"Those boys didn't stand a chance," Mossman said. "Paine and that lot shot them to pieces . . . not that I'd spill any tears over the likes of a man like John Shaw . . . and then they buried them in what was left of the cemetery and rode back to Winslow to spread the news and celebrate."

Paine and the rest stood in the same Winslow saloon that Shaw had robbed, and, once well in their cups, the deputy exclaimed: "You know what's a shame, boys. John Shaw and that greaser never got to finish their drinks!"

Thus Paine led the drunken gang of ruffians back to the ambush site, where they proceeded to dig up the bodies and pour whiskey into the mouths of the two corpses. They even propped up the bloody bodies, dirty, one ring finger chopped off, pockets turned inside out, for a couple of Kodaks and other photographs taken by a professional photographer on his way north.

"No matter what John Shaw was, nobody deserves that," Mossman concluded.

More silence.

"You knew Ollie Sinclair well, Mama says," Mossman said, persistent.

Just a nod.

"Ol' Corb out there, he says Ollie was the one outlaw who never showed yellow. Is that true?"

Garrett concentrated on buffing the saddle, allowed his head to bob once.

Mossman finally muttered a feeble good bye and said: "Maybe next week we can make that drive, sir."

The door shut, and Garrett looked up, tears welling in his eyes, partly for Holly, partly for old Oliver Sinclair. He had lied to Daric Mossman, a white lie. He was getting good at those. Ollie Sinclair had showed yellow.

Once.

Chapter Six

Few things intimidated Lin Garrett, but the land here often left him unnerved. Cañon walls splashed with vermilion and other colors—red, orange, black, brown, gray, turquoise amid splotches of green—a blue, cloudless sky that stretched into eternity, broken wedges of sandstone, water-smoothed rocks and wind-carved boulders, singing rattle-snakes, towering cliffs, biting wind, and the roar of the Colorado River rapids, loud enough to drown out a battery of artillery. The country could just swallow a body up. Men could disappear in the vastness forever, and they had, some lost, others, in all likelihood, murdered.

The sun had disappeared beneath the cliffs, immediately bringing a chill to the air, and he dismounted. He opened a saddlebag, and reached inside, filling his pockets with .44-40 cartridges for his Winchester, then withdrawing the hobbles for his buckskin stallion, already slaking its thirst from a pool along the river's edge.

Garrett drank as well, filling his canteen with the water cascading over the rocks, careful not to let the powerful current sweep the container from his grip. He corked the canteen, slung it over his shoulder, and crept along the rocky banks, crouching, slowly climbing until he could see the stone fortress several hundred yards ahead in the gloaming.

He knew Ollie Sinclair would come this way. Predictable, the old fool. Ollie always ran north when in trouble. He would cross the river, head over the Kaibab and into Utah. Not that he had much of a choice.

Lee's Ferry had been in operation since the early 1870s. Old John D. Lee himself once ran the ferry, charging an amount that seemed obscene, but it was the only safe crossing for hundreds of miles in either direction, so Lee got away with it. Then the law had finally caught up with Lee in Utah and hanged him about ten years back for the massacre at Mountain Meadows. Lee's family still ran the ferry, though, and a Mormon son like Ollie Sinclair would be treated like family.

Has Ollie already crossed?

Garrett would find out soon enough. He studied the corral, teeming with horses, a curious mare sniffing the air and pawing the dirt. She whinnied—at least Garrett thought she whinnied—but the only sound audible came from the bellowing river.

The Colorado ran high, furious for this time of year, and he forced himself back toward the bank and crept upriver until he saw the ferry. No, Ollie hadn't crossed. Most likely, he and the Lees were inside waiting, eating a big supper before bed. They'd be back at first light to repair the busted ferry and lines torn apart by the rampaging river. Or . . . ? Garrett pursed his lips. The Lees could have destroyed their ferry themselves, after spiriting Ollie Sinclair across, stopping any pursuit.

Not likely, though. Destroying a ferry, here, in this wilderness, that would be downright criminal, like poisoning a well or stealing a man's horse. Besides, no one, not even a cautious man like Ollie Sinclair, would have expected the law to follow one of three train robbers this far from Williams. Typically posses turned back long before they even saw Echo Cliffs. Anyway, Garrett would find out soon enough if he had guessed right. He went back downstream, finding a good spot, where he could see his buckskin and the main building, a long, uninviting mass of rock walls that matched the red earth.

An impatient man might charge in at night, bust through the door, catch the men sleeping, but not Garrett. A passel of kids and women likely called this home, and, if it came to shooting in a darkened room, some innocent Mormon might get killed. He wouldn't have that on his conscience. Waiting till morning, finding out if Sinclair was here—that seemed a better plan. Garrett pulled down his hat brim and settled in for the night. Dead tired from such a hard ride, he drew the Winchester closer. He'd need his strength come morning.

A squawking chicken awakened him shortly after dawn. At least, he thought so at first, then understood it must have been a dream. No way he could hear anything, not with the thundering rapids just a few yards behind him. Still, he peered above the boulder and studied the coop for a second, saw nothing, and tried to remember the dream, only couldn't. It was as far away as the water that had roiled over the rocks here last night.

Movement to his right caught his attention, and he spotted two men studying the river, one shaking his head as he gripped the ferry line, the other skipping rocks over the deep water before the current began to speed out of control. They talked a bit, then headed back to the stone building. Smoke drifted out of the chimney, and a cat snaked its long body atop the flat roof. Garrett lifted his rifle as the men walked on, oblivious to his presence. He aimed at the taller man's broad back, knowing he couldn't miss, not at this range. It would have been so easy, but he lowered the rifle, allowing Ollie Sinclair and the Mormon ferry master to close the door behind them.

For a moment, he thought he smelled breakfast cooking, but dismissed that as readily as he had the idea of a squawking chicken. He backed away from the house, telling himself that he was not growing soft, that he had not just made a potentially fatal mistake, and returned to the stallion, removing the hobbles, tightening the cinch, and lifting his leg, pointing the boot into the stirrup. He swung stiffly into the saddle, and gave the buckskin a gentle kick.

Farther from the river, he could hear clearly as horses milled around in the corral, the cat on the roof screeched out a warning, and hens and a rooster took up the alarm. Hoofs clopped on the hard rock until he fingered the reins gently and stopped the buckskin. He dropped the reins over his saddle horn, kept his left hand free, his right gripping the rifle, cradled across his lap, hammer cocked, finger against the trigger.

A woman opened the door and stepped outside, holding a baby girl in yellow calico against her chest. The woman could have been anywhere between fifteen and fifty, her face as weathered and beaten as the rocky hills behind her. She said nothing, nor did the baby, and Garrett refused to dismount without an invitation. Instead, he tipped his hat.

"Ma'am, would you mind asking Ollie to step outside for a minute?"

He could smell the food now—definitely not his imagination—and his stomach rumbled. He hadn't eaten a thing other than cold cornbread and jerky, and nothing since yesterday morning. The woman gave him a malevolent stare, but a voice muttered something behind her, and she retreated, disappearing in the darkness.

For a couple of seconds, the door remained open, before Ollie Sinclair stepped into view. With a grin, he closed the door and walked into the sunlight, stopping a few feet from Garrett.

The buckskin snorted.

"You're a long way off your range, Lin." Sinclair had crossed his arms, hooking his thumbs inside his gun belt, still smiling. He hadn't shaved in weeks, and his red hair looked grayer, unkempt as always.

"Never was one for fences, boundaries," Garrett said.

"No, I reckon you wasn't." Sinclair had always been a big man, with a paunch that strained against his shirt and belt, pockmarked, cold eyes, about an inch taller than Garrett. Ladies usually found Ollie Sinclair handsome, or at least they seemed intrigued, downright mesmerized by him, although Garrett and Ol' Corb considered him uglier than sin.

"Besides," he added, tapping his badge, "I'm federal now."

Ollie Sinclair made no reply.

"I told you not to come back, Ollie. After you killed Dunlap. You give me your word."

Sinclair sighed. His hands moved. Garrett held his breath, tightening his finger against the trigger, almost bringing the rifle up, but Sinclair wasn't reaching for his revolver, not yet, at least. He actually looked hurt, maybe even a bit ashamed.

"I didn't know you were back, Lin. I'll swear that on a stack of Bibles. Didn't know you were back. Thought you and Ol' Corb were still up in Wyoming or the Dakotas or wherever it is you went." Sinclair's eyes swept past Garrett, scanning the riverbanks and boulders strewn over the ground. "Where is Corb?"

"Somebody had to look after Flagstaff while I was gone. Where's your brother? And Harry Prudhomme?"

"Split up. They went west. Me . . . well, you know me."

He didn't speak for a while. He kept his eyes on Ollie Sinclair, but made sure he could see the door, and the sides of the building. He had no way of knowing how many men were inside, likely a brood, and for all he knew, Troy Sinclair and Harry Prudhomme hid in the rocks, lining Lin Garrett in their rifle sights.

After the robbery, the three bandits had ridden west, but separated after a couple of miles, two galloping toward California, the other north. Probably hadn't even had a chance to split up the loot, what little there had been. Garrett had sent the ten men riding with him, including the railroad detective and the Williams marshal, west, and had turned north alone. Of course, Troy Sinclair and Harry Prudhomme also could have doubled back. He considered this for a moment, then decided, no, that wasn't likely. It was just him, and Ollie, and the family inside.

"You still broke your word," he said finally, "but that don't mean nothing right now. You robbed the Atchison, Topeka and Santa Fe at Williams, Ollie. I have to take you in. You want to come in peaceably?"

His friend shook his head, more animated now, angry. "We got thirty-seven dollars and sixteen cents, Lin. That's all we got from that train. Don't hardly seem worth it, does it? And you come riding up here, bold as brass, to take me in . . . *for thirty-seven dollars and sixteen cents?* Would you let them hang me, your old friend, for thirty-seven dollars? That ain't what pards do."

"If they hang you, it'll be for Jed Dunlap."

"Dunlap got what he deserved, Lin. If I hadn't killed him, you would have." He shook violently, and, for a second, Garrett figured this was it, the final meeting, where the two old friends blew each other to graves, but, when Sinclair raised his arm, the only thing he pointed was a finger.

"What galls me, Lincoln Garrett, is you. You wouldn't ride this far for the railroad, even with a federal lawdog's appointment, wouldn't follow a man for thirty-seven dollars this far north, exceptin' that I broke my word to you, told you I wouldn't come back to Arizona Territory, and I did. That's the only reason you're here. Don't seem fair. It ain't fair! Only reason I rode down with Troy and Harry was because what they been sayin' about me, printin' lies in the papers again. Near five years, Lin, five long years it's been since I shot Jed Dunlap, and them writers bring it all up again, after it's almost forgotten."

"Senator Dunlap died a few months back. Gives them something to write about."

"Yeah . . . well . . . ."

Garrett cut him off. "I never read newspapers much, Ollie. You shouldn't, either."

Sinclair lowered his arm, resting his hand on the gun butt. "I could have shot you ten times when you come ridin' up here."

I could have put a bullet in your back, he thought, but only nodded in agreement. "No need in innocent folks getting hurt. I'm glad you come outside. Now, I'll ask you once more. You coming in peaceably?"

Sinclair's right hand moved again, but toward the buckle. "This is the last time, Lin. Only reason I'm doin' this is because, well, like you said, ain't no call in lettin' anyone else get hurt." The gun belt dropped in the dust, and the cat leaped from the roof and began brushing its body against Ollie Sinclair's legs.

The $37.16 stayed with the family at Lee's Ferry. At least, Garrett assumed it did. He didn't ask, and Ollie Sinclair never volunteered, swearing, a few weeks later, that the two men riding with him had taken the money. Naturally he would tell everyone except Lin Garrett that he didn't know his partners in the robbery, claiming they were just a couple of saddle tramps he had met in California.

They rode south slowly, out of the desert eventually and into forested hills, stopping at Red Mountain one evening on the pretext of resting their horses. Garrett let Sinclair visit with Holly Mossman, while he stayed by the corrals talking to that retired Army officer she had married, a fellow who yapped more than Ol' Corb but never said one thing slightly interesting. Garrett felt relief when Mossman announced that he needed to check on something in the barn, but then he saw Holly heading his way, leaving Sinclair in their cabin, bouncing Holly's daughter on his knee.

Although heavy with child, she moved with agility, and purpose, and Garrett braced for her assault. Another mistake, he figured, stopping here. Should have just ridden on to Flagstaff. No, then Holly never would have forgiven him.

"Are you that mule-headed, Lin? Is your pride so great . . . ?"

"I'm paid to uphold the law, Holly. Ollie broke it."

She spit out a mouthful of five-dollar words, as he knew she would, trembling, but not in rage, but fear. Garrett had been doing his job. Sure, he might concede, if forced, that he probably wouldn't have dogged that trail if the Sinclair brothers and Harry Prudhomme hadn't been identified as the robbers. Ollie Sinclair had broken his word. Five years back, Lin Garrett had let Sinclair cross the Colorado at Lee's Ferry, after making him vow he would stay in Utah, or, at least, out of Arizona Territory.

"Ollie says he won't let me testify," Holly said weakly now, dabbing her eyes with her sleeves, forced to lean against the corral fence for support. "Says I shouldn't . . . if they charge him with Jed Dunlap's murder. Jed . . . ." She shuddered, and Garrett had to stop the urge to reach for her.

"You always made up your own mind, Holly," he said at last, and, when she looked up at him, the venom was gone, and he knew he had said the right thing.

"You'd let me . . . ?"

"I don't own you, Holly. Ollie don't. Ben Mossman don't. You don't need nobody telling you that, either."

"I won't embarrass Ben," she said.

"You don't have to," Garrett said. He had been thinking about this since Lee's Ferry, probably even before.

In the end, Holly Mossman didn't testify, not before a jury, at least. She met with the territorial solicitor, and told them about Jed Dunlap, and why Ollie Sinclair had killed him in 1883. Nobody would have cared one whit about Jed Dunlap if that snake-in-the-grass's daddy hadn't been a territorial senator from Prescott, one of the old stalwarts who had pushed for the charter after the War of the Rebellion to build the Atlantic & Pacific Railroad and open up northern Arizona. Even a simple man like Lin Garrett could remember that the A&P had barely gotten out of Kansas, and had been forced to sell its charter rights to the AT&SF, so Senator Dunlap wasn't near as big as he, or some newspaper editors, thought he was. And his son wasn't worth spit.

Amid a few outcries of injustice, the Territory of Arizona allowed Oliver Sinclair to plead to manslaughter and train robbery, and he was sentenced to twenty-five years at hard labor. Troy Sinclair and Harry Prudhomme made it across safely into California, although both remained wanted for their part in the Williams train robbery, despite Ollie's statement that two saddle tramps had planned the crime with him. Later, Troy and Prudhomme were indicted for a bank robbery at some Colorado River town and a stage-coach hold-up near Bisbee.

By stage, train, and a rented jerky, Lin Garrett took Ollie Sinclair to Yuma, arriving on a blistering July afternoon. Here, the sun baked the ground, the wide Colorado River rolled slowly, its blue surface reflecting sunlight, and the sand burned Garrett's feet through his boots. There were no vermilion cañons and cliffs, no roaring rapids, no end-less sky, just scrub and desert and a stone and iron prison that, like the rugged terrain near Lee's Ferry, could swallow up a man, and had, indeed, swallowed up many convicted felons.

And it was here, before Deputy U.S. Marshal Lin Garrett turned over his prisoner, that Ollie Sinclair showed yellow.

Staring at the iron gate and thick walls, Sinclair paled, shuddering uncontrollably as Garrett unlocked the metal handcuffs, which fell to the ground. Garrett put his hands on Sinclair's shoulders, squeezing, steadying the big man.

"I wish . . . they had hanged me," Sinclair said in hoarse, broken sobs. "Twenty-five years . . . Lin . . . I don't know . . . ."

Garrett searched for the right words, but said nothing,

just squeezed harder, and pulled Sinclair close into a bear-like embrace.

"You should have killed me, Lin. I should have . . . made . . . ."

Garrett choked off the rest by hugging tighter. Finally he pushed Sinclair away, aware of the approaching guards, the warden, even a couple of journalists.

"Buck up," he said at last. "You're Ollie Sinclair. Remember that. Twenty-five years . . . that ain't nothing."

"I am scared," Sinclair whispered, wiping his eyes. He smiled grimly, and spun to face his crowd, firing out a string of curses, laughing callously, giving the newspapermen what they expected from such a murderous beast. Sinclair carried himself with pride, tall, erect, as the prison guards led him inside.

One of the ink-slingers tried to get a few comments from Garrett, but he just stormed away, and didn't stop until he found a miserable *cantina* in Yuma.

Chapter Seven

Spring and winter fought for dominance over the next few days. Ol' Corb's daddy undoubtedly had some saying about such weather, and Corbett was probably resurrecting that Missouri proverb, or about to, in the parlor, but Garrett hadn't seen much of his friend lately. Hadn't seen much of anybody, other than the county-supplied doctor, a balding man from Flagstaff's *real* hospital, and only then at the superintendent's insistence.

Most days, he spent alone in his room, cleaning the saddle again and again, even manufacturing *tapaderos* accented with brass rings he had bought in town, cheap enough for him to afford as they were covered with green tarnish. A cowboy these days didn't see many *tapaderos* fastened to stirrups, but Gus Ghormley had sworn by them. "If they don't keep your feet from freezing, they'll at least keep the toes of your boots from getting scarred," the saddle maker had said.

The leather he had found among the dead cowboy's traps, although not as dark as the rest of the saddle. Colorado soil, rich in iron oxide, had worked its way into the leather's pores, turning the saddle into a rich mahogany, the crevices from the carvings now practically black. The leather for the *tapaderos* was paler, newer, but good enough to do the job, and he polished the brass rings till the green almost disappeared and turned golden again. Even Daric Mossman commented on the workmanship when he made his weekly visit.

Not that Holly's son spent much time lauding Garrett's saddle-making abilities.

This time, the young peace officer had brought a photograph of Benji, his nephew. Nine years old now, Mossman said. Hard to believe his sister and brother-in-law had been dead seven years.

Penny, Daric's older sister by five years, had always been the spitting image of her mother. He could visualize her again, the little spitfire, being bounced on Ollie Sinclair's knee that late autumn day in 1887, then could see her again, right before the turn of the century, almost mistaking her for Holly. Hard to believe she had become a mother, even harder to believe that she was dead.

"How was it she died again?" Garrett found himself asking.

"Influenza. Took her and Charley both. Mom's been raising Benji since. I help out when I can, but can only get away once a week."

He tried to picture Holly taking care of Penny's boy, not yet a teen, and coping with her invalid husband before he was called to Glory. Of course, Holly had always been a fighter.

She had come out with the Arizona Colonization Company with designs, she had often told him, on becoming a schoolteacher, but the rules society demanded from women schoolmarms didn't fit her pistols at all.

Teaching children, filling the lamps with coal oil—bought from her own salary—and cleaning the chimneys, that was well and good, but the rest . . . . He remembered Holly reciting the rules, remembered it as clearly as he recollected anything.

★ ★ ★ ★ ★

" 'Male teachers may take one evening each week for courting purposes, or two evenings a week if they go to church regularly,' " she read to him one night after the colonization project had been abandoned and she had moved south to Prescott. "That's what it says, Lin. But then, listen to this . . . 'Women teachers who marry or engage in unseemly conduct will be dismissed.' Dismissed! Men can court, but we women can't even get married and still teach."

"Maybe you should think about Wyoming," he said. "They allow you all the vote up yonder."

It had been a stupid thing to say. For one, Garrett didn't want Holly to leave Arizona Territory. More importantly he certainly didn't care for the look she gave him.

The glare passed, and she read another rule. " 'Any teacher who smokes, uses liquor in any form, frequents pool or public halls, or gets shaved in a barber shop will give good reason to suspect his worth, intention, integrity, and honesty.' "

"Reckon I'd have to draw my time was I teaching," he said, and she laughed, the glare now history.

"Here's one, Lin. 'Every teacher should lay aside from each pay a goodly sum of his earnings for his benefit during his declining years so that he will not become a burden on society.' " Lowering the page of rules, she peered at him with a look Lin could not read. "I suppose that should apply to lawmen as well as teachers."

Garrett handed the photograph back to Daric, Holly's words echoing in his ears. *A burden on society.* Well, he certainly had become that.

"He's a handsome boy," Garrett said, and prepared himself for Daric's invitation to Red Mountain. It came, and he quickly rejected it.

70

"Mom's starting to say you think she has the plague," Daric said glumly.

"It ain't that. I just don't ride so well these days." At least, that wasn't a lie, Garrett figured. The pain in his bones, the cramping muscles, had worsened, although he hadn't dared tell Doc Steinberg that, fearing the superintendent would bring that pill-pusher from Williams with his cathode-ray, pain-inflicting apparatus.

"Are you sure?"

"Yeah."

"Maybe next week then."

"We'll see."

The image of Holly appeared again, in the parlor at the cabin in Red Mountain, years after she had decided she would never teach school, not with the rules the board of education demanded. She had asked Garrett something, although he couldn't remember what, and he had answered: "We'll see."

Holly's glare resurrected itself. "*We'll see* means *no*, Lin Garrett, at least when you say it."

He had stopped working on the saddle, figuring if he kept at that saddle, he'd rub all the leather off and whittle down the tree. Instead, Garrett pulled out his revolver and cleaned it, always in his room, knowing that the opium addict and the crazy old lady would throw a conniption if they saw him with that old Colt. Not to mention Doc Steinberg and his missus.

Fools would probably think he was about to stick the barrel in his mouth and pull the trigger, and, truthfully, the thought had crossed his mind a time or two, although never seriously. A man's death was the second-most important thing he had, next to his life, and he sure wouldn't spit on his seventy years by killing himself like some coward. He would not end his life the way Jude Kincaid had, be compared to that squat assassin.

When cleaning the revolver no longer satisfied him, when the dreary gray walls began closing in on him, he at last left the confines of his cell and wandered into the lobby, reappearing for the old, the vagrants, the addled, and the dying.

"Winter's over," Ol' Corb announced from his rocking-chair throne. "The bear's come out of hibernation."

He helped himself to coffee, listened to the meaningless chatter among the patients and staff, then, bored immensely, walked outside, heading to the stables to visit Scarlet Knight.

The horse snorted, suspicious again, but he held out his hand, palm up, and waited as the blood bay gelding pranced and stamped until finally recognizing Garrett's scent and came over.

"Afraid I don't have a carrot or nothing for you," he said.

Another voice from the past came, Holly Mossman's once again, and he saw her in the 1890s, when Penny could ride better than boys ten years her senior and Daric was just a toddler, saw her as the successful ranch woman at Red Mountain, breeder of horses, thinking of the future.

"Horses like people, Lin," she had told him. "I think horses need people. They need companionship." She had looked at him again, not glaring, though, just staring at him, hurt, maybe unable to comprehend. Or maybe she finally understood Lin Garrett at last, knew him better than he knew himself.

"I'm not sure any of that fits you." He had waited for her to explain, although Lin Garrett needed no explanation. He knew what she meant.

You don't like people. You don't need people. You don't need companionship. And you never needed me.

Yet she didn't say another word, just looked at him with those sad eyes.

The last time they had ever spoken. He wasn't mad, couldn't ever be angry with Holly, but he had left a few days later. Left for what? Come back to what? To be what?

A burden on society.

He walked to town three times a week after that, to build his strength, he told Doc Steinberg. Looking for a job, he told Ol' Corb, and sometimes Corbett came with him.

He didn't really seek employment. By jacks, Flagstaff had little to offer a seventy-year-old lawman nobody remembered. Nor did any other burg he had seen over his lifetime. Often, he tinkered with the notion of hopping one of the freights, maybe letting Ol' Corb tag along with him, leaving Flagstaff and all of her memories, heading west, or east, to something new. Only, he knew, there was nothing new for him, not now, not at his age. Flagstaff held the same future as Kingman or Winslow, Santa Barbara or Fort Smith. Instead, he would sit around sipping coffee in the Weatherford Hotel or one of the cafés in town, killing time, mostly, or resting up after looking at the wares in the window of the Babbitt Brothers store or watching the activities at the depot.

Once, alone at the Weatherford, he listened with amusement while a salt-and-peppered mustached man in a bowler hat and black Prince Albert told a story about Ollie Sinclair, a stretcher that would have rivaled anything Ol' Corb could make up.

"This is the story my father told me, and it's true, although not many people know about it," the man began,

73

enjoying his audience. Men and women trying to keep dry crowded into the lobby that overcast, damp morning.

"My father's mother was alone in her cabin over on the Blue River, not far from Springerville, when a stranger came riding up, and asked if he could spend the night in the barn," the storyteller continued. "Grandma said yes, she'd never turn anyone down, and told him, if he'd split some wood, well, she'd feed him breakfast. The next morning, the man sat at the table, and she fed him biscuits and gravy, and then she broke down in tears.

"She owed money to the bank, and Grandpa had took the fever and died the previous fall. She was going to lose the place if she didn't come up with six hundred dollars. Then she apologized, said she had no right to blurt out her personal problems to a complete stranger. But sometimes, you know, it's easier to tell a stranger what troubles you than a friend, or even family.

"Well, the man he walks outside and comes back. 'I ain't' never been one to ride the grubline,' he told her, and handed her six hundred dollars in gold coin. Freshly minted. Grandma gasps, but the stranger told her to give this to the banker, but make sure she got a receipt. Grandma refused, but the man insisted, saying he didn't need the money, that she reminded him of his own mama. Well, the stranger rode out, and a few hours later, the banker showed up, and Grandma gave him the money, got a receipt, and then that cock-of-the-walk banker rode back to Springerville, happy as fox in a chicken coop.

"Only a few miles after he crossed the Blue, he got held up by a masked bandit, who took that six hundred dollars, plus the banker's watch and his own wallet.

"That was Ollie Sinclair, friends, and that's a story you can take to the bank as gospel."

When Garrett snorted out a laugh, the man got riled, asking what was so funny.

"Heard the same story said about Jesse James, Sam Bass, the Daltons, even Butch Cassidy," Garrett said calmly. "Guess it was only a matter of time before Ollie latched onto it."

The storyteller's face flushed, and he stood over Garrett, arms trembling. "Well, mister, I guess my grandmother knew Ollie Sinclair better than you."

He felt the stares, realized his mistake, his dilemma. He couldn't very well fight the drummer, although, even at seventy years old, he felt certain he could beat the pasty man. So he'd have to leave, and never return to the hotel for coffee. They'd think him a coward, or just some blow-hard, an old fool—a burden on society.

"I reckon so," Garrett said. Setting his cup aside, he stood and walked outside into a misting rain.

Chapter Eight

Flagstaff overflowed with chaos on that chilly April morning when Garrett walked to town alone. He found himself standing at the depot, his mouth agape, staring at the insanity all around him. He hadn't seen this much movement, this much madness, since the early days of the War of the Rebellion, at Wilson's Creek and Pea Ridge. People ran to and fro, most of them lawmen, and a great, black locomotive belched steam and smoke as engineers, conductors, and firemen shouted orders. Across the street, in front of the iron and brick buildings, citizens gathered, their faces masked with a mix of bewilderment, shock, and curiosity.

Perched in his Classic Six, Mayor Fox—at least, Garrett guessed it was the mayor—barked orders to Police Chief Bell, who had to leap onto the Chevrolet's running board to keep from being mowed down when a swerving Ford sedan, filled to capacity with sheriff's deputies, slid to a muddy stop in front of the depot. Deputies piled out, lugging rifles, shotguns, bedrolls, and bandoleers of ammunition, while Bell screamed obscenities at the county sheriff for driving so recklessly. Ignoring the police chief, the sheriff pointed a pudgy finger at the train, directing his deputies to board the train, although none responded promptly. Some moseyed toward a passenger car coupled behind the tender. Others fired up cigarettes and checked their rifles. A few just stood there like idiots, gaping at the crowd, the confusion.

He caught snippets of commands, of conversation, but could make little out of discordant voices. A train was just robbed. Something about Williams, the town due west on the AT&SF line. Pandemonium. A dead body.

"Where's Paine?" someone bellowed during one lull in the noise.

"Drunk or gambling," came an answer, and then another: "I don't know."

"Well, we ain't waiting for him," the sheriff was saying. "There will be another train tonight. If you see Paine, send him on his way then, along with them boys from Winslow. Smithfield, get my train moving!"

"What about horses?"

"Telephone Marshal Carol in Williams. Have two dozen mounts saddled and ready at the station. Tell him we're on our way now! Let's move, Smithfield, move! A . . . ."

The Baldwin's screaming whistle washed out the rest of the sheriff's sentence. He nodded at something the mayor had shouted into a megaphone and made a beeline for the train with the rest of this posse of fools, hurrying when they realized Smithfield had the train moving, and it was about to leave them.

Somehow, all managed to climb aboard the train before it pulled away, and the police chief borrowed the mayor's megaphone, ordering folks to go about their business, that everything was all right. Slowly sanity returned to the streets.

"What's happened?" Garrett asked a bespectacled man, but the only answer he got came with a slow shake of the head before the gent disappeared inside the depot office.

"This is bad, this is bad, this is . . . ," Mayor Fox mum-

77

bled inside the Chevrolet, shaking his head. "The tourists . . . what will . . . ?"

The train whistle blared again.

When the sound died down, Garrett overheard two words spoken by a Mexican railroad worker.

Ollie Sinclair.

His mouth turned dry, and he stood there shaking, suddenly enveloped by the insanity that earlier had gripped everyone else in town. *Ollie Sinclair? It couldn't be.* Yet something gnawed at the pit of his gut, and he found himself in control again, marching into the depot.

"What's going on?" he demanded, speaking to the back of the bespectacled man who was talking into one of those wall telephones.

"Shut up," the man told him. "I'm talking to the governor!"

Garrett started for him, thought better of it, and checked his rage, let the man finish speaking into the mouthpiece, then slam down the receiver. When he turned around, Garrett blocked his path.

"I asked you a question, mister," Garrett said. "What's going on?"

It must have been the burning anger in his eyes, because the railroad man took two steps back. "Ollie Sinclair and his gang robbed the Grand Cañon Railway," the man said, "about two hours ago, north of Williams."

Garrett answered with a curse of contempt and doubt.

"Couple passengers recognized him," the railroad man said. "And he introduced himself. Conductor killed one of them. Now . . . if you'll excuse me."

He had stepped aside, not really knowing it, and maybe he mumbled his thanks as the man walked by, wiping sweat on his striped trousers. Garrett wasn't sure he had said anything, if he were even capable of speech.

Another man worked the telephone. Garrett hadn't even noticed him in the depot. This gent screamed into the mouthpiece, likely telling a newspaper editor or lawman the particulars, repeating pretty much what the railroad man had just told Garrett, but with more information. Ollie Sinclair and six or seven others had held up the Grand Cañon Railway at milepost Nineteen north of Williams. Exact amount stolen undetermined might be more than $80,000. One gang member assaulted a woman, but the conductor killed him, and the rest of the outlaws fled, riding west. The woman was badly shaken but unharmed. No one else was hurt. It's the biggest crime since statehood!

Garrett looked down, found his hand, clammy, gripping the doorknob. He still refused to believe this fantastic story. Sinclair had just been released from prison. He wouldn't have had time to form some gang, ride to Williams, rob a train. Would he? It was April 1st, maybe the 2nd. Living at the poor farm, Garrett had lost track of time. When had Ollie been released from the state pen in Florence? Maybe it had been long enough to form a gang—Handsome Harry Prudhomme and Sinclair's no-account brother Troy would likely have had some hardcases in mind, men unafraid to pull a trigger or—*assault a woman?* Not Ollie.

Had to be a mistake, he told himself, and walked outside.

The mayor had driven away in his Chevrolet, and Police Chief Bell had disappeared as well, along with most of the bystanders, but Garrett found a familiar face, and hurried across the street, catching Daric Mossman as he rounded the corner.

"What's this all about?" he asked the young policeman.

His face must have told the story, because Mossman said: "You've heard?"

"Heard some nonsense about Ollie Sinclair, but . . . ."

"It's true."

"I don't believe . . . ."

"Ollie Sinclair stood up in the smoking car, introduced himself, pulled an automatic pistol, and fired a round into the ceiling. The emergency cord was pulled, the train stopped, and four others rode out of the piñons, pulling four extra horses. Three others were on the train as well, one in each car."

He started to speak, stopped, let Mossman continue.

"They robbed the passengers, tourists mostly, a few miners, took four payrolls, too. We don't exactly know how much they got."

Garrett sucked in air, remembering the man on the phone in the depot and his estimate of the robbers' take: $80,000. Sam Bass had not scored that much when he had pulled his train robbery over in Nebraska back in 1877 or 1878. Ollie Sinclair had never stolen that much, either, had never stolen anything except some cattle and $37.16 when he, Troy, and Handsome Harry had robbed the Atchison, Topeka & Santa Fe at Williams in the winter of 1887.

"Sinclair and those men rode west, so we've wired the sheriffs in Mohave and Yavapai counties, as well as the U.S. marshal," Mossman said. "That's all I really know. Now, if you will excuse me . . . ."

"It couldn't have been Ollie," Garrett argued.

"He introduced himself, sir, and people recognized him. Tall man, pockmarked, skinny as a rail with graying hair, thin, almost bald, and a rough mustache and beard."

He started to say—"There, that proved it wasn't Ollie . . . ."—but just stood, lips quivering, feeling foolish.

Ollie Sinclair was anything but thin, must have weighed nigh 200 pounds, and his hair was thick, red like some character in a children's storybook. Only that had been years ago. He closed his eyes and pictured Ollie Sinclair again, back in 1887 at Lee's Ferry, saw that graying hair then, the rough beard, the hollow eyes. Better than two decades had passed, so certainly Ollie Sinclair had changed, gotten older, lost weight, maybe gone a little mad.

"Are you all right, sir?" The voice sounded distant, muffled, but Garrett shook his head, snapping the trance.

"Why aren't you on that train to Williams?" he asked urgently.

"It's not my jurisdiction, Mister Garrett. Sheriff Oldridge is leading a posse. I'm a city policeman. My job's here."

Without thinking, Garrett reached forward, grabbed Mossman's coat, and jerked him forward. "Your job's protecting your mother. Ollie Sinclair always runs north, boy. You haul your butt over to Red Mountain. *Pronto!*"

"I can't," he heard Mossman saying as he turned away, heard the young man mumbling something about the mayor's concerns that Sinclair would strike again, rob a bank or train here in Flagstaff, that the outlaw was plumb crazy.

Plumb crazy. Yeah, that was the size of it.

Now, he had no doubts. Ollie Sinclair had robbed the railway, to prove a point, make a statement, strike back at that idiot newspaper editor with the *Sun*. It was that ink-spiller's fault, writing that garbage, provoking Sinclair with those lies about Mountain Meadows, the Danites, ravishing women. *Ollie Sinclair may be free, but he is not welcome in Coconino County. Go back where you belong, Mr. Sinclair, which is Hades, where the Devil spawned you and your evilness. Leave us alone.*

No, Garrett thought, moving faster, despite the shortness of breath, his racing heart. *I'm thinking like Ollie now, blaming everyone else but me.* He cursed Ollie Sinclair but, by the same token, had to admire the old man's sand and sass. Sinclair would be laughing at that journalist's words now, riding west with designs to turn north, leaving Coconino County some $80,000 richer. He had Flagstaff's mayor worrying about tourists, fearing Ollie Sinclair would turn Flagstaff into another Mountain Meadows, even if Garrett knew that wasn't Sinclair's style, not even Troy's. Well, good old Ollie had turned at least Flagstaff, and probably Williams as well, into bedlam.

It all made sense. By jacks, there must be better than thirty mines in Coconino County alone, or had been, years ago, rich deposits of copper that assayed out at sixty-five percent around Anita and elsewhere. When Buckey O'Neill and others had pushed for the building of a railroad out of Williams, they had not been thinking about hauling tourists to some giant hole in the earth. Old-timers had often re-peated the legends of Coronado searching for Quivera in these parts, and, while no one had ever found some city of gold, many had struck pay dirt. The railroad had been born for the mines. Granted, most of those lodes had played out over the years, but if that train had carried $80,000 in pay-roll money for the mines . . . . ..

He paused, correcting himself. Daric Mossman hadn't said mine payrolls, just payrolls. Probably not only for the remaining mines, but the national monument, even the rail-road itself. By thunder, for all Corbett knew, some dude from back East had already opened a bank at Grand Cañon National Monument.

$80,000! He let the thought drift and stood on the shoulder of the road, waiting for a Model N to pass before

crossing the street and heading to the poor farm.

In the middle of the street, he stopped, staring at the distant snow-capped mountains. Holly Mossman would be at Red Mountain, and Ollie Sinclair would be heading there, no matter what those railroad fools and lawmen thought.

Ol' Corb looked incredulous.

"I thought the same thing," Garrett told him, "but it's true. It's got to be true."

"Eighty thousand dollars? There ain't that much money in this whole county, Lin."

"That's what the man said, Corb. I figure it's not just the mines, but the railroad and the national monument, all them other things they've built up at Red Lake, Prado, Valle."

"And Ollie done it?"

"With Handsome Harry, Troy, some others. Eight in all. The conductor killed one messing with a woman, and that sent the rest skedaddling. Riding west, but you know Ollie. He'll be turning north, lighting a shuck for Utah."

They stood outside the stables, alone, the pines rustling in the wind that had turned colder.

"Ollie's like you and me, Lin, old enough that our cinches is frayed." Ol' Corb expelled a mouthful of tobacco juice. "It don't make a lick of sense."

"Sure, it does. Ollie robbed that train in 'Eighty-Seven because he was mad about the newspapers bringing up his killing Jed Dunlap again. Figured they owed him, Ollie did, and that was always his nature. Always figured the world owed him something. Well, the newspapers did it again, printing that mean-spirited story about him after he got out of prison. It all rings true, Corb. By jacks, I should have known it before, should have figured Ollie would pull this thing as soon as I saw that copy of the *Sun*."

Corbett shook his head. "Ollie must be off his nut. That ol' fool. Things ain't the same. Telephones. Horseless carriages. Like my pappy would say . . . 'He's close enough to hell to smell smoke now.' They'll catch Ollie by morn, I warrant, or kill 'im."

"We'll catch him," Garrett announced, almost in a whisper.

Corbett shifted the tobacco bulge to the other cheek. "Now, you're off your nut, Lin."

"Like your pa always said . . . 'When a gent's got nothing to lose, he'll try anything.' We're going after Ollie. Them fools will ride west, but you and me know where he's going. Maybe see Holly, then go to Lee's Ferry."

The gray head shook. "How do you expect us to chase him, Lin? Afoot?"

Garrett tilted his head at the stables. It had all come to him on the walk back to the poor farm. "These are county horses, Corb, and you are a special sheriff's deputy. Remember? I say that justifies our borrowing them."

When Corbett laughed, Garrett spoke louder, with more urgency. "I'm serious, Corb. We can get supplies at the Babbitts', ride to Red Mountain, be waiting for Ollie when he gets there. Or keep riding north till we catch him."

"You think you can saddle a horse like that, Lin?" Corbett argued. "Because I'm a-thinkin' we ain't gonna catch up with Ollie by morn. We're talkin' 'bout days and nights in the saddle, in the cold, Lin. You really think you can do that, pard, at your age, the way your back, your legs keep a-tormentin' you so?"

"I ain't never quit, Corb," Garrett shot back. "And I don't hurt that much." Neither was exactly the truth.

There came another explosion of tobacco juice. "Yeah,

and you said . . . what was it . . . eight men robbed that train? Eight men. Two of us."

"Seven. One got kilt. And they'll likely split up," he argued. "Besides, I expect them boys, with the exception of Prudhomme and Troy, ain't worth spit . . . no better than them half-wit deputies chasing them."

"Ollie wouldn't hurt Holly. You know that."

"I don't know nothing any more, pard. One of them boys assaulted a woman on that train, and, if the conductor hadn't killed him, Lord knows what might've happened. Ollie's been in prison for a quarter century, Corb. Maybe he ain't the man he once was."

"Who is?"

"I'm going after him," he said firmly.

Corbett just stood there, working his quid, staring but not speaking, and Garrett quit arguing, burning daylight like that. He left Corbett outside the stables, made his way into the hospital, and went into his room. He buckled on the gun belt, tied his coat to the back of the cantle, and picked up the saddle, not caring if Mrs. Steinberg, the superintendent, anyone saw him as he made his way out the front door, lugging the saddle, which seemed heavier now, sending spasms of pain up and down his back, into his gut. Biting his lip, grunting, blocking out any doubts, he passed Corbett, who had not moved, and found Scarlet Knight in his stall.

He'd have to borrow a saddle blanket, plus oats for the gelding. Garrett worked with a purpose, filling a sack with oats, which he stuffed in one of the cantle bags, and saddled the horse, which snorted impassively. Catching his breath, Garrett smiled, pleased. He had saddled the big blood bay, showed Ol' Corb something. *I ain't never quit*, he had said, but he couldn't remember how long it had been since he had last saddled a horse. Well, he'd need a bridle, too, but he found one in the next stall, slipped the old Army bit into the gelding's mouth. No rifle, and only four rounds in his old Colt. He'd get the rest on tick at the Babbitts', be riding out before nightfall.

"There are two sides to any man's argument . . . his'n and the wrong'n'."

Garrett studied Corbett in the shadows.

"That something your pa told you, too?"

"Actually, it was Bob Clagett, our first boss. Remember?"

Garrett didn't answer, simply led Scarlet Knight out of the stall. He thought about making one final plea, telling Ol' Corb he was free to sit on his rocking chair and make Mrs. Aikin laugh at his jokes, fill the brains of opium addicts with his hogwash, rock and rot and die like some cripple. He kept quiet, though, and, grunting, struggling, put his foot in the stirrup, grabbed the big horn, and pulled himself up.

Garrett rocked the saddle to his right, adjusting it, and almost chuckled with pleasure. He looked down at Ol' Corb, wondering how he would say good bye, if he should.

"That sorrel over yonder looks like a good mount," he heard his friend saying, and Lin Garrett grinned, with relief and admiration, as Ol' Corb hefted a saddle off the rack and entered the nearest stall.

Chapter Nine

Low, gray clouds, ever darkening, had followed the cold wind, and Garrett's bones ached, partly from the miserable weather, the threat of snow after a few days of spring-like sunshine, but mostly from the ride to town. Scarlet Knight had an easy lope, a smooth walk, but the gelding's hard trot would break a man's back. During the ride, he recalled the last ranch he had worked at, some place for dudes up in Wyoming a few years back, not that he had done much work, just mucking out stalls and cleaning out chamber pots for $10 a month and found. At this ranch, though, he had heard some wrangler telling gyps from Dayton and Chicago and Buffalo about posting trots. *Posting?* The first time the wrangler mentioned posting, Garrett had thought he had been talking about mending fence, only to learn it had something to do with matching a horse's trot. Fools bounced in their saddles at that Wyoming spread, and not just the cads from the East, but even the wrangler and other cowhands. He'd never seen the like, always figured a man's rear end should never raise an inch off his saddle seat. That's the way he had always ridden, the way his pa had taught him.

But as mean as the blood bay gelding trotted, he might have to learn to post after all. Else he might never walk again.

The sight of that massive red sandstone building made him glad, and he swung down into the muddy street in front of the Babbitts' store. His left foot, however, caught on the inside of the *tapadero*, almost sending him over the hitching post before he caught his balance, pulled his boot free, and struck solid land. He felt stiff, and he had ridden only a couple of miles.

His friend's irritating cackling got his dander up, but, after wrapping the reins around the cedar post, Garrett realized Ol' Corb hadn't been funning him. Corbett was merely pointing out where they had hitched their county horses—between a Model T Ford and a mud-splattered Buick White Streak roadster.

"My pappy always said that age will make a fellow a stranger in his own country," Corbett said, shaking his head. "Look at them things, Lin. Never would have dreamed this in all my days. My pappy also said . . . ."

Muttering—"Did your pa ever *shut up?*"—Garrett walked stiffly into the Babbitts' mercantile, where a smirking boy in sleeve garters promptly greeted him and the trailing Randolph Corbett, busy fastening his badge to the lapel of his winter coat.

"This is Deputy Sheriff Randolph Corbett," Garrett said, stepping aside to let the boy see Ol' Corb polishing the ancient tin star. "Need to pick up some ammunition and stuff for the trail."

"You with that posse coming from Winslow?"

"We're lawmen, sure enough."

"Pretty exciting day, huh? Gang waylaying a train. Feature that, eh?"

"Uhn-huh. Let's get the hardware first."

"What in tarnation is that?" the boy said from behind the cherrywood counter.

"It's an Army Colt, son," Garrett replied impatiently. He surveyed the store, but the big building looked practically deserted. Seems everyone was staying home, fearing that maybe Mayor Fox was right, that Ollie Sinclair would ride into town and sack it like Quantrill at Lawrence or Custer at the Washita.

"They still make those? No, jiminy, that thing's older than . . . ."

"Two boxes of Forty-Fours, son. It still shoots." He fought the temptation to add: *Want me to prove it?*

He stared at his six-shooter, old sure, but still solid, shining after all his cleaning at the county hospital, remembering yet again the newspaper editor calling his choice of weapon "antiquated" almost thirty years ago. His father had given him the revolver, told him to use it with honor when he went to save the Union, and the .44 had been with him since. Old, sure, but antiquated? He didn't think so. He saw himself shaking his father's hand on that day, not really knowing that he would never see his pa again, that what his mother called in a letter "cerebral apoplexy" would call his father to Glory in the winter of 1863. No, sir, he'd never trade in that old Colt for some new model, one of those automatic pistols or something shiny. He had let a gunsmith in Tucson convert it from cap-and-ball to cartridges, but that was all he would allow.

"Antiquated," he said aloud.

"How's that?" the clerk asked.

"Two boxes of Forty-Fours," Corbett repeated.

The kid picked up a box from behind the counter, pushed it in front of Garrett, who, fighting the urge to leap over the counter and brain the idiot, slid it back. "Colt, boy. Not Russian. And two boxes, not one."

When the boy finally got it right, Garrett began filling

the empty loops with the brass cartridges, then nodded at a Marlin rifle in the long rack. The boy handed the repeater over the counter, explaining that it was a Winchester '94, used smokeless powder in .30-30 caliber, about the most popular rifle in northern Arizona next to the .30-40 Krag.

"It's an Eighteen Ninety-Five Marlin," Garrett corrected. "And it shoots Forty-Five-Ninety ca'tridges. I'll take it, and two boxes of shells . . . Marlin shells, son," repeating the caliber in an exaggerated drawl so the kid would make no more mistakes. By jacks, he'd be here all night.

"All right," Garrett said, satisfied with his arsenal. "Need some bedrolls, slickers and a coat, and grub."

"We don't sell food, excepting peppermint candies and some chocolates."

"Lin . . . ." Ol' Corb looked like a toddler about to burst into tears. "I need something to shoot."

Garrett swore, asking about that tiny little Smith & Wesson and the Winchester .25-35, then silenced his friend before Ol' Corb could tell the clerk that he had left his weapons back at the poor farm.

"Give him that Colt Bisley and a 'Ninety-Four Winchester," Corbett barked before storming across the store to examine the bedrolls.

When they had loaded their plunder on the front counter, the clerk pulled out his pencil, licked the tip, and started his ciphering. Calmly Garrett put his hand on top of the pad when the boy lifted the pencil to wet the lead again.

"I told you Corbett here's a special deputy sheriff. He's on county business."

The kid blinked dumbly.

"When I was your age, son," Ol' Corb added, helping out for once, "folks didn't charge peace officers for meals and the like. Called it a courtesy, they did. Shoot, son, up at Northfield, Minnesota, they passed out weapons from the hardware store and shot the Younger boys to bits on the streets. That's the way things worked in our days, as lawmen, and that's one courtesy that ain't changed with the new century."

"Mister Edward says . . . ."

"Put it on my bill, Leonard."

Garrett spun at the voice, swallowed down bile, recognized the scent of Rowland's Macassar Oil. Near a stack of dime novels, Deputy Sheriff Evan Paine stood grinning, running his fingers through his thick mane of black hair.

"Yes, sir, Mister Paine," the boy said respectfully, finished the last of his tallies, and handed the receipt to the brazen lawman. Paine pretended to shove the paper into the pocket of a heavy coat, but in reality let it fall behind the penny dreadfuls.

"The last train for Williams is about to leave," Paine announced. "You two deputies coming with me?"

They stopped at David Tate's liquor store on the way to the depot, where Evan Paine bought three bottles of Cedar Brook Whiskey, and Ol' Corb, ignoring Garrett's glare, bought one—on Paine's credit. They procured no grub, however, not even coffee or jerky, and slowly led their horses to the depot, where a black railroad worker loaded the horses into a stock car.

"Follow me, deputies." Sarcasm laced Paine's voice as he walked to the smoking car and climbed up. In silence, Garrett and Corbett followed, surprised to find the car empty.

"Boys from Winslow never showed," Paine announced as he fired up a cheroot, flicking the match to the floor instead of toward the spittoon. "Reckon it's just me and you two. Have a seat, gents. We're in this posse together."

Taking a pull from his bottle, Ol' Corb settled into the seat opposite the deputy. Slowly Garrett sat beside his friend.

"I got roostered last night," Paine said, "and, when I learned what had happened, what I had missed, I was mighty upset, but now, the way I figure things, this has all worked out mighty fine, mighty fine. You two old boys rode with the Sinclair boys for a spell, right?"

"Just Ollie," Garrett answered dryly.

"I'm guessing you know him pretty good, know where he's going, or apt to run. That's why you decided to go after him yourselves."

Silence.

"You two codgers got sand, that's one thing I can say about you-all," Paine added with a slick grin. "Once we get to Williams, what then?"

When Garrett didn't speak, Paine laughed and blew a smoke ring into the air. The whistle blared, and the train lurched forward. "I can always put you two gents in jail in Williams," the deputy continued, his voice losing some of its friendliness. "Now, let's not be unsociable. We're deputies, lawmen, chasing a gang of killers." He seemed to find his good humor again. "Yes, sir, the way I figure things, the man who brings in Ollie Sinclair after this little caper, why, he's got the election for Coconino County sheriff wrapped up. Don't you agree?" The smile vanished. "Where do we go after Williams?" Paine repeated testily. The man's emotions went every which way.

Garrett cleared his voice. "Talk to the conductor, the one who shot the gang member on the Grand Cañon train, see what he knows, what he saw."

"Oldridge got a few hours' head start on us," Paine said. "I'd hate for him to catch them Sinclairs."

"He won't," Garrett said icily.

As the train picked up speed, the deputy flicked the cigar out the window. "How much money did they get?"

"A right smart," Ol' Corb blurted out, and Garrett's face flushed, the whiskey loosening Corbett's tongue like that, turning him into an old fool. "Eighty thousand."

Shaking his head, Paine cackled and let out an oath. "Not hardly."

"It's the truth," Corbett said. "Lin heard some railroad dick a-tellin' the governor hisself on the telephone."

Garrett snatched the bottle from Corbett's grasp. "Don't be the hog, Corb," he said, took a pull, and passed the bottle toward Paine, who caught it, corked it, and slowly rose from his seat.

"Eighty thousand? Well, then, I think it's most definite that the man who brings that rapscallion in will become the new sheriff, and that man's bound to be Evan Paine. Thanks for joining up with me. I'll make sure the conductor knows that he better do everything but bust a boiler to get us into Williams *muy pronto.*"

The smell of Macassar oil and cigar smoke faded as Evan Paine walked away. The dread in Lin Garrett's stomach only worsened.

"Recollect how my pappy used to say somethin' 'bout a-suppin' with Satan," Ol' Corb said, his voice uncharacteristically sullen, a few minutes later.

"Paine don't change our plans," Garrett answered sharply. "Besides, you said yourself how Ollie's got us outgunned with six boys riding with him. Having Paine join us, that just evens things out, more or less. He's a top hand with a gun. Remember what Paine did at Cañon Diablo."

"Ain't likely to forget," Corbett said.

Nor am I. Garrett sighed. "It's still good," he added minutes later. "Besides, I'd rather take the train to Williams than ride there, cold as it's getting . . . ."

"We wasn't a-goin' to Williams, I thought," Ol' Corb interjected. "Seems you was bound and determined to get to Red Mountain afore daybreak."

This reminder, Garrett had expected, and he was waiting for the chance to defend his plan. "No, I've been thinking on it, and you were right. Ollie wouldn't do a thing to Holly, but them boys he's riding with, well, they might have other notions."

Corbett's chuckle irritated him. "Holly's a grandma, Lin, not one of them handsome lasses in the flickers to cause men, even badmen, to turn downright prurient."

He didn't know what *prurient* meant; that annoyed him, too.

"Them boys made off with eighty thousand dollars," he shot back, "and that might provoke some to violence. So the way I see things, clearer now, Ollie's bound to make a wide loop around Red Mountain, just to keep Holly safe. He wouldn't want to ride there."

Ol' Corb laughed again, harder now, like he was drunk, and he had only managed a few swallows before Evan Paine left with the bottle. "I think I got it figured out, too, ol' pard."

"How's that?" Garrett asked, although he had not meant to say a bloody word.

"You're scared, Lin. You're scared of a-seein' Holly after all these years. You're the one who don't want to ride to Red Mountain."

Garrett mumbled a curse, and pulled his hat down, hoping the rhythmic swaying of the train would rock him to sleep. Even more, he wished Evan Paine had not taken Corbett's bottle with him. He had the sudden urge for a drink.

Chapter Ten

Shortly after their arrival in Williams, they found the body of the dead train robber propped up in a pine coffin outside the Harvey House. The heroic conductor, they learned, was, even money, holding court at Kilpatrick's Saloon two blocks up.

"Thunderation!" The swamper at the depot addressed Evan Paine, paying scant attention to Corbett or Garrett. "Just about every elected or appointed official in the county's been worrying about what this robbery and killing will do for business, but I think Ollie Sinclair's done more for us than Teddy Roosevelt. Fella telephoned from Prescott not two hours back, says he's sold two omnibuses full with folks who want to come see him in the morn." He nodded at the corpse. "By golly, things are booming."

"Reckon so," Garrett said, frowning at the dead man.

They had done the same to the Yavapai Kid back in 1882, only the citizens of Flag had shown some decency. At least, they had left the Kid's shirt on, and placed silver dollars over his eyes. Maybe that tin-horn photographer had charged two bits for viewing and $1 for each print he sold, but Bob Clagett had run him out of town after one day, even got a priest to bury the Kid before his corpse grew ripe.

"Trains are coming in from Holbrook and Kingman,

providing the weather don't turn on us," the man continued. "Even heard that the governor is gonna make a special trip up here from the capital, but I ain't sure that's the gospel."

"Know who he is?" Garrett asked.

"Nah," the man said, after studying Garrett for a moment. "Marshal reckoned he came from California, somehow figured that out from the saddle the boys found on a horse a mile from the tracks after the robbery. Guess it was this boy's."

Boy was right. Kid couldn't have been older than Daric Mossman, probably a great deal younger. Buckteeth, one capped gold, which would probably be pulled by some slob if they kept him on display much longer, a nose that had been broken often during his short life, missing left ear lobe, and a wicked scar that ran from the left nostril to midway underneath his jaw. A short, violent life. Ending the same way. He had been shot four times in the chest—which was why the shirt had been removed; showing off the fine grouping of bullet holes—and twice more in the forehead, from the little powder burns, at a considerable distance.

"Mighty fine shooting for a conductor," Ol' Corb said, which evoked a chuckle from Paine.

"Maybe we should see if he'll join our little posse," the deputy announced, and pivoted, gathering the reins to his horse, a dapple gray, and leading it up the street toward Kilpatrick's Saloon.

Well in his cups, conductor Bryan Crowne barely could clutch the pocket Smith & Wesson he kept trying to jerk from his coat pocket. The little pistol waved wildly in his trembling hand as he pulled the trigger, the metallic *clicks* lost among the cackles and hurrahs inside the smoke-filled bucket of blood.

"You wanted to talk to him!" Paine yelled over the din of drunken laughter and shouts. "Well, talk to him!" Paine put his right foot on the brass rail underneath the bar and shouted at the bartender for a whiskey, leaving Garrett to interrogate the town's newest celebrity. Ol' Corb stood beside the nearest spittoon.

Tobacco smoke stung Garrett's eyes, and his head hurt, worse than his bones now. He wondered what time it was, how long Ollie Sinclair had been on the run. Another round was bought, and Conductor Crowne's empty glass in his left hand was replaced by a full one, although it didn't stay full for long. The walking whiskey vat spilled half of it on his boots while shoving the Smith & Wesson back into his coat.

Garrett had no patience to let the man perform his reënactment again.

"Name's Lin Garrett," he said, stepping in front of the conductor. "Deputy United States marshal." Well, he had been. Come to think of it, he didn't think he had ever tendered a resignation or anything like that.

"Bryan . . . ." The conductor struggled, as if having to recall his last name.

Someone answered for him. "Crowne."

The saloon rocked with laughter.

"Crowne," the conductor repeated.

"I'd like to talk to you about the little fracas this morning."

"Awe," one of the nearby vermin complained, "Crowne's talked to practically ever'body. Newspaper reporters, the governor, Marshal Carol, railroad men, Pinkerton men, Sheriff Oldridge. Let us talk to him for a spell, old-timer."

97

When the conductor smiled at this defense, Garrett leaned over closer, and whispered in Crowne's ear. "You're coming with me outside, mister, or I'll show you for the miserable liar you are, right before I tear you apart."

Paling, Crowne looked suddenly sober. "It's all right, boys," he said, slurring his words. "Be back directly."

As soon as Crowne stepped outside the saloon, trailed by Paine and Corbett, Garrett spun him around and snatched the .32 revolver, ripping the pocket. "What, the . . . ?" the conductor began, but never finished. Garrett shoved him hard in the chest, almost knocking him over the hitching post. He didn't have patience to walk this big-mouth fool all the way to the Harvey House.

"You say you killed that kid over yonder?" Garrett demanded.

"Well . . . ."

He took one quick sniff of the barrel, then tossed it to Ol' Corb, who didn't even bother to see if the weapon had been fired recently. Corbett had known, probably the moment he saw the dead man. Ol' Corb might be long in tooth, might pull a few too many corks, but he wouldn't be played for a fool. Not him. He hadn't changed that much.

Paine looked uncertain, but he took the revolver from Corbett and held the barrel underneath his nose.

"All right," the deputy said, pocketing the revolver. "He didn't use this gun."

"No, he didn't." *And any man with half a brain and half sober would know that.* The dead man had been shot with a large-caliber pistol, probably an automatic given the fact you could cover the chest wounds with a poker card, by a man better than thirty feet away. Six bullet holes, too; the pocket .32 only held five rounds.

Garrett wrenched the conductor's arm behind his back

and shoved him into the alley, overturning one trash can that startled a cat as the drunk fell to the ground and tried to stand up, but his legs refused to co-operate.

"Grand Cañon Railway would frown upon a conductor putting a woman's life at risk," Garrett said. "At that range. Don't think the railroad wants its employees armed no how."

"Well . . . ." The conductor began to weep.

"What happened?" Paine demanded. "What really happened?"

Garrett, and most likely Ol' Corb, had already guessed it.

As soon as the train had stopped, the bandits began herding everyone into the smoking car, figuring it would be easier to have all the passengers in one place, under guard, while the rest of the gang hit the combination mail and baggage car.

When a gunman shoved two other passengers inside, the old man, the conductor said, the one who had introduced himself as "Ollie Sinclair, the scourge 'of Coconino County," asked a silver-mustached fellow he called Harry if that was everyone.

Harry, Bryan Crowne remembered, shook his head and mumbled something underneath his breath.

"I was standing right there, at the door," Crowne told them, "couldn't hear what was said, but I could read that old man's eyes, I know that much. Sinclair, I mean. He cussed something fierce, and knocked me into the next car, pushing me through the door, hollering at me to get out of his way, then shoved me over one of the seats. That's how come I was there."

The slurring of words decreased as the conductor, still

lying atop the refuse, continued his story.

One of the bandits had the car to himself, just him and a raven-headed woman he had pinned against the wall, pawing her with his left hand, pistol in his right, running his tongue across the lady's neck and ear. She was sobbing, begging, choking.

"Sinclair told the boy to stop it right now or he'd kill him," Crowne said, "and the boy started to spin. God as my witness, I never seen a man shoot so fast. Blood spattered everywhere, and I figured Sinclair had killed them both, but, when I could see clearly, I found only the dead man on the floor, and Ollie Sinclair was escorting the woman into the room, telling her everything would be all right."

Evan Paine spit on the ground. "So you figured to steal the glory."

"Well, about that time, the robbers outside was shouting. I guess the gunfire spooked them, so the bandits left, and folks was asking me what had happened, and then, well, I reckon I had picked up the dead man's pistol. Don't recollect doing it, but they saw me with that little gun, and, then . . . . W-well, I mean, it wasn't like nobody was gonna question that lady, upset as she was. I just . . . well . . . I mean . . . it just seemed . . . ."

"Yeah," Garrett said, and walked away.

"Wait a minute!" The conductor pulled himself to his feet, and staggered into the street. "You-all ain't gonna tell nobody . . . I mean . . . ."

Garrett kept walking.

"I can get you-all a train!" the conductor shouted. "Run you-all up north. Save time! If you'd just . . . *please.*"

Paine, of course, had argued, questioning why they would want to take Bryan Crowne up on the offer, why they needed to head north by rail when everyone knew the train robbers had ridden out west. He had seen little point in questioning the conductor, too, he said, only agreed because Williams was in the right direction and maybe those slow-moving fools from Winslow would catch up with them, give them more guns.

"What's the point?" Paine asked. "You think them boys want to take in the wonders of the Grand Cañon with their eighty thousand dollars? Figure they plan on joining the Navajos and raising sheep?"

"You want to part company, we ain't stopping you," Garrett said. "Ride on west. You'll likely catch up with Carol and his posse by morn."

Paine smirked. "No, I reckon I'll play this hand, boys. Something about you two . . . ."

Powered by one Baldwin 2-6-0 locomotive, the train—if you could call one smoking car and a double-deck stock car a train—pulled out of the roundhouse at 11:10 that night. Garrett had to give Bryan Crowne credit. The conductor was a hero, and barely had to prod an engineer and fireman to fire up the No. Eight and take these lawmen north.

He stared at his reflection in the black as midnight window, not sleepy despite the grueling day, half listening to the *clicking* of metal and steel as the train rolled forward, thinking of Ollie Sinclair and Red Mountain. Up by the stove, Ol' Corb sat with the conductor, drinking coffee. He knew Evan Paine sat closer. He could smell Macassar oil and cigar smoke.

A cigar stub *pinged* in the spittoon, and Evan Paine spoke. Garrett knew he would, sooner or later. The deputy had tried threats, tried sarcasm. Now he opted for charm.

"All right, Garrett, I figure you don't like me, figure I'm

just in this for my own political career. And you're absolutely right. But you got your own reasons for chasing Sinclair and this gang, and I'm not prying. Let's just say you-all got your desires, and I got mine. But we're together, for better or worse."

The window was frosting over, cold to the touch. Garrett looked up and pushed back his hat, finding Evan Paine seated across from him, trying to look ever so sincere.

"I've read a mite about you, sir," Paine said. *Sir?* Now wasn't that something. "Jude Kincaid . . . Yavapai Kid . . . Ollie Sinclair. You made a name for yourself back then."

"Reckon you made a name for yourself, Deputy, at Cañon Diablo."

Paine's head shook, and his fingers searched his pockets for another cigar. "I wasn't full growed in 'Aught Five, Mister Garrett. I made my share of mistakes, rode with some fellas I shouldn't have, drunk too much rye, and talked too much. But if you're asking me if I'm ashamed that I had a hand in stopping them no-accounts, well, I ain't. No more, I reckon, than you wish the Yavapai Kid had killed you, or that you hadn't took Sinclair to Yuma."

Garrett simply stared.

"We don't have to like each other, but I warrant we should at least trust each other. All I want is to bring them robbers in, and that payroll. So why are we riding north?"

Garrett took a deep breath, held it, let it exhale. He thought he saw his own frosty breath, wished the conductor or Ol' Corb would crank up that stove some. Kept getting colder, or maybe he was just getting older. He studied Paine again, and nodded slightly.

"Ollie was raised in Utah," he said. "When he gets into a peck of trouble, he hightails it north, back home. Kind of a habit with him." He considered telling Paine about Lee's

Ferry, but decided against it. He'd trust this slick lawman only so far. Besides, if Evan Paine had read enough, he would know that Garrett had captured Sinclair back in 1887 at the Colorado crossing.

Paine remained silent for a few minutes, finally withdrawing a cigar. "All right," he said, biting off an end and spitting it onto the floor. "Let's hope you're right, else you won't get your name in the newspapers again, and I won't get elected sheriff."

He slammed hard into the ground, shoulder throbbing, head pounding, cursing Ollie Sinclair for that jackass prank, mumbling that he could have been killed. Horse might have kicked out his brains.

Then, his vision clearing, he heard someone else cursing, and the fog lifted from his mind. He wasn't in Colorado, and Ollie Sinclair had not put six burrs underneath his saddle blanket. Must have been a dream. No, just a memory.

He lay on the floor, and his shoulder did hurt, as did his back. The train had slammed to a stop, and Evan Paine stood somewhere in the car cussing out the conductor for trying to kill them all.

"You all right?"

Slowly Garrett held out his hand, let Ol' Corb pull him to his feet. He shook his head clear, nodding gingerly as Corbett repeated his question.

"Yeah." He rubbed his shoulder. Nothing broken, likely not even a bad bruise. His pride had been hurt more than anything, just like the time Ollie Sinclair had pulled that prank on him over at the Flying V spread along the Picketwire.

Paine had stopped screaming at the conductor, turning

his frustrations to higher powers. He cursed God, cursed his luck, cursed Arizona, and his own stupidity. Conductor Bryan Crowne had hurried over to Corbett and Garrett, muttering his apologies to Garrett, praying that he had not hurt himself in his fall.

"I'm fine," Garrett snapped, embarrassment rising. "What happened?"

Paine screamed the answer, cursing the snowdrift that had stopped the train.

"A blizzard!" Paine bellowed. "A damned blizzard in April!" Paine's laugh held no mirth, and he slammed his hat against a frozen window.

Chapter Eleven

Dawn broke over a sea of white, a wet, heavy snow blanketing piñons, chamisa, scorched earth, and, most importantly, the steel rails of the Grand Cañon Railway. Towering drifts had stopped the old locomotive, which now *hissed* and *creaked* while the engineer and fireman tackled a six-foot mound with shovel and pick.

"We'll have a snowplow here directly," conductor Bryan Crowne said. "Don't worry. You'll be after that gang of black-hearts directly. Why don't you-all step back inside, warm yourself by the fire? Not much to do out here."

The fireman and engineer must have had the same idea, realizing the futility of their labors, and returned the hardware and themselves to the warmth of the locomotive's cab. Outside the smoking car, Deputy Sheriff Evan Paine spat out his contempt at the conductor. "*Directly?* Mister, by the time that . . . ." He stopped, shaking his head, knowing he couldn't change a thing.

Corbett and Paine stood on the rear platform of the smoking car, while Garrett stepped into the snow beside the conductor.

"We ain't the only folks a-bein' caught by this storm," said Ol' Corb, warming his hands on a mug of coffee. "Ollie Sinclair ain't a-goin' nowhere, neither."

Running a gloved hand over his whiskered face, Lin Garrett stared east. Clear blue skies and a warming sun meant the snow would disappear, except in a few shadowy crevices, in two days or so. Granted, it would take more than just "directly" for the railroad's snowplow to make it here and clear a path for the Baldwin. By then, Ollie Sinclair would be out of reach. Yet Ol' Corb had also made a valid point. Sinclair had been stopped by the blizzard, too. He would not stay put, though, would light out quickly. The way Garrett saw things, at this very moment Ollie Sinclair was saddling his horse. He'd plow through snowdrifts to get to Utah. Had to.

Yet the train had taken Garrett a fair distance north, miles past the robbery site. Maybe far enough.

"Conductor," Garrett said softly as Crowne gripped the metal railings and started to climb up the steps.

The man turned toward Garrett, uncertain.

"Open the stock car," Garrett ordered. "Reckon we'll be taking our leave."

"Surely you can't be serious!" Crowne stepped back in dismay. "Drifts are four feet high in places. You'll fall in an *arroyo*, break a horse's leg . . . ." His voice trailed off, and he clucked his tongue, glancing at the stock car. On the other hand—Garrett could see the conductor's mind working—it would be much better to be rid of the posse, to send away the lawmen who had figured out the conductor's lie about the previous day's events.

"Well," the conductor drawled, "if you are sure."

"Pretty sure," Garrett said, pulling up his collar.

With a groan, Corbett emptied his coffee cup. Anxious, Evan Paine had no reservations about riding out, no matter the risk. Anything would be better than waiting aboard a stalled train. Inside the stock car, they saddled their mounts before easing them down into the snow, tightening cinches, then mounting.

"Where do you think?" Paine asked. Ol' Corb didn't have to ask; he already knew.

"Red Mountain." Garrett pointed a gloved finger at the horizon above the rolling, piñon-studded hills.

It made sense. Ollie Sinclair might have tried to steer clear of Holly Mossman's place, but the storm would have forced him to seek shelter.

"Red Mountain?" Paine sounded skeptical. "That's pretty near Flagstaff and the law."

"Ollie's guessing the law's still riding west," Garrett said. "Besides . . . ." He was dead right, knowing Sinclair the way he did.

"All right." Paine fished out one of those thin note pads Garrett had seen ranchers carry lately, watched as the lawman scratched out a note and handed it to the conductor, telling him to make sure it got delivered to the right people. Sheriff Oldridge, Garrett assumed, or someone else with the main posse.

Garrett kicked his horse into a walk, giving Scarlet Knight plenty of rein, letting the gelding pick its own path through the snow.

The pain in his back and legs felt little short of murder, and the trail they cut all that day worsened Garrett's agony. A burning sensation struck both feet, Garrett's first thought being frostbite, but then he could recall that doctor, not the Williams ruffian but the pleasant gent from Flagstaff, giving him his verdict back at the poor farm. "Peripheral neuropathy" the doc had called it. A couple of $10 words, Garrett figured. Garrett knew what was ailing him. It came from seventy years of a hard life.

"You all right?" Ol' Corb asked.

"Fine," he said.

"Well, I gotta pee." Corbett hollered at Paine, riding ahead, to hold up, and he reined in the sorrel and swung from the saddle into knee-high snow. "You need to, too?"

Garrett shook his head.

"Then hold my reins. And don't stare at me while I'm a-tryin' to lessen this load in my bladder. Takes me forever these days."

That had never been a problem for Garrett. Fact was, he should have joined Ol' Corb on the ground, unbuttoned his fly, and emptied his kidneys, but he could hold it for a spell. Urinating didn't trouble him as much as the prospect of getting back on Scarlet Knight.

His bones ached—docs called this another high-dollar word, "osteitis"—his muscles cramped easily, he had trouble breathing from time to time, seemed to be suffering from a touch of jaundice of late, had developed a red, bumpy rash on his left forearm, and now his feet felt like they had been set afire. Yet for the first time in years, he felt suddenly alive.

This is what his life had been about. Not riding the rails with tramps, scraping by, almost begging for hand-outs. Not mucking stalls for Easterners at some Wyoming ranch. Not mending an ancient saddle in a hospital for the indigent. Not swamping out a saloon or grocery for a meal. Not contemplating stealing a Chevrolet for three bucks. He felt like a lawman again, trailing a band of desperate men, and this gave him purpose, even if one of the men he intended to bring back or kill had been one of his best friends.

"Thanks," Ol' Corb was saying, taking the reins from Garrett, struggling to find a stirrup and mount the big sorrel.

"You deputies finished?" Paine asked impatiently.

With a snort of contempt, Ol' Corb kicked the horse forward, Garrett following close behind, always looking ahead.

Pushing through banks of melting snow, carefully climbing in and out of gullies, maneuvering through trees, brush, and boulders, the three men made little progress all that morning and far into the afternoon. Several times, much to Garrett's displeasure, rugged terrain and tired horses forced them to dismount and lead their mounts through the snow, which by mid-afternoon had decreased to only boot-high. The blizzard had played itself out by the time it got this far east.

Once, Ol' Corb's horse stumbled into a deep depression, leaving only the sorrel's head and Corbett's head and torso sticking out of the white snow. Corbett had laughed at his predicament, recalling a bit a propaganda some newspaper, the *Daily Star*, Ol' Corb remembered it, had printed back in the late 1880s.

" 'Why come to Arizona? Because there are neither blizzards nor tornadoes, earthquakes or inundations, snowstorms or cyclones. Because there is health in every breeze, and strength and vigor under its cloudless skies.' Well, it's like my pappy used to say . . . 'Only believe half of what another man tells you, and nothin' in no newspaper.' "

The sorrel picked its way out of the hole, lunging the final hurdle, and they rode on. For the next few hours, no one, not even Ol' Corb, spoke.

"How far?" Paine finally asked, but Garrett could only shrug. The burning had left his feet—perhaps from snow freezing his boots—and, much to his delight, he had no trouble mounting the gelding when they finally decided to ride again.

The wind had picked up that afternoon, cold, violent, unrelenting, and the sun began dipping low into the horizon. Night would be brutal, maybe not snowing, but icy, moonless. Garrett dreaded that. His bones dreaded it. He could picture Ollie Sinclair a few miles northeast, sitting in the cabin at Red Mountain, bouncing Holly's grandbabies on his knee, sipping coffee that had been sweetened with whiskey. No, not now. Ollie Sinclair had left Holly by now, was slugging his way northeast, through Cedar Wash, likely as tired and miserable as Garrett felt.

"I say we ride all night," Paine declared as they picked their way through a piñon forest. "Snow'll make it like daylight with the moon and all."

"What moon?" Ol' Corb said. "Ain't you checked your almanac, Deputy?"

Garrett blinked once they cleared the trees, unbelieving. They had made better progress than he had realized. On the other hand, they had been in and out of the saddle for the better part of twelve, no, fourteen hours. His body certainly felt it. He pointed a trembling finger down the hill.

"Might not need the moon," he said. "There's the road."

Parallel tracks stretched northward in the snow-carpeted road. No hoof prints, nothing but those two lines, except a few slices in the snow from a coyote and jack rabbit or two. So only one horseless carriage had made its way from Flagstaff toward Red Mountain after the blizzard.

"Looks like somebody left Flagstaff to go sightseeing," Paine said, pointing northward.

"Automobile ain't none of our concern," Ol' Corb reminded them. "Men we's a-chasin', they be on horses."

And the snow had covered all of their tracks.

"Let's ride," Garrett said.

★ ★ ★ ★ ★

Paine saw the yellow truck first, the front end buried in a ditch, icicles dangling from the red wheels and hard rubber tires. The truck, Paine said, was an International Harvester, cost about $900 brand-new, and what a waste, wrecking it like this. "Always wanted one of them things for myself," Paine said, with a menacing laugh. "Then I'd run that idiot of a mayor off the road in his highfalutin Chevrolet."

"Maybe you can take this one," Ol' Corb said.

Although night was coming fast, Garrett looked beyond the truck, detecting no footprints. The driver had to be inside, so he quickly swung down, ground-reining the gelding, and hurried toward the International Harvester.

"Come on, old man!" Paine yelled. "We've no time for this."

Inside the truck, the man slumped forward, head against the steering wheel. That's all Garrett could see. He fished a match out of his coat pocket, struck it on his thumbnail, ignoring Paine's shouts that the driver was no concern of theirs, that the cad had gotten what he deserved. The truck had no doors, was as open as an old Studebaker wagon, and likely the truck's owner had already frozen to death. Wind blew out the flame, but Garrett had seen enough. Gasping, he leaned inside, praying as he grabbed the body, pulling the crumpled figure onto the road.

A low moan escaped the driver's lips, and Garrett let out a quick prayer of thanks.

"We need a fire!" Garrett bellowed. "Warm this boy up, get his blood circulating."

"He's dead," Paine fired back.

"No!" Garrett yelled. Doubt crept in. Had he only imagined the moan? Leaning forward, he pressed his cheek close to the lad's mouth and nose, pulled off his gloves, tried to find a heartbeat.

"Get off your horse," he now heard Ol' Corb ordering, "afore I drag you off, Paine. I'll get some firewood, while you figure out how to steal some gasoline out of that there thing. That way, it'll be sure to burn. Move it, man! Time's a-wastin'."

Garrett could feel a pulse, and breath on his cheeks. He pushed himself back, jaw firm, eyes thankful, staring down at the young man, half frozen, an ugly bump on his forehead covered with dried blood, and a city policeman's badge pinned to the lapel of his coat.

Daric Mossman was still alive.

The fire felt good, even if Garrett didn't care for the stench of gasoline. He massaged Daric Mossman's hands and fingers while Ol' Corb rubbed the boy's toes. Paine just sat in front of the fire, sipping whiskey and hating the fact they had made camp here, just off the road a few feet from the International Harvester, and not closer to Red Mountain and Ollie Sinclair.

"You're one lucky boy," Garrett said warmly.

"I feel like a bloody idiot." Mossman's teeth chattered.

"What were you thinking?" Garrett said. "Driving like that, after a blizzard?"

Bundled beneath the three saddle blankets, wet sides up, the young lawman tested his head, wincing at the pain, and gently shook his head. "Thinking about Mama. About what you said."

Garrett looked away. Back in Flagstaff, after the robbery, he had goaded young Mossman, preached about duty, protecting his mother, argued how he should head to Red Mountain, keep his family out of harm's way, out of Ollie

112

Sinclair's way. In doing so, Garrett had almost gotten Daric Mossman killed. Undoubtedly the lad would have frozen to death had not Garrett and the others happened by, and that had been pure luck.

"Well," Garrett said after a moment, "reckon you might keep all your digits."

"And Ollie Sinclair will keep his eighty thousand dollars." Whiskey slurred Evan Paine's speech.

Mossman's eyes squinted. "What did he say?"

"Pay him no mind." Garrett reached over, grabbed a coffee pot, and refilled Mossman's mug. Pot, mug, and Arbuckle's had been found inside the International Harvester. Paine's supplies consisted of a few sacks of jerky and a handful of bottles of Cedar Brook Whiskey, and the whiskey would be gone directly.

Suddenly Mossman giggled, spilling coffee onto the saddle blankets. "Looks like you're going to see Mama, Mister Garrett," he said lightly. "Feature that, sir. I got you to Red Mountain, after all."

Chapter Twelve

Colorado and Arizona
1876

He hadn't even noticed all those Easterners pouring off the train in La Junta. Ollie Sinclair had, though. So drunk had Garrett and Ol' Corb been, they never realized their pard had left them inside the Rusty Rowel until he came sauntering inside with a smug grin and a harebrained scheme only three inebriated, unemployed cowboys would call sound.

"Boston?" Garrett sniggered after Sinclair revealed what the sodbusters planned. "And they're going . . . where?"

"San Francisco Peaks," Sinclair answered, then had to explain that those mountains lay in northern Arizona, a pretty good haul—especially considering that those sodbusters planned on walking that distance, using old prairie schooners to transport their farming implements, tools, and necessities.

"In February?" Ol' Corb refilled Sinclair's tumbler.

The way Sinclair explained it, forty-seven men and three women had delusions of farming along the Little Colorado River, and that was only the beginning. Another party of fifty would be coming right behind them in the next few weeks, conscripted by the Arizona Colonization Company of Boston, Massachusetts. A lot of jackasses, Ol' Corb labeled them, and Garrett agreed. Somebody in Boston, likely a gang of confidence men, had a pretty good deal going, charging idiots for a part of country most sheepherders even avoided. Not that he had ever been to the San Francisco Peaks, not even Arizona Territory, but he had heard enough accounts to know that the only folks who dared settle in that patch of desert were Navajos and ne'er-do-wells.

"They figure on *farming?*" Garrett laughed, reaching for the bottle till he saw it was empty. He started to flag the bartender over, but remembered they were out of money, and Seamus O'Rourke had less inclination to give credit to out-of-work cowboys in February than any other whiskey peddler in southeastern Colorado did.

"Farmin' ain't the half of it, Lin," Sinclair said. "You should see how wide their eyes get. Not only do they think they can make a living on some quarter section, they figure the creeks and mountains are ripe with gold and silver, for the pickin'."

It was Ol' Corb's time to laugh. "Like my pappy once tol' me . . . 'You can't talk sense to no fool.' "

"They're fools, maybe, but no one in this town's eager to send them home. They're practically runnin' Silverman's Mercantile out of merchandise, fillin' up wagons they bought from Mister Best. Bought horses and oxen at Bookbinder's livery to pull them wagons. And here's the rub."

Eyes sparkling, and not from O'Rourke's forty-rod, Ollie Sinclair pounded his elbows on the table and leaned forward, pushing back his big hat to reveal that unruly red hair. Garrett had seen that look many times over the past three, four years, usually to his regret.

"You remember Ted Cutter, don't you?" Sinclair asked.

115

Cutter had worked on Wallace Johnston's spread along the Picketwire for a spell, before the big Scot let the worthless saddle tramp go. Afterward, Cutter had done a few odd jobs around La Junta, everything from shooting antelope for the café to dealing faro for O'Rourke, till his luck ran out when he consumed five fingers of bad whiskey (not at O'Rourke's). A spinster found him in her cistern the next morning. That had been the biggest event of the past year until the first greenhorns from the Arizona Colonization Company showed up a few hours ago.

"Sure," Ol' Corb answered. "We was pallbearers, remember?"

"Well, Cutter had been employed to guide these folks to the Little Colorado, him and a couple of pards, though nobody knows who them pards would be." Sinclair's smile broadened.

"If you're a-thinkin' . . . ," Ol' Corb began.

"Seventy-five dollars a month," Sinclair said, "for each of us. That's what I'm thinkin', and that's what these Yankees have agreed to. They was willin' to pay Cutter that, so they'll pay us in his stead."

Garrett saw Ol' Corb staring at him, and slowly shook his head. "I'm not one to lead a bunch of greenhorns to their ruin or deaths, Ollie, because that's all that'll be waiting for them in Arizona." Actually he was also thinking about his father, and wondering about Ollie Sinclair's real motive.

"Besides," Ol' Corb added, "what would we do once we got to Arizona?"

Sinclair's booming laugh rocked the table, knocking the empty bottle onto the dirt floor, and he leaned back, his big head shaking. "Don't you boys want to see the elephant? Cattle's big in Arizona. Prescott's boomin'. We could find work cowboyin' in no time, at better wages, too, I warrant. Not only that, but it's a whole lot more promisin' than this god-forsaken patch of nothin'."

"Yeah, but guiding them? Criminy," Ol' Corb said, "we ain't never been to that part of the country. How could we guide 'em?"

"I've been there," Sinclair announced. "Grew up in Utah, boys, after my folks got run out of Missouri, cut my teeth on red sandstone. Drifted down to Arizona many a time. Not much country I don't know between the Virgin and Salt Rivers. And if these Yankees are payin' that much money for guides, no tellin' what else they might have to offer us."

"I ain't a-doin' nothin' I can't do from the back of the horse," Ol' Corb announced.

"You'll stay on your horse, Corb. Only them sodbusters will be walkin', walkin' behind those rickety Conestogas Mister Best couldn't sell for kindlin' . . . till today."

Sinclair's eyes locked on Garrett. While Randolph Corbett's father had said many things, Garrett had learned over the past decade, he found himself thinking about one of his father's offerings, wondering if it applied to Ollie Sinclair.

If a man's never had a chance to steal, that doesn't mean he's honest.

"Lin, if you're happy riding the grubline till spring, hoping old man Johnston will hire you back for twenty-five and found, that's fine. I just think you ought to listen to what these Bostonians have to say."

That's what lured Lin Garrett out of the Rusty Rowel, that and the fact that he needed fresh air, plus money unless he wanted O'Rourke to throw him out.

He stared in disbelief at the commotion in the streets,

young men in striped britches and woolen coats loading a handful of relics of wagons with flour and bacon and seeds for grain. Fools. The lot of them.

A broad-faced man with a flat-crown straw hat crossed the wide street and vigorously shook Sinclair's hand, then Corbett's, and finally Garrett's, arm pumping like a thirsty man at a well, with a vise for a grip, introducing himself as Timothy Coyne.

"I'm glad you're with us, gentlemen," Coyne said in a brogue Garrett could barely understand. "When I heard of the late Mister Cutter's fate, I felt the burden of Moses on my shoulders, but now I know we shall see the Promised Land, after all. Glory to God!"

"There's nothing promising about Arizona," Garrett said, "no glory, certainly no God." He hadn't meant to say a thing. Whiskey had done the talking. Coyne stared at him, his ecstatic face replaced by a grimness, leaving Garrett wishing he had taken his chances with Seamus O'Rourke in the saloon.

A new voice turned his head. "Have you ever been there, Mister . . . ?"

He saw her then, and suddenly felt sober, or maybe ashamed, as he swept off his hat, only to drop it at his feet, then clumsily stood on it to keep the wind from blowing it to Texas.

"Well . . . ."

"A simple question, Mister . . . ?"

He remembered his manners, and his hat, telling her his name while he grabbed the Stetson and slammed it on his head, tightly, before looking at her again.

Her hair blew in the wind like a horse's tail. Sandy brown, Garrett observed, her eyes a shade lighter. Of slight build, she stood rather tall, and wore a close-fitting red and black plaid dress covered by an unbuttoned greatcoat of Union Army issue. Unlike most recruits of the Arizona Colonization Company, she spoke with no thick accent. In fact, she talked pleasantly, even if her eyes could not conceal her lack of respect for the drunken cowhands swaying before her.

"You haven't answered my question, Lincoln Garrett," she said.

"Well, no, ma'am, I haven't exactly been there, but . . . ."

"Then how do you know a thing about it, sir? And why, pray tell, is my uncle paying you and your colleagues one hundred dollars apiece to guide us?"

Garrett wanted to pull the hat even lower, but something about her comment registered, and he shot Ollie Sinclair a cold stare. That reprobate had mentioned $75, figured on pocketing the rest for himself. Now, Sinclair focused on his own dusty boots.

"I'm waiting, Lincoln Garrett," the woman said.

He tried to find the right words, but he had never been comfortable talking to strangers, especially women, yet, once he managed to straighten, he summoned his courage.

"Well, ma'am, it's like this. This ain't Boston, this ain't Missouri. This is the West, not meant for farming. And if there was gold out there, I reckon somebody would have discovered it by now. That's all I'm saying. Was I you, I'd turn back."

Coyne spoke, saying they were determined to make their community a success, lauding the perseverance of the chosen settlers, that they would employ the most modern methods of farming, turning this Great American Desert into paradise. They would divide the land into lots, form their own government, and grow wheat, fruits, and vegetables. They would transform the Little Colorado River into a garden, a paradise.

"We'll see," Garrett said stubbornly.

The woman laughed. "We'll see," she repeated, shaking her head. "You are set in your ways, Lincoln Garrett," she added before walking away. She looked back, however, and Garrett thought she might have even smiled at him. That, too, was most likely a whiskey-induced illusion. Yet Garrett knew then, the moment she looked back, while Sinclair explained to Coyne that *he* most certainly had been to Arizona, that he would help lead the party West.

Garrett didn't learn her name, though, until they were two weeks on the trail.

"You were right, Lin," Holly Grant told him a few months later.

It didn't make him proud.

They had reached Leroux Spring on May 1, 1876, and Coyne's volunteers went to work, attacking the meadows with back-breaking work, turning Fort Valley into gardens, building homes and barns of logs, working harder than any cowboy Garrett had ever known. Since he had began cowboying after the war, he had disliked sodbusters, disapproved of their jeans and dirty hands, hated their use of the land, yet now he had to respect them, for their effort, their own pride, their resourcefulness, their dreams.

He had seen a lot of Holly Grant, too, more than he had seen his partners. Ol' Corb had taken off less than a week after he had been paid, said he had a hankering to visit Prescott and maybe get a real job, a cowboy job. Sinclair had stayed longer, dancing with Holly as many times as he could during Saturday night hoe-downs, but left after the first hard freeze.

A few days later, the second freeze hit, and this one killed the remaining crops, killed the hopes of the settlers from the Arizona Colonization Company. Nor did they find any gold or silver in the mountains, just wolves and a few Spanish-speaking sheepherders with less tolerance for greenhorns than cowboys.

The weather's unpredictable nature had not surprised him, but the land managed to cast its spell. This wasn't the desert Garrett had imagined at all—although crossing eastern Arizona had certainly been desert, and brutal. Past Cañon Diablo, however, the country began to change, and under the shadow of the San Francisco Peaks, the travelers had found spectacular country: alpine meadows, thick forests, bubbling creeks, and stunning vistas. There was water, too. Only problem, you couldn't control it. It might come as three feet of snowfall, or in a raging thunderstorm with stinging raindrops and hailstones the size of a man's fist, crushing crops and dreams. Melting snow pack atop the mountains transformed creeks into frightening walls of water. On the other hand, rain might not fall for months.

Fit country for cattle and sheep, sometimes, but never for farmers.

Within weeks after the second killing freeze, most of the Bostonians had left Fort Valley for Prescott, but Holly Grant stayed. She was there in early July when the second group of fifty homesteaders arrived from Massachusetts. Tumultuous creeks spilled from their banks shortly afterward, and a devastating hailstorm followed. Finding little more than ruined fields and deserted homesteads, the last group of settlers, and Holly Grant, decided to forsake the Arizona Colonization Company and try their luck in Prescott.

"I wanted you to see this," Holly told him.

They had ridden north, at Holly's suggestion, several miles from the failed farming community, out of the pines and to a patch of red earth lined with piñons and junipers. She pointed to the mountain in the distance, not really a mountain, just a foothill compared to the San Francisco Peaks. The top and sides were verdant, but the middle looked as if some monster had taken a bite out of the mountain, corduroying it with pockmarks and palisades of more red earth.

"Ollie took me here once," Holly told him, and Garrett felt a pang of jealousy. "A few days before he left." She laughed. "I think he wanted me to run away with him to his Zion, but that's his Zion, not mine. This is mine."

"I am sorry, Holly," he said. He meant it, too. By jacks, the only reason he hadn't ridden off to see the elephant was because of Holly. He wanted to be with her, dance with her, and he didn't want to see her fail.

"They call it Red Mountain," Holly said.

"More green than red," Garrett observed.

She smiled, not with humor yet not without mirth, either, and walked back to her horse. "I wanted you to see it, Lin. I wanted you to know that this is going to be my home. Maybe not today. No, I know that can't be, but I'll be back here, and I'll make this my home."

"We'll . . . ." He stopped before saying *see,* studied her as she mounted one of the horses the farmers had bought in La Junta. "I believe you will, Holly," he said.

"We should get back," Holly said. "Independence Day is the day after tomorrow, and I dare say there will be a celebration on our way to Prescott."

He swung into the saddle. "What will you do in Prescott?" he asked.

"Teach school," she said. "Or something. Something that will bring me back here. And you?"

"Punch cattle, I reckon." He followed her down the trail.

Chapter Thirteen

He had punched cattle, too, Garrett remembered as he tossed another piece of wood on the fire, holding his hands out toward the dancing flames. Behind him, over the whipping wind, came Corbett's snores. Paine had also fallen asleep, or passed out, and Daric Mossman had finally drifted off. Surprisingly Garrett felt wide awake. Doc Steinberg and that Muller X-ray tube–wielding Eli Meredith had cautioned Garrett that he would probably become more and more drowsy, that he'd become difficult to wake, but none of that had happened. Nor had other symptoms, leading him to believe, partly, that those sawbones were as worthless as the Union medical corps he had seen during the rebellion. Sure, he didn't have much of an appetite any more, especially compared to Ol' Corb, but he felt alert, and he certainly thought clearly, especially when he remembered those old times.

Holly had told him that he'd be a fine, honest cowboy, and he had been, for a while. Then Ollie Sinclair had ridden back into his life, talking Corbett and Garrett into punching other men's cattle with a wide loop and a running iron. That had brought Sheriff Bob Clagett into their lives, turning Corbett and Garrett into lawmen and sending Ollie Sinclair on the run.

He slept fitfully that night, tormented by the cold and

his memories, and, perhaps, an uneasiness about what the morning would bring. When the others began stirring in the grayness before dawn, Corbett tossed off his bedroll and began stoking the dying embers, putting the coffee pot on top while checking to see that the contents had not frozen during the night.

"Up," he said, kicking Ol' Corb's boots. "We're burning daylight."

"You sound like old man Johnston," Corbett grumbled, but slowly climbed to his feet, stretching and yawning, his breath frosty.

The first thing they had to do, Garrett told them, was to get Daric Mossman's truck out of that ditch, see if it would still run, and they had better tackle that *pronto*. Snow would be melting fast today, turning the road into a Missouri swamp. It would be a lot easier to drive that International Harvester while the road was still frozen.

Mossman chuckled. "You've never driven on ice," he said.

"I'm not sure we need to be taking that truck with us," Paine said. "If the Sinclairs are still at this kid's ma's, the truck will give us away. Horses are quieter. Faster, too. That thing can't run more than twenty miles an hour, and that's not over an ice-coated road."

"Barely reach fifteen miles an hour, maybe sixteen," Mossman said.

Both Mossman and Ol' Corb looked at Garrett, seemingly agreeing that Paine had a legitimate concern, and the point was valid—if the Sinclairs remained at Red Mountain.

"Ollie's not taking a vacation," Garrett said, irked by their doubts. "My guess is he saddled up and headed north about the time we were leaving the train yesterday morn. *If* he even stopped at Holly's. My thinking is this. We send in the boy here in his truck. We watch from the trees. Plenty of trees at Holly's place." At least, there had been. "The boy drives up, goes inside. If he comes out and gives us a wave, we know it's safe. If he ain't out in five minutes, then we make other plans."

He liked the plan, which had come to him while he shivered in his bedroll. Ol' Corb, to his surprise, looked doubtful.

"If Ollie or some of those vermin are still there, Lin, you could get him kilt."

"That ain't gonna happen!" he snapped. "Holly wouldn't let that happen."

"I'm game," Mossman said, ending any argument. "Let's get Mama's truck . . . hope it still runs."

It did. Getting the International Harvester back on the road proved uneventful. Two ropes, two horses pulling, Ol' Corb pushing, and Mossman inside at the wheel, they had the truck back on the road in a matter of minutes. It took longer to start, cold as it was, though, and Garrett's concern mounted that Paine had taken too much gasoline from the tank last night to fuel the fire.

He sat on Scarlet Knight, fretting, scratching his head while kicking free of the stirrups, waiting, praying, when finally the engine caught with an explosion that sent smoke out of the exhaust like an old rifle in the days before smokeless powder. That was the only thought that registered. The next thing he knew, he lay on his back, spread-eagled in the road, eyes bulging, trying to get his lungs to work while Scarlet Knight kicked and snorted and came close to smashing Garrett's head with its forehoofs.

"You all right?"

Mossman knelt beside him, lifting Garrett gently, until

he sat upright, wheezing, trying to make his legs to stop shaking. His feet burned again, too, but at least the gelding had not crippled him. As his vision began to clear, he sucked in precious air, exhaled rapidly, until he knew he wasn't going to die. Wouldn't that have been a story! *Lincoln Garrett, dead at age seventy on the road to Red Mountain, killed when bucked off a horse boogered by a backfiring horseless carriage.*

"I'm . . . fine." He pushed himself to his feet, using Mossman's shoulder as leverage. "Where's my horse?"

Ol' Corb had caught it, stood a few rods away trying to calm that old star-gazer. He swayed when he finally stood, fighting a wave of dizziness, ignoring the protests of Corbett and Mossman as he walked toward the gelding, determined to mount up, prove he was just as ornery as he had been fifty years earlier.

Doubt stopped him, though. Doubt and pride. He knew his legs might not work, and he wasn't about to let Ol' Corb or one of those young lawmen give him a boost into the saddle. Mossman kept arguing that he should ride in the truck, that it was only three or four miles to his mother's place, give him time to make sure he hadn't busted anything on his insides, and give that crazy old horse of his time to get used to the yellow truck.

"Well," Garrett said. "Maybe you're right. We'll stop when we're a mile or so from Holly's. That'll give us time to get in position before you drive on up. Give me some time to tell you what to do just in case it comes to a shooting."

He settled into the strange seat inside the International Harvester, legs pulled up in front of him, the floorboard cold. Never had he stepped inside one of these automobiles, and, when Daric Mossman, wearing goggles and a woolen scarf, released the brake and pressed the accelerator,

Garrett's knuckles tightened. It felt cramped in one of these things, nothing like the freedom he experienced when sitting in a saddle, even if the wind whipped his face.

"It's a two-speed transmission," Mossman explained, his hands sawing the wheel as the truck slipped and sputtered across the icy road. Garrett longed to be horseback. His stomach felt queasy. "New model, came out only last year. I bought it for Mama for Christmas."

Christmas. That was another change he had seen during his lifetime. Before the war, few folks gave presents at Christmas, saving them for New Year's Day. He remembered something Paine had said, something about the price of an International Harvester.

"Nine hundred dollars . . . that's a right smart of money," he said, closing his eyes as the truck slid down a hill, sideways, picking up speed in its descent. Garrett figured they would flip over, but Mossman managed to regain control and straighten the wheels once the road leveled out.

"Mama's worth it. Anyway, I got a loan at the bank."

He stopped himself from snorting with contempt. Banks? Loans? He had never stepped inside a bank except as a lawman or as a customer wanting to change a gold piece, never had much use for banks. He laughed at himself. *Never had any money to put in a bank.*

"If you got it for your mother, why are you driving it?"

Garrett figured he knew the answer, hoped he did, anyway. *Holly Mossman raised horses, by jacks, had no interest in some horseless carriage.* That wasn't the answer, however.

"Oh, Mama has me keep it during the winter, bring her supplies from Flagstaff, that kind of thing. Besides, she has an old Ford Model N."

Holly Mossman with two automobiles! Hard to picture, hard to stomach, but then Holly had always been one to see the future, to look ahead. At least, she still raised horses.

He summoned enough courage to look at Mossman, and decided he liked the view better than staring out the front, seeing every tree and boulder the truck could slam into. He found himself staring at Holly, blinked away the illusion, and noticed the badge pinned on Mossman's coat.

"Better take off that badge, boy," he said. "Just in case Ollie ain't worn out his welcome."

He regretted those instructions, biting his lip when the young lad lifted his right hand off the steering wheel and unclipped the badge, controlling the truck with only one hand until he tossed the tin star on the dash and returned his right hand to its proper place on the black, ugly wheel.

"Thanks," Mossman said.

"What made you become a lawman, boy?" Garrett asked unexpectedly.

"I'd like to say it was because of you, sir. Though I scarcely remember you. You rode out when I was just a boy, but Mama, even Pop, had many stories to tell about the great Lin Garrett and Randolph Corbett. But, if you want the truth, well, it's the only job I could find."

He grinned, knowing that feeling.

"How about you, Mister Garrett? What made you pin on a star?"

"Ollie Sinclair," he replied, and chanced a look at the snowy road.

For two years, he had cowboyed around Prescott. Holly had tried to become a schoolteacher, then, disliking the board of education's restrictions, had slung hash and stitched clothes before becoming a laundress at Camp Verde, soon to be promoted to Fort Verde, about thirty-five miles east on the Verde River's west bank. It was there that Holly met a young second lieutenant with the 6th Cavalry. Ben Mossman had wide shoulders and a ramrod straight back, pretty nice-looking lad, although his toes stuck inward so much he practically wobbled around like a duck. Garrett never dreamed that Holly Grant would take a liking to such a prig.

Yet Ben Mossman was an officer and a gentleman, a man building a reputation in this man's army, too, had distinguished himself when the troops had moved almost 1,500 Apaches from the Verde reservation over to San Carlos back in 1875. Yes, sir, folks said, Ben Mossman would be a fine catch for some lady. Could give a woman a future in this wild region.

Ben Mossman might have been the reason Lin Garrett had agreed to join Ollie Sinclair.

Sinclair had shown up in Prescott with another crazy scheme. No sense in letting those ranchers get wealthy while Garrett, Corbett, and other cowboys broke their backs for $30 a month. By thunder, the ranchers wouldn't even let cowboys own their own horses, and that was criminal. They'd just take a few head, Sinclair said, and it wasn't really stealing. Half the cattlemen between California and Texas, even old man Johnston, had thrown a wide loop at one time. That's how they had built their herds. Ranchers here wouldn't miss a few head.

"Where do we sell them?" Ol' Corb had asked.

"My brother Troy," Sinclair had answered. "He knows some ranchers around New Harmony who ain't too particular. We sell them to Troy in Utah, he takes over from there."

"And how do we get them beeves to Utah?"

"Got some friends of the family at Lee's Ferry. Won't be easy, herding cattle through that country, but the law won't be expecting that. They'll figure we'll go south or west."

Of course, the law didn't have to figure it out. A posse jumped them while they were slapping a running iron onto one of Senator Owen Dunlap's heifers. Ollie Sinclair had reacted first, leaping into his saddle and spurring away while Ol' Corb and Garrett had found themselves staring down barrels of several rifles.

"What happened?" Mossman asked.

"Figured they'd hang us," Garrett replied, enjoying the memory. "Probably would have, too, only Sheriff Bob Clagett looked us over, must have seen something he liked. He asked us who we'd been riding with, said if we told him that they wouldn't string us up, just give us a day to light out of the territory, but we didn't say a word. Clagett must have liked that about us, too. I mean, we could have lied, could have said any name, even Jed Dunlap, the senator's son. That snake wasn't beyond stealing from his old man. But we just kept our traps shut. So he, Clagett, I mean, says, and I ain't making this up . . . he says . . . 'All right, gents, I'll give you a choice.' "

Thirty-five years later, he still couldn't believe that offering. Clagett had held out a pair of badges. *Ride with the law, or ride a rope to hell.* That was the choice. On that day, Lin Garrett and Randolph Corbett had sworn to uphold the law. They had become deputies, rather than be hanged.

"Best pull over here," Garrett said.

"You remember the way!" The International Harvester slid to a stop, and Garrett climbed out of the truck. Yeah, he remembered Red Mountain, every detail. He felt a bit stiff, bruised from the fall, and waited for Corbett, leading Scarlet Knight, and Paine to ride up.

His boots crunched snow as he walked away, took the reins, grabbed the horn, and fought the agony as he climbed into the saddle, moving slowly, gingerly, keeping his body close to the horse. With a grunt, he rocked the saddle to his right, and gave Mossman a final nod.

130

"Give us ten minutes, boy. Then drive on up the road. Don't do nothing fast, just in case. Just act like you were calling on your mother for Sunday dinner. We'll be in the woods over yonder. You got a pistol?"

Actually Mossman had two: a 1890 Remington revolver holstered on his left hip, butt forward, and a 1900 .38 automatic he slipped into his coat pocket. "I figure if they see the Remington, they won't look for the Colt," Mossman said.

Garrett nodded approvingly. Boy was smart, and had more backbone than most folks his age.

"Be careful, boy," he said.

"Just one thing," Mossman said. "The name's not boy. It's Daric."

Garrett couldn't stop the grin as Mossman climbed into the truck, waiting for the riders to move out.

Chapter Fourteen

Maybe he was losing his faculties, turning as loony as one of those opium addicts back at the poor farm. Garrett's heart pounded when he spotted the International Harvester weaving over the road leading to Holly Mossman's spread. Foolish, it was, sending that boy down there, alone. If Sinclair and his cut-throats were still there, Garrett's plan might wind up getting Holly's son killed. He felt cold, not necessarily from the biting wind.

He stood underneath a snow-laden piñon, Scarlet Knight hobbled several rods behind him, Evan Paine crouched somewhere on his left, and Ol' Corb on his right, scattered about, all with a clear view of the ranch and trading post, the Flagstaff road, and Red Mountain.

The yellow truck slid to a stop between the cabin and corrals. After removing his driving goggles and scarf, Daric Mossman stepped out cautiously. The policeman looked around, suspicious, nervously unbuttoning his coat and—Garrett cringed—placing his right hand on the butt of his Remington.

"Don't do anything fast, boy," Garrett whispered, and braced the Marlin against his shoulder, pointing the barrel toward the windowpane nearest young Mossman. He muttered an oath. Stupid, he was, a worthless old man. Oh, sure, he could see Daric Mossman as clear as he could have fifty years ago; however, the rifle sights blurred. Doctors had treated him for his myriad ailments, or tried to, but nary a one had given him anything to improve his vision. Just a pair of spectacles. That's all he needed, though, prideful as he was, he wondered if he would have worn them. Definitely he longed for them now. If it came to shooting, at this distance, he'd be practically blind, firing on instinct.

Holly's ranch and trading post lay nestled between thick groves of piñon and juniper, snow-capped Red Mountain looming behind it. He remembered the ranch vividly, clearly; only the trading post was new. Shortly after the turn of the century, she had added that little adobe hut a quarter mile from the main ranch, just off the turn-off from the road leading toward the national monument. She sold Navajo blankets, leather items, jewelry, and, these days, gasoline. A hand-painted sign creaked beneath a wooden Indian, about the only thing at the post that wasn't authentic, but, Garrett assumed, it would stop the tourists. That and the gasoline.

Garrett concentrated on the main ranch. He couldn't visualize Ollie Sinclair hiding in that trading post, even to lay an ambush. For that matter, Sinclair had never been one for ambuscade. He'd want you to know who killed you, and make sure you didn't catch a bullet in the back. By jacks, Jed Dunlap, even that squirt on the Grand Cañon train, they had been facing Sinclair when they died. In that regard, Ollie Sinclair had always been a fair man.

Horses snorted and pranced around in the corrals, and others whinnied from inside the barn. Lot of mounts, but that didn't mean a thing. For nigh thirty years, Holly and Ben Mossman had raised horses here. Running as many as 140 head was not unusual, another factor that might have brought Ollie Sinclair this way. Garrett almost grinned, thinking back to one spring day back in '85 or '86 when Holly had said: "Horses are like family." And Ben Mossman, in a rare display of wit, had quipped: "Yeah, but we could use less family."

His middle finger pressed against the trigger, index finger stretched out just beneath the side ejection and behind the loading gate, the case-hardened metal cold to the touch. He had removed the glove on his right hand, for a better feel, never understanding how some men could pull a trigger, accurately, wearing gloves.

Young Mossman had started moving toward the cabin, hand still on the revolver, picking his way across the slush and patches of ice. Melting ice dripped onto the brim of Garrett's hat, thumping rhythmically. The deputy gripped the railing and placed a boot on the first of three steps, climbing, then turning, hearing something, spinning, falling. Garrett heard the noise, saw the movement, spun himself, part of him watching Daric Mossman, making sure he was all right, while trying to draw a bead on the speaking figure emerging from the barn.

Almost immediately he released pressure on the trigger, lifting the barrel just to be safe, calling out—"Don't shoot!"—to Corbett and Paine, echoing Daric Mossman's own cries. The door to the cabin burst open and a gangling boy rushed outside and leaped into the sprawled lawman, who had apparently slipped on the ice when he heard the voice from the barn.

Slowly Garrett rose, staring at the woman silhouetted inside the barn door.

"Come on down, Lin!" Holly Mossman shouted, looking directly toward him although she couldn't possibly see him. "I've been expecting you!"

He didn't know what to expect as he led Scarlet Knight down the road, which was beginning to show more red mud than dirty snow. Holly moved from the barn, helped Daric and her grandson to their feet, and ushered them inside, but not before she made Daric pull off his muddy boots. In the doorway, she peeled off her coat, scarf, and hat, then waited.

At the corrals, one pen was empty, the gate open, water trough full, so Garrett led the gelding inside, took off the bridle and loosened the cinch. Holly had been expecting them. "Put your horses in here!" he told Ol' Corb and Paine, and, still carrying the Marlin, covered the last few yards, his stomach queasy, legs shaking. At the foot of the steps, he stopped, looking up, trying to figure out what he should say.

She was older, Garrett knew, a little heavier, the sandy brown hair coarse and gray, her once pale Boston skin bronzed and creased from years underneath Arizona's blistering sun. Her eyes hadn't changed, though, still brown, capable of dancing with laughter and love—or burning hotter than a cathode ray tube. She remained pretty, especially when her thin, chapped lips slowly turned upward into a smile.

"Hello, Lin. Been a . . . ." She paused. Holly had never been one for making banal statements. "Coffee's boiling. You and your deputies come inside." She shot a glance toward Corbett and Paine, looked back at Garrett. "That all you got with you?"

Before Garrett could respond, she quickly looked back at the corral, her eyes brightening, smile growing, and she stepped forward.

"Randolph! Randolph Corbett . . . is that you?"

"It's me, Holly. Hope you still got that rockin'

something to sweeten up your lousy coffee."

Her laugh hadn't changed a bit, either. Still musical. Yet when she looked back at Garrett, the laughter had vanished, and her eyes hardened. "What are you doing, Lin, bringing that old man out on this fool's errand?"

His tongue refused to co-operate, not that he had any defense, and he didn't much feel like arguing with her, especially in front of her blood kin, Paine, and Ol' Corb. Besides, he could smell the coffee, and, unlike his partner, he had always found Holly's coffee rather satisfying. Not only that, but his bones ached. By jacks, even that rocking chair sounded good right about now.

Ol' Corb came to his rescue. "Hey, little lady, I'm younger than that ol' man. Let's not stand out here and catch frostbite. Holly, this here is Deputy Sheriff Evan Paine. Deputy, meet Missus Holly Mossman."

Paine made some sort of grunt, didn't even tip his hat.

"Boots stay on the porch," Holly said as she turned. "Hats and coats you can hang up inside. Oh, yeah, leave your hardware on the porch, too." Her voice raised. "That goes for you, too, Daric! You know better than bring a gun under my roof."

"Where I go, my guns go." Paine spoke to Holly's back. "It's policy."

"Then you stay outside," Holly said without turning around. "That's policy."

Over coffee and biscuits, they learned that Ollie Sinclair had indeed stopped during the blizzard: Ollie, Troy, Handsome Harry Prudhomme and two other men Holly didn't recognize. She didn't learn their names, either, nor had she wanted to. They had ridden out yesterday shortly after dawn.

Garrett felt vindicated. He had been right.

Paine, however, lashed out angrily. "Rode out on fresh horses!" he snapped. The deputy had relented, leaving his weapons on the porch, the lure of whiskey-sweetened coffee and a warm fire greater than his policy. Garrett wished the lawman had stayed outside. "You swapped fresh mounts for his winded horses."

"Seemed like a good trade to me," Holly said. "Horses they took are still green."

She sat across from the others, resting in a colorful tête-à-tête, trimmed with worsted fringe, pretty fancy for a log home and out of place amid all the other rough-hewn furniture. The boy, Penny's son, lay on her lap, eyes closed. He had tried to stay awake, had kept his eyes focused on Garrett, but eventually exhaustion overtook him.

"Well, the state of Arizona and Coconino County might think otherwise, ma'am. It's called aiding and abetting train robbers."

She snorted. "Deputy, if you want to arrest me, go ahead." She held out her hands as if awaiting the manacles. "You can take me back to Flagstaff, send Garrett and Corbett on after the rest. All I know is what I read in the newspaper, and that's that Ollie Sinclair was freed from prison, having completed his sentence. I knew nothing of any train robbery when I traded for their horses."

She was lying, Garrett knew, had always been good at lying, but Paine backed down, interested in another point. "You said there were five men?"

"Yes."

"Well, eight robbed that train. One's dead. So where are the other two?"

Garrett answered. "Split up. Other two probably rode west, give Oldridge something to chase."

"What if one of those two has all that money?"

"Oh," Corbett offered, "I'd bet they already split it up. Ain't like the olden times. Outlaws don't trust each other these days."

That seemed to satisfy Paine, who announced that they should get moving, quit wasting time while the Sinclair gang got closer to Utah. He left without another word, the slamming door punctuating his departure.

Daric Mossman rose next, rubbed the sleeping boy's hair, told his mother to tell Benji good bye for him, and walked out, followed by a slow-moving, coffee-slurping Randolph Corbett.

After finishing his coffee, Garrett walked toward the corner rack, grabbing his coat and hat, waiting for Holly to call out his name. She did, and he turned.

"Ollie knows you're coming after him." Her smile and laugh held little mirth. "I told him you wouldn't, but I knew you would."

He waited for the men outside to put on their boots and gun belts and move toward the corral before speaking.

"Ollie likely robbed that train because he knew I was here."

The eyes blazed again. "You know better than that, Lincoln Garrett. He didn't even know you were in Flagstaff until I told him. He robbed that train because, well, because he's Ollie. You know that. But when I told him about you, you should have seen his eyes. He's changed, Lin." Her head shook away the image, or maybe she was trembling. "I hardly recognized him. Almost cried when I saw . . . . Anyway, he said you'd be coming after him, said that's the way things should be."

Maybe he's right. Garrett buttoned his coat, then remembered he would have to unbutton it to strap on his gun belt.

His fingers worked the buttons again. Perhaps he was just stalling.

He looked around the cabin, pretty spartan, just a few pieces of furniture, a crucifix hanging on one wall, a cracked mirror on another, and in one corner, a small table, full of small candles surrounding an old photograph. Holly was Catholic. As a backsliding Baptist, Garrett didn't know what you called that display of photo and candles, but it had to be some kind of memorial. The photo was a wedding picture of Holly's daughter and her son-in-law, both killed during the influenza outbreak a few years back. All the candles had been lit, probably after Ollie Sinclair had ridden out.

"Troy and Harry I know," Garrett made himself say. "What about those other two riding with him?"

Holly shrugged. "About the same as that one riding with you."

When she wanted to, needed to, she could rake him with spurs. That part about her hadn't changed, either. He could tell she wanted to get up, maybe to hit him, maybe to hug him, but didn't want to wake her sleeping grandson, pinned down on that piece of Sears, Roebuck and Company furniture that belonged in Boston, not Red Mountain.

"He'll be waiting for you. You know that."

Garrett nodded. Likely at Lee's Ferry, if he wasn't there already. He'd send Troy and the others on into Utah, out of Arizona jurisdiction, then sit and wait. Wait to gloat. Wait to kill. Wait to die.

"Why go after him, Lin?" Now, he knew she was about to cry. "Why not let him be?"

He didn't know why; at least, that's what he tried to tell himself. Maybe he was selfish. Maybe he needed to track down Ollie Sinclair again, to prove he could still act like Lin

139

Garrett. Maybe he had been a lawman too long to let a man like Sinclair get away. Or maybe this was a suicide, for both of them, what Ollie Sinclair and Lin Garrett desired. They'd find each other, meet one more time, just like they had at Lee's Ferry in February of 1883 and again in December of 1887. Only this time, neither would back down. They'd kill each other. And, maybe, that's the way it should be.

"You keep Daric safe, Lin. He's all I have now, him and Benji." She rubbed the boy's hair.

She wouldn't ask Garrett to send her son home, not Holly. Besides, Daric Mossman seemed as stubborn as they were, and, as a man sworn to uphold the law, he wouldn't turn back, even if ordered to. Holly knew that as well as Garrett did.

Outside came Paine's voice, urging Garrett to quit dawdling or they'd go on without him. The tear finally broke over its dam—Holly couldn't hold it forever—and slowly rolled down one cheek. She didn't try to hide it, to wipe it away, just looked away from Garrett and stared at her grandson.

He knew why he was determined to bring in or kill Ollie Sinclair.

Benjamin Coyne Carter really didn't look that much like Holly, or Penny, or even Jasper Carter, the boy Holly's daughter had married. He was the spitting image of Oliver Lee Sinclair.

"I don't know why you always protected him," he said. Immediately he regretted those words, and the anger in which he had said them. Holly didn't bother to look up, didn't flinch, acted as if she hadn't heard him, although Garrett knew she had. She just stroked the boy's hair.

Hating himself, Garrett stepped out of Holly's home and into the cold.

Chapter Fifteen

Even crazy old Mrs. Aikin back at the poor farm could have followed Ollie Sinclair's trail out of Red Mountain. Wasn't Sinclair's fault, exactly, having to travel fast and unable to control the weather or make even an attempt to hide his route. Five men on horseback cut a swath through the white landscape, and, when the melting snow finally began disappearing, the marred red mud pointed Garrett's posse in the right direction.

"Won't last," Ol' Corb announced, as if reading Garrett's mind. "You know it. Moisture'll get sucked down right soon, turn this swamp into hard rock again. Then Ollie won't be so easy to track. I've knowed Apaches who couldn't follow a trail in this country."

"I don't need an Apache to follow Ollie," Garrett said.

The riders turned off the road around Cedar Wash. Any tourist puttering along in his horseless carriage would thank Ollie, too, for his consideration, making the road passable from here on to the national monument.

Cedar Wash toward the Painted Desert, then up along the Little Colorado toward the confluence, skittering along Marble Cañon, and on to Lee's Ferry and the Vermilion Cliffs, on through the thick forests north of the cañon, then up the Kanab and into the Virgin River country of Utah.

He could read Ollie Sinclair like a book. Always had. Well, almost always.

The cold front had passed, and spring finally emerged, windy but warm. By late afternoon, most of the snow had vanished, except in shadows and deep ravines. Ollie Sinclair's trail kept moving northeast, though, as Garrett predicted. If he knew of another way, some short cut, some way he could lope ahead and be waiting for the train robbers before Lee's Ferry, Garrett would have taken it, but there was nothing here, nothing but juniper and thick red mud. Too easy.

I should have known better.

That was Garrett's first thought when the shots rang out, one lead ball splintering a juniper branch and peppering his face with bark. He dived out of the saddle as Scarlet Knight pitched forward, snorting, bucking, bolting down the wash. Garrett had reached for the Marlin, tried to jerk it free of the scabbard, but the gelding was too bronchy, scared witless, and Garrett crashed into the quagmire, rolled over, moved for cover, cursing his own stupidity.

His next thought: *Ollie never bushwhacked anyone.*

Yet Holly had warned him, and he remembered her words as he hugged the earth behind a rock and a dead juniper, drawing the Colt from its holster, blowing on the cylinder, making sure the revolver remained free of mud and dirt.

. . . when I told him about you, you should have seen his eyes. He's changed, Lin. I hardly recognized him . . . .

He cursed louder, looked up, his mouth turning to parchment, heart pounding. A bullet sent him back to shelter, mud staining his mustache and sunburned face. It tasted like pure brine.

A rifle popped to his left, and he chanced a glance, relieved to find Ol' Corb a few yards away, spitting round after round from his Winchester, unharmed but wasting lead.

"Don't shoot, you old fool!" Garrett blared. "Not until you see someone to shoot at!"

Corbett actually grinned at him. "It's like my pappy once tol' me . . . ."

"I don't want to hear it!"

Rolling to his right, he hugged the earth, pulled the Colt to full cock, and peeked over the wet earth, holding his breath. "Boy? . . . Daric?"

The answer made him heave a sigh of relief. "I'm all right, sir."

"You ain't hit?"

"No, sir."

"You sure?"

"Yes, sir. Nothing but scared."

Thankful, he licked his lips. *Scared.* He sure knew that feeling.

"Paine?" Garrett called.

No answer.

He tried again, but the result remained the same.

Garrett lifted his head, sweating, ducked after another round, and reached to take off his hat. Only, he wore no hat. He had lost it during the first few shots. He smelled sulphur, brimstone, as if he had passed through the gates of hell. Maybe he had.

"Paine!" He spoke with more urgency, but still heard nothing.

Slowly, carefully he peeked over a rock. He could make out his horse, a quarter mile or so down the wash, right before the bend. Lucky for him Scarlet Knight had stopped there. As much as that horse had bucked when the shooting started, the gelding could have run all the way to Marble Cañon or back to Flagstaff. Daric Mossman's bay mare, which he had borrowed from his mother, was nowhere to be found, either hightailing it back toward Red Mountain, dead, or galloping to parts unknown. He didn't see Ol' Corb's horse, but heard it snort, and knew his partner hadn't forgotten one thing. He had taken care of his mount first. Although prone to burn too much powder, Randolph Corbett had always been level-headed in a shooting affair.

Feeling light-headed, Garrett sank deeper into his bit of cover, and looked for a wound. His feet burned, his legs shook out of control, but he detected no blood, felt no pain he hadn't felt before.

"Paine?" he tried once again, knowing the deputy wouldn't answer.

"Lin . . . ," Ol' Corb called out in a dry whisper.

He looked toward his friend.

"Paine's mount is dead," Corbett said. "In the middle of the wash."

"You see Paine?" Garrett asked.

"Nothin'. Could be behind his hoss. Or there's a whole tree that collapsed from the snow. Could be behind that, too. Could be dead or a-dyin'. Or a-playin' the 'possum."

He chewed on his lip. "Paine!" he yelled for the last time, then decided the bushwhackers had scored one hit. They had killed Deputy Sheriff Evan Paine, or wounded him. Not that he ever cared much for the lawman, but Paine had sand, and ambition. Maybe Paine didn't do things the way Garrett would, and certainly Garrett could never trust a gunman like that, but he would always respect the badge the man wore.

The gunshots had died down. Not even an echo now, not a sound other than Garrett's rapid heartbeat, the creaking of limbs, and an occasional snort from Corbett's sorrel.

"Bit of a pickle," Ol' Corb said.

He had been in worse, though. The rifle shots had come from the other side of the wash, and likely the assassins remained hidden behind those boulders, scrub brush, and junipers. Garrett tried to recall the gunfire, see if he could detect how many rifles had been blasting. Two, he thought. Maybe three. If they had killed Paine, that still left the odds dead even. He didn't think those assassins would move from their position, unless to mount up and ride away, which would be the safe, practical thing to do. They had stopped the posse, killed one mount, likely one rider, scared the devil out of two other horses. Garrett and his men wouldn't be going anywhere for a spell, at least, anywhere near Ollie Sinclair. They'd have to limp back to Red Mountain.

The sun cast long shadows. All Garrett had to do was be patient, sneak out after sunset, move through the mud and muck, drag his sorry arse back to Holly's. Only thing hurt was his pride. And Evan Paine.

Patience—he never had the knack.

He decided to take a different approach.

"Ollie?" he yelled.

Nothing.

"Come on, Ollie. You know it's me, Lin Garrett. Let's talk!"

When no one answered, Garrett pursed his lips. Cold mud soaked his britches, and his legs finally stopped shaking. He studied the old Colt, nodded at his decision even before he knew he had made it, and quickly rolled to his right, sending a round toward a juniper across the wash. Immediately he rolled back to cover, as a deafening roar of gunfire erupted, splattering his pants legs with mud as bullets ripped into the ground.

The echoes slowly faded.

"Ollie!" he yelled again.

A bullet popped the juniper above him.

So, Ollie Sinclair wasn't among the assassins. That reprobate liked to talk as much as Ol' Corb, and he had never been one for ambush. Well, that would work out just fine. Lying on his belly, he crawled through the mud, brush, and patches of snow toward Corbett, reached into his shell belt, and pulled out a fresh cartridge. He didn't speak until he had ejected the spent shell and replaced it.

"Still keep that one chamber empty, I see," Ol' Corb stated.

"I'd like to keep all my toes." Garrett holstered the Colt, figured to keep it clear of mud until reaching the other side of the wash. Six-shooter, for Garrett, was a misnomer; he always kept only five beans in the wheel. He looked up. "How many you figure?"

Corbett raised two fingers.

"Ollie's not one of them," Garrett whispered.

"Not hardly. Else we'd be dead."

"I'm going to crawl around, get behind them. Want you to talk to 'em, pretend like Ollie's there. Keep 'em occupied."

"Why don't you talk and let me crawl?"

"Never had your gift for gab." He thought about adding—*And your big arse makes an inviting target.*—but let the thought slide, never having been the type to crack many jokes. Instead, he left before Ol' Corb could protest, moving slowly, picking his way a quarter mile down the country, then across the wash. He bellied up the side, and stopped, out of breath, sweating, his vision blurred, mouth dry.

Slowly Garrett reached into the shadows and grabbed a handful of dirty snow, filled his mouth, enjoying the coolness as the snow melted. Swallowing, he scooped up another bit of snow to slake his thirst. *Not too much,* he told himself. *Don't want them fingers to get numb.*

Behind him came rambling stories and laughter from Ol' Corb, spitting out yarns as if Ollie Sinclair could hear him.

"Remember that time back in Trinidad? You was drunker than a peach-orchard sow. And me and Lin bet you that you couldn't ride your hoss down Front Street, buck naked, and leap into that water trough out front of Langston's Saloon? You done it, though, you measly rapscallion. Probably wouldn't have busted your leg and arm, neither, had Lin tol' you that the water was frozen solid. 'Course, them busted bones likely kept you out of jail."

After crawling another 100 yards, Garrett stopped, rising slowly, shielded by a rise of rocks and cactus. Ol' Corb finished another story, then announced his throat was parched, that he needed a sip of water, but would be happy to hear any stories Ollie or one of those other boys wanted to tell while he swallowed some whiskey. Garrett drew the Colt again, and slowly cocked it, covering the hammer with his gloved left hand to try to diminish the metallic *clicks.*

Voices. Whispers only, but the sound carried, and he moved slowly, picking his path carefully, pistol extended, ready. He saw the two men a second before they spotted him, saw them turning, raising their carbines, one cursing, the other yelling. He didn't recognize them, not at first, then one's face registered. He pictured that bearded face from that night at the Flagstaff depot when he had first arrived, one of the three toughs, the one who had kept his hands in his coat pockets, on the revolver he had hidden. Riggs. Joe Riggs.

The other was just a boy, really, not out of his teens.
Both Winchesters swung in his direction.

He fired at Riggs, rushing his shot, jerking the trigger, knowing he had missed. Then dived for cover before the carbines tore him in half.

Rolling, picking himself off the ground, chancing another shot, launching himself behind a boulder. Riggs came after him, shooting from the hip, like an idiot, while the boy tumbled down the embankment, into the wash, heading toward Corbett and Daric Mossman rather than his horse. Out of Garrett's line of fire, though.

Garrett had troubles enough.

A bullet burned his shoulder blade, and he rolled again, heard Riggs coming. Garrett's right arm was pinned underneath his side. Couldn't get a clear shot. Knew it didn't matter for Riggs was upon him. Garrett realized he was a dead man.

Only Riggs staggered before he could finish smiling, his Winchester only half raised, and he turned away from Garrett. The carbine fell from his hands, banged on the rocks, and the burly man tumbled backward. Bullets ripped into his chest and stomach, and, with a final pivot, Riggs crumpled, his eyes rolling back in his head as he fell across Garrett's body.

Garrett kicked, dragging himself from beneath Riggs as the big man shuddered, soiling himself as he died. Garrett pulled himself to his feet, uncertain, and finally noticed Evan Paine grinning at him from the bushes.

"Reckon we had the same idea, old man," the deputy said.

Garrett tried to think, but heard another sound, a voice from the wash, and his face turned ashen as he remembered the second assassin.

"Halt! Halt, I say, in the name of the law!" Daric Moss-man's voice.

The reply was the heavy report of a .30-30.

Chapter Sixteen

Moving quickly, Garrett bumped past Evan Paine, who didn't seem to care a whit about the gunfight taking place down in the wash. Paine merely grinned as he approached the bullet-riddled body of Riggs, probably hoping he had killed Ollie Sinclair. He would be disappointed.

When another gunshot boomed below, Garrett's face tightened. He reached the edge, leveled the Colt, gripped a twisted juniper branch to support himself, and looked down, his gun arm sweeping, trying to find the second ambusher. All he saw was Daric Mossman, standing in the open, the .38 Colt automatic waving in his right hand. The boy looked pale as a ghost, but at least he was still standing.

From this angle, the kid with the .30-30 remained hidden behind the collapsed juniper at the bottom of the wash, near Paine's dead mount. Garrett kept his revolver pointed in the general direction anyway, although he couldn't take his eyes off Daric Mossman.

"Get out of the way, boy! Get out of the way!" Ol' Corb kept shouting, running into the open, his own Winchester cocked, ready.

If Mossman would move, Ol' Corb might have a clear shot at the second bandit, only Mossman just stood there, finger tightening on the automatic's trigger. Garrett cringed. He had little use for automatics, figured they would jam up on you in the middle of a gunfight. He didn't care much for a Remington, either—which the boy had kept holstered on his hip—but at least the 1890 model borrowed extensively from Sam Colt, and it was a revolver, a whole lot more reliable than those new, fast-shooting side arms.

"Get down, boy!" Garrett barked, praying that Mossman would obey, flatten himself in the mud, let a veteran lawman like Randolph Corbett do what needed to be done. *Get down—or shoot!*

The boy took a tentative step forward. Garrett started to slide down the embankment, but Mossman's voice stopped him.

"Don't do it!" the boy yelled. He followed that with an oath, took another step, and practically cried: "Son, I can't miss at this range!"

Neither will that kid with the Thirty-Thirty, Garrett thought.

The whole episode had taken only seconds, almost as fast as Garrett's brain could register everything happening. The automatic bucked twice, and Garrett lost his grip on the tree, accidentally or by design, he couldn't be certain. He was sliding, finger still against the Colt's trigger, cactus spines biting into his trousers, waiting for that awful sound of a Winchester rifle.

Once he reached bottom, he tried to stand, only to slip in the mud, tried to take in everything. Ol' Corb, although out of breath, kept running, and the boy, Daric Mossman, stood unsteadily, mouth open, eyes tearing, only a few feet from Garrett.

Garrett still couldn't see the second train robber.

Suddenly Daric Mossman charged, screaming as he ran, emptying the Colt. "What were you thinking?" Mossman's cracking voice carried above the echoes of gunshots. "I told you . . . I told you . . . what . . . *why?*"

By now, Garrett couldn't see Mossman. He scrambled to his feet, lunged forward as Ol' Corb raced past him, wheezing, only to stop a few feet behind Daric Mossman, and lower the rifle. Holly's boy stood numbly, empty Colt hanging at his right side, finally slipping from his fingers, swallowed by the mud. Garrett wet his lips, lowering the hammer on his Colt and slipping the old revolver into its holster.

The second bandit, the kid, even younger than Mossman, lay spread-eagled, face up, sightless eyes staring into the cloudless sky, rifle cradled against his blood-soaked chest. One of the bullets from Mossman's automatic had splintered the stock of the '94, likely when Mossman had emptied the Colt in anger, fright, or shock, after he had killed the boy.

Garrett moved past Mossman. Deliberately he used his body to shield the dead kid from the Flagstaff city policeman, kneeled, knees popping, and tossed the .30-30 aside, then closed the boy's eyes. Two bullets had hit the boy in the chest, another in his stomach. Mossman's other shots had gone wild, but none of that had mattered. The first two shots had killed the boy. He peeled off his coat, used it to cover the kid's face. Finally he rose, stiffly, and walked back to Daric Mossman.

"You all right?" he asked. Stupid question. He knew the answer, could still taste the bile in his own mouth from killing the Yavapai Kid thirty years earlier.

"What . . . why did he do that?"

"Boy had sand," Ol' Corb said. Having caught his breath, he squatted to retrieve the Colt from the mud. "Give him credit. He died game."

"Our city policeman showed grit, too," Evan Paine

bragged. "That's some mighty fine shooting, Mossman. Mighty fine."

Garrett frowned. He hadn't even noticed that Paine had made his way down the wash. Paine held out Garrett's mud-stained hat, which he had picked up a few yards back. Garrett ignored the hat for the time being.

"Two dead," Paine added, dropping the hat by his side. "That leaves only three we're trailing. Our odds keep improving."

"But our luck ain't," Ol' Corb said. "Your horse is dead, the boy's and Lin's both scattered. We ain't a-goin' nowheres in a hurry."

None of that mattered to Garrett. He moved closer to Mossman, wanted to reach out, take hold of the boy, but didn't know how. He felt sick. Holly had asked him to look after Daric, keep him out of harm's way. Well, the boy looked fine, physically, but two men were dead, one, a mere teen-ager, at Daric Mossman's hand. Self-defense, sure, and the policeman had given the kid more of a chance than Garrett or Corbett or, certainly, Evan Paine, would have. Didn't help, though. Garrett understood that.

"Well, I found two horses picketed up yonder," Paine was saying, although Garrett scarcely understood a word. "Good mounts, too, lot of bottom. I'll say that for the boy's mama. She raises good horseflesh. Green mounts, my ass. And Garrett's horse didn't run too far off. I reckon we'll be riding out fairly soon."

"Well," Corbett said, "what about them two dead . . . ?"

"Shut up!" Garrett snapped. "The both of you!"

His right hand reached out, hesitantly, uncertain, and he grasped Mossman's shoulder, steadying him. He started to tell Mossman he had done the right thing, that he had no other choice, that he was alive, and there was no dishonor in that. The words couldn't form, though, no matter how hard he tried, and then a new fear briefly gripped him. He jerked his hand off Mossman's shoulder, looked at the warm, sticky blood staining his fingers.

Daric Mossman saw the blood, too, his own blood, and his eyes rolled backward. Garrett stepped forward just in time to catch the lad before he dropped into the mud.

"Bullet went clean through." Ol' Corb spoke evenly, nodding with satisfaction at his assessment, while Garrett sat on his haunches, rocking back and forth. "Don't think it hit no bone, neither, nor artery." Ol' Corb had packed both entrance and exit wounds with snow and mud, said the mud would draw out any poison, that the snow would probably hold good now that the sun had set and the temperature kept plummeting.

"Reckon, though, if we want to keep on Ollie's trail, I could heat up my knife . . . ."

"No." Garrett stopped rocking. The moon had risen, bright, silvery, big. "We're taking him back to Red Mountain."

He expected an eruption from Evan Paine, and the deputy started to protest, but something made him stop. It couldn't have been Garrett's stern look. Garrett never looked away from Daric Mossman, who lay still, lips tight, face drained of all color, but conscious, alert, brave.

"I don't want . . . ," Mossman bit back pain. Shock had helped the boy at first, but that had begun to wear off. Mossman needed a doctor. Right now, Lin Garrett would have welcomed any old sawbones, even that louse, Eli Meredith and his X-ray machine.

"It'll be fine," Garrett told Mossman, forcing a smile.

"You'll lose Sinclair's trail," Mossman protested.

154

"Wouldn't be the first time," Garrett said. "But we'll catch him, sure enough." He made a vow to himself to do that, too. Ollie Sinclair had broken the rules now, had waylaid them. Maybe Sinclair hadn't been there, but Garrett still held him accountable for that bullet through Mossman's shoulder. Holly had been right: Sinclair had changed. One of those sayings Ol' Corb kept attributing to his father played through Garrett's mind: *Crooked trees never straighten their branches. They just keep a-twistin' and a-turnin' till they finally break.*

Even if he had to follow Sinclair all the way to New Harmony, Garrett would find Ollie Sinclair, kill him or capture him, make him pay for spilling Mossman blood.

"We'll get you back to your mother," Garrett said softly, "maybe trade for fresh horses, then lope out after Ollie."

"Mama will raise Cain." Mossman spoke through clenched teeth.

Ol' Corb chuckled. "Son, she'll raise more than that. Likely she'll lift our hair."

They'd move out at once, Garrett figured, use the stars to guide them back to Holly's trading post, take advantage of the night's cold to slow Mossman's bleeding. He turned after rising, staring at Paine, waiting for the confrontation. That there hadn't been any argument yet surprised him.

"You can ride on, Paine," Garrett said. "We'll catch up."

"No." That wasn't a shock. Odds would be three against one if Paine traveled alone, and the Sinclair brothers and Handsome Harry Prudhomme possessed a whole lot more skills with a gun than the two dead men in Cedar Wash ever did. "Kid needs a doctor," Paine said, "at least a bed. Besides, we can store them two carcasses . . . ."—he hooked a thumb at the bodies of Riggs and the boy—"at his mama's

155

place." Paine grinned wickedly. "Maybe the railroad has already posted a reward. I'd like to make some profit, just in case Sinclair and the rest are already in Utah."

Earlier, while Ol' Corb tended Mossman and Garrett fretted, Paine had ridden out on Corbett's sorrel horse, caught and brought back Scarlet Knight, but had no luck finding Mossman's horse. Likely, by now, that bay mare had loped halfway back to Red Mountain. Another reason to take the boy home. Holly would be worried sick, wondering if she had lost another child.

They packed the two dead men on a leopard appaloosa that one of the robbers had ridden, and fashioned a travois out of blankets and juniper branches for Mossman, which Garrett pulled behind him on Scarlet Knight. Travois poles made Garrett's ride even more uncomfortable, but he would not complain. Ol' Corb led the wretched cargo of corpses, while Paine took the point, riding a buckskin, cradling a Winchester across his lap and whistling one bawdy tune after another.

Even traveling all night, they wouldn't reach Red Mountain until well past mid-morning. Garrett felt stiff, cold, angry, ashamed, worried during the ride. They kept a slow pace, good for Mossman's comfort, equally helpful to Garrett's joints. By dawn, Paine had run out of tunes to whistle and, exhausted, fell into a thankful silence.

Six or seven miles north of the Red Mountain trading post, Scarlet Knight's ears pricked forward, then flattened against its head. Garrett quickly reined up, and dropped his right hand to the Marlin. "Easy, boy," he said softly. "What is it?"

He heard the sputtering almost immediately and looked down the road. Seconds later, the yellow International Harvester topped a hill, slinging mounds of mud, digging furrows like an old plow from the Arizona Colonization Company. Scarlet Knight's ears flicked forward again, less threatening, and Garrett swung from the saddle.

"It's your mother, boy," Garrett said. Mossman, fast asleep, didn't stir.

The truck slid to a stop, and Holly Mossman leaped outside, her face masked with fear.

"He's all right!" Garrett shouted, and Ol' Corb repeated the information, but Holly didn't hear. She just ran toward them, struggling through the mud.

Chapter Seventeen

Holly hadn't traveled alone. When Garrett saw the other figure, bundled up inside the high-wheeled truck, a small head barely visible over the dash, his stomach soured. Holly had brought her grandson, young Benjamin Coyne Carter, with her. She hadn't had much choice, Garrett figured, couldn't very well leave the nine-year-old alone at the ranch and trading post, although Garrett wished she would have. The boy would see his uncle, shot through the shoulder, barely conscious. Not only that, two bloody bodies draped over a horse. Criminy, they hadn't even bothered to cover the dead men.

"Stay inside!" Holly shouted as she ran.

Petrified, the boy didn't move.

"Daric's all right," Garrett said again, but had to step aside, let Holly run past him. She dropped to her knees, crying, and reached down, stroking her son's hair, then checking the makeshift bandage and poultice Ol' Corb had concocted.

"We got bushwhacked," Garrett explained, wishing Ol' Corb would do the talking. He had always been better at this kind of thing, but, for once, Randolph Corbett turned mute. "Boy took one through the shoulder, but he's all right." When he looked at Mossman again, however, he felt uncertain about his statement. Mossman had turned feverish. Garrett had seen corpses with more color.

"The killer that shot him, your son shot dead," Paine said, as if that would comfort Holly.

Holly rose, her face tight. "Move him to my truck," she ordered.

Once they had transferred Mossman into the back of the truck, and covered him with blankets, Garrett said they would follow her to Red Mountain, that Ol' Corb could ride along if Holly wanted, to keep Daric comfortable. While he spoke, he stared at Benji Carter, his eyes bulging from beneath his uncle's driving goggles that were several sizes too big for any nine-year-old.

"You're coming, Lin," Holly snapped, and Garrett knew better than to argue. "Benji, you ride back there with Mister Garrett and your Uncle Daric. Just hold Daric's hand, Benji, he'll be all right. Tell him that you love him." She spoke rapidly, nervously and fumbled trying to crank the International Harvester's engine.

Once the truck sputtered back to life, she hurriedly whipped it around, and raced over the hill, plowing through the muddy road, the blasting wind almost whipping Garrett's hat off his head. He followed Benji's lead, took Daric Mossman's other hand in his own, patting it, but never taking his eyes off Holly's grandson.

They had moved Daric to Holly's bed, Garrett and Benji, while Holly telephoned a doctor in Flagstaff. He felt utterly useless, a miserable, worthless old man, needing a nine-year-old's help to carry Mossman inside the house, Benji struggling while holding his uncle's feet and Garrett trying hard not to aggravate the shoulder wound, or his own back.

As soon as she hung up the telephone, Holly went to

work, mumbling a few oaths about Randolph Corbett's ideas of medicine, cleaning the bullet holes with alcohol and stuffing them with clean strips of bandages. Garrett, still feeling like a louse, just stood in the doorway, hat in hand, cognizant of the blood- and mud-splattered coat he wore. Horses snorted outside; Ol' Corb and Paine had arrived.

"Benji." Holly did not look up. "Go outside. Help them stable their horses."

Garrett pursed his lips, considering. He didn't think the boy should go outside at all. The kid had seen enough today, and maybe Holly had forgotten about the two dead men they were packing. He held his tongue, however, deciding Holly knew what was best. This was her grandson, and none of his business.

As soon as the boy tromped outside, almost before the door had slammed shut, Holly Mossman rose and slapped Garrett so hard, his hat slipped from his grasp and rolled across the bedroom floor.

"How could you, Lin?" she bellowed, reared back, and whacked him again. The second time, Garrett almost rose his hand in self-defense, then decided to take his punishment, let Holly vent her anger. He deserved it. "Are you that vain? Is that it? You have to prove you're still the man you were thirty years ago?" She cursed, stepped back, then charged, banging her fists against his chest, hitting until, exhausted, she collapsed against him, sobbing, muttering Daric's name over and over.

He eased her onto the edge of the bed. "That's my son," she told him. "That's . . . ." He couldn't understand the rest of her statement, not that it mattered.

In silence, Garrett picked up his hat and walked out of the bedroom, softly closing the door behind him. Hearing the thundering of hoofs, he hurried outside. Too soon to be that sawbones from Flagstaff, and too many horses. When he reached the porch, he spotted Corbett and Benji tending the stock while Evan Paine walked toward a half dozen riders loping down the road.

"Took you boys long enough!" Paine said, and Garrett's stomach tightened.

I am an old fool. A pathetic old fool.

Maybe the doctors were right, and he was losing his faculties.

Evan Paine made introductions, but Garrett didn't remember any of the names, didn't care to know any of these lawmen. The posse from Winslow, maybe the same vermin who had dug up John Shaw's corpse back at Cañon Diablo in 1905. Garrett recalled the note Paine had handed the conductor back on the Grand Cañon Railway. He had figured the message was for Sheriff Oldridge, but should have known better. Plus, these six men, heavily armed with whiskey and iron, were why Paine had not objected to returning to Red Mountain after getting waylaid. He had underestimated Evan Paine. Hell, Paine knew how to play politics better than many lawmen, had a ruthless streak in him, and very well might win election after election as county sheriff, although he would never earn Lin Garrett's vote. What was that Ol' Corb had told him down in Flagstaff, about supping with the devil?

From the corral, Ol' Corb gave Garrett a cold stare. Garrett told the new batch of deputies to wait outside. He wouldn't have them inside Holly's home.

"Who are they?" Holly stared out the window in the kitchen, working the pump to fill a pitcher with water.

"More deputies," Garrett answered, and looked inside

the bedroom. Daric was awake, not moving though, not really aware of anything, just staring at the ceiling.

The front door banged open, and Holly instructed Benji to take off his boots and coat first, then informed him that his Uncle Daric was awake, and he should go see him. She finished working the pump, and faced Garrett, light brown eyes darker, rimmed red.

"I'm sorry," she said.

So am I, he wanted to say, yet only stood there like an oaf.

"You didn't shoot Daric, and I couldn't have stopped him if I wanted to. Thanks for bringing him back to me."

He remained as silent as that silly wooden Indian out front of the trading post.

"And I didn't mean that about you being vain. I don't think you have an ounce of vanity, Lin." She placed the pitcher on the kitchen table. "I still . . . ."

She didn't finish, but he knew what she meant. *I still don't know why you want to keep at this foolish idea. Let Ollie go, Lin, just let him go.*

"Ollie's changed," she said. "I think Randolph has changed. I know I have. Sometimes . . . ." Tears welled again. "Sometimes I wish you could."

Often wish I could, too, he thought, yet, one more time, he couldn't voice those feelings.

"Daric's thirsty." She brushed away a tear. "That's a good sign. Let's take him this to drink."

He sat in Ol' Corb's favorite rocking chair, which Holly had moved from the parlor to her bedroom, sat talking to Daric Mossman and Benji Carter while they waited for the doctor to drive up from Flagstaff.

"Were you scared?" Benji asked. He thought he was

162

talking to his uncle, but the kid was looking right at Garrett, those blue eyes wild with curiosity, his red hair unruly from his morning adventures.

Garrett's head bobbed slightly.

"Grandma says Uncle Daric was brave."

"Sure was," Garrett said.

"Bet he was brave as Wyatt Earp."

Another nod. "Braver. Far as I know, Earp never got shot."

The boy's eyes brightened. "You knew Wyatt Earp?"

"Met him a time or two." Mostly at the card tables, though, he remembered, at the Weatherford Hotel and over in San Diego, trying to buck the table at Earp's faro layout and never having much luck. But that was just like Earp. Even while wearing a star, he had always seemed more interested in his business ventures, his gambling operations, than in preserving the peace and protecting citizens.

"How about Wild Bill Hickok?"

"Not really," he said, although he had seen Hickok a couple of times when he had first started cowboying, trailing a herd of beeves to Abilene back in 1871. He hadn't cared much for Hickok, either.

Truth was, most of the lawmen kids remembered weren't much better than the outlaws made famous in those half-dime novels—no, they cost a whole dime now, or even more. Hickok courted cards and whiskey, spent more times in cribs and gambling parlors than in the marshal's office. Earp wasn't a drunk, but whenever he swore to uphold the law, what he really meant was to protect himself and that clannish family of his. Pat Garrett belonged on the other side of the badge. Bill Tilghman, like many others, had first been on the other side of the badge. The real lawmen, the ones who did serve and protect, hell, nobody even remembered their names. Tom Nott—Bob Clagett—even Lin Garrett.

Two hours later, the doctor pulled up in a 1909 Maxwell Model A, and how he managed to get that roundabout up the muddy road, Garrett couldn't even fathom a guess. He remembered the pill-roller, knew the doctor remembered him, the way he twisted his mustache and stared at Garrett while Holly explained what had happened to her son.

"You left the hospital, sir," said the doctor.

"Been deputized," Garrett said, then he remembered the doctor's name. Magruder, the one who had told Garrett all about "peripheral neuropathy" and the like.

"I see." He released his mangled mustache. "Well, let me see your son, Missus Mossman."

Garrett moved to the kitchen window, frowning as Paine and his deputies saddled fresh mounts. They hadn't bothered asking Holly for permission, and he started to go outside, give them an earful, but Holly took his arm. "Don't bother," she said. "I'll send Curt Oldridge a bill for rental. Then I'll vote him out of office."

"Might not like the other name on the ballot." He tilted his head toward Paine.

"Maybe you'll run again."

He smiled, but lost the grin when Holly kept holding his arm, then slipped down and clasped his hand, interlocking their fingers, giving him a squeeze.

"I . . . ." She took a deep breath. "Did you ever read Cooper's Leatherstocking Tales?"

He shook his head. He'd never read any book. Well, his mother had made him read Bible passages back in Missouri, but he didn't think he ever made it all the way through, and his father had considered *Nick of the Woods* one of the best books ever written, and had cited passages by the fireplace, but Garrett couldn't remember a word all these years later, couldn't even name the author. Holly didn't wait for him to reply; likely she knew his answer.

"You're a lot like Natty Bumpo. I guess I'm not."

"You see ahead," Garrett said.

"That I do. When we moved out here, Uncle Timothy and me, we saw Arizona as a place to farm, but it didn't take me long to see the error of our ways. I thought this would be horse country, though, good country. To be truthful, I never thought we'd see things like that Ford in the barn and those two trucks parked outside, but they're here, Lin, and they aren't going away. So now I know horses and cattle aren't going to last forever. You know what I think is the future of the West, not just Arizona, Lin, but the whole West?"

"What?"

"Tourists. They come to see the Grand Cañon. Or Yellowstone. Some of them even come to see cowboys. They devour those penny dreadfuls about Wild Bill, they hear those stories about Wyatt Earp, they go see Buffalo Bill Cody and his Wild West exhibitions, and they read about the Rocky Mountains and the Apaches and the Navajos."

She was right. All those tourists coming to Flagstaff. All those city folks visiting that ranch up in Wyoming.

"And, just like Natty Bumpo," Holly said, "they crowd you out. You, and Randolph, even Ollie."

A moment later, before Garrett could absorb Holly's comments, Magruder came out of the bedroom, looking grim like every doctor Garrett had ever met, twisting the other end of his mustache. "He lost a lot of blood," he pronounced once he had stopped playing with his gray handlebar, "but the wound's clean. Don't let him move around too much, ma'am, keep him in bed. Infection is the main thing. Change his bandages frequently, and he should be fit in a few weeks. I'll drive up day after tomorrow to check on him, but call me if he takes a turn."

The doctor studied Garrett. "And how are you?"

"Alive," Garrett answered.

A silence hovered inside the house like a heavy fog. The doctor reached for his mustache again, thought better of it, and asked Holly to bring her son some soup, try to get some food into him. When she headed for the pantry, Dr. Magruder inched closer to Garrett, who braced for the assault, figuring that that old pill wanted to interrogate his former patient, maybe cart him back to the poor farm, mention that he knew all about those horses Garrett and Ol' Corb had stolen. Only, instead, Magruder whispered: "I can patch up his bullet wound. But I'm asking you to try to fix him up . . . here." He tapped his temple.

"Run along, boy," Garrett said. "Go help your grandma fix your uncle some grub."

The kid relinquished the rocking chair, and bolted outside, and Garrett closed the bedroom door. Mossman stared at the ceiling, seldom blinking, and Garrett headed toward the chair, then veered to the bed and sat down, uncomfortable.

"I can't get that boy's face out of my mind." Mossman squeezed his eyes shut. "I just can't . . . ."

Grinding his teeth, Garrett loathed Doc Magruder. What did an old cowhand-turned-lawman know about this kind of thing?

"Does it ever go away?" Mossman asked, eyes open, tears welling.

"Not really," Garrett said, and then he recalled something else. "You learn to live with it. Better than dying with it."

Chapter Eighteen

He found Ollie pounding rye whiskey, for Ollie never sipped anything, over at Pratt's Saloon, a rawhide wooden affair down in Old Town that would not be missed when it was consumed during the Great Conflagration three years later.

Somehow, over the past four years, Ollie Sinclair had managed to keep his name off the Wanted dodgers, although many people suspected him of being rather free with other folks' cattle, and a story had made the rounds that Ollie and Troy Sinclair had killed a couple of miners down around Jerome a year or so back, a story neither brother ever bothered to deny. He kept his nose clean in Flagstaff, though; that was all Garrett really cared about.

What troubled Garrett on that hot afternoon was that Ollie Sinclair would be brooding, looking for a fight, with no intention of staying out of trouble. That's what brought Garrett down to Old Town after hearing that Sinclair had ridden in shortly after dawn, and was coming close to drinking Paul Pratt out of business. Garrett understood why. By jacks, he had already downed a couple of whiskeys in the town marshal's office, and it wasn't yet two o'clock.

That didn't count the shots he had consumed since Corbett brought him the news from Fort Verde.

Railroad laborers and mill workers had piled into Pratt's. Ollie Sinclair had always been one to draw a crowd, most of them expecting either a pretty good fistfight or at least some stupid prank Ollie would volunteer. Despite the smoky haze, Garrett recognized that shock of red hair among all the bearded and sunburned faces, and moved to the edge of the warped plank bar.

"Buy you a whiskey." Sinclair slapped a greenback on the bar, slurring his words, without even turning around to face his old friend. Like he had been expecting Garrett.

You never turned down Sinclair hospitality, Garrett had learned over the years. To do so was to invite a go of fisticuffs. Besides, the beer-jerker had filled a mug and slid it skidding down the uneven piece of pine before Garrett could accept or reject the offer.

"Beer?" Sinclair said contemptuously. "Have a man's drink, Marshal." He topped the mug with a finger of rye.

Sinclair's mood had soured. There would be no fun-loving pranks, but the odds of a fistfight, an outright brawl, seemed better than even money.

"You've heard." Garrett reached for the drink.

"Read it in the paper down in Prescott." Sinclair had long since shunned the shot glass in front of him, gripping the bottle by the neck and drinking the last of the rye.

"That's why I don't read newspapers." Garrett drained his own drink.

The whiskey bottle shattered against the wall, but the only reaction Sinclair received came from the barkeep, who slid a full replacement toward him. Almost immediately, the cork went to the floor, and after another long pull, Sinclair wiped his mouth with the back of a dirty shirt sleeve, and spit out a curse.

"Engaged. Can't figure out what she sees in that little Yankee bootlicker."

Letting that comment slide, Garrett motioned the bartender for a refill.

"You probably done it yourself, Garrett." Sinclair staggered closer. "Filled her with lies about me. Thunderation, maybe I should have stayed with you and Corbett over in the valley back in 'Seventy-Eight. Then Bob Clagett would have pinned a tin star on me. Maybe . . . ."

You ran out on us, Garrett thought, but drank his beer to keep from picking at Sinclair's festering wound and giving him reason to throw the first punch.

"Holly Grant turns out to be nothin' more than a . . . ."

His patience had evaporated. "Shut up, Ollie!" Garrett turned quickly, leaving the mug of beer on the bar. "You got better manners than talk about a lady in a saloon. She made her choice, so let it lie, because if you say one more word . . . ."

Sinclair shuddered with laughter as he squared himself, and the saloon turned fairly quiet. Hooking one thumb in his gun belt, he laughed again and flicked a finger with his free hand against the badge pinned on Garrett's vest, then let that hand drop, hooking the other side of his gun belt.

"You think you can take me, Lin?"

"You may beat me," Garrett answered, "but I'll whip you of the habit."

They stared at each other briefly, and then Sinclair cackled again, breaking eye contact first, staring down the bar at the beer-jerker. "In that case, Sam, I rescind my offer. Marshal Garrett will be buyin' his own drinks, includin' the two he just had."

Nervous laughter filled Pratt's Saloon. Garrett fingered a coin from his vest pocket and flipped it onto the bar, drained his beer, and turned to leave. "Stay on this side of the deadline, Ollie," he said.

"Absolutely, Marshal."

He hadn't reached the batwing doors when a timid little clerk from the depot ran inside, screaming at Garrett, between gasps for breath, that the Yavapai Kid had just killed a man over at the Palace Restaurant in New Town.

When he had accepted the position of Flagstaff marshal in March, riding the legendary status he had achieved after his run-in with Jude Kincaid back in December, Lin Garrett had taken advice from Tom Nott and Bob Clagett.

Keep New Town respectable, and nobody would really care how much blood got spilt in Old Town. Garrett had seen enough Kansas cow towns to realize there was truth to that. Most of those woolly burgs had a deadline, separating the town proper—where no civilian went down the streets packing a gun—and no man's land, where anything went. Abilene had its Devil's Addition. Fort Worth had Hell's Half-Acre.

Flagstaff had Old Town.

"Lawman can only do so much," Tom Nott had said. "You try to preserve peace in Old Town and they'll plant you right beside the fella you're replacing. In time, those places will burn themselves out."

Three years later, Old Town and New Town would almost burn Flagstaff out of existence.

On that day in 1882, Garrett had decided that Ollie Sinclair could terrorize Old Town all he wanted, as long as he kept his trap shut about Holly Grant and her engagement to Ben Mossman, but the Yavapai Kid had just killed someone in New Town, right across from the depot.

"Where's Corbett?" Garrett asked as he hurried down the boardwalk with the clerk.

"Don't know. Wasn't in the office or courthouse."

He remembered then. He had sent Corbett on some fool's errand to Winslow, just to get him out of town, to keep him out of his hair, so he could brood and drink alone. *Don't do nothin' foolish, Lin,* Corbett had told him. *"I knowed I shouldn't have tol' you about Holly. I . . . .*

"Stay here," Garrett ordered the clerk.

He could see the Yavapai Kid on the street, waving a pistol in his left hand, turning, shouting something in broken English and border Spanish, then firing a round through the window of the Flagstaff Mercantile.

"Kid!" Garrett called out, resting his right hand against the butt of his Colt as he stepped onto the street.

Newspaper accounts, and at least one half-dime novel, would later describe the Yavapai Kid as a burly Mexican bandit wearing a serape and carrying a brace of Walker Colts and a couple of machetes, a villainous ruffian without morals or fear.

Lin Garrett knew better. Like the name implied, he was a kid, just a boy, from Yavapai County, barely nineteen, and the only gun he carried was an old double-action Starr flecked with rust and dirt. Of course, the .44 remained deadly. Enrique Francisco Javier Castañeda had proved that by killing a man—Stephen Bier, Garrett would later learn— over at the Palace.

"Put the pistol down," Garrett commanded.

"Mi corazón." The kid said a lot more, but that was all Garrett understood.

"He stole her," the boy sobbed in English. "He stole Florencia from me, so, *sí,* I killed him, the *pendejo.*" He tapped his chest. "Inside, I am empty."

"Lot of that going around," Garrett said, surprised he had said anything. *I am empty, too,* he thought, thinking this might end without more bloodshed, but a second later, he detected that flicker—anger, fear, dread, longing, hopelessness; he'd never know for sure—in the Yavapai Kid's eyes.

"Don't do it!" Garrett yelled, drawing his Colt.

When they finally got around to burying the Kid, Garrett found himself back in Pratt's Saloon. He didn't know how long he had been there, for Pratt's never closed, but it had taken Enrique Francisco Javier Castañeda, shot in the belly from Garrett's .44, two days to die. Afterward, undertaker Jason Longmont had laid the Yavapai Kid in a coffin, displayed the "most perfect greaser corpse" at the depot for all the travelers to see. An itinerant photographer named Chris Hornbostel took photographs of the dead man, setting up a tent office beside the coffin and selling prints to anyone aboard the AT&SF line for $1.

By jacks, Garrett realized, the folks of New Town didn't want anyone packing a gun that side of the deadline, but, once there had been a killing, they sure loved the business it drummed up. Bob Clagett put a stop to that, though, when he passed through town, throwing the tinhorn photographer on the next eastbound train and paying a priest—some say at gunpoint—to bury young Castañeda.

All of this, Garrett overheard at Pratt's.

"You're a sorry lot."

Garrett looked up, saw the red hair, finished his whiskey, then motioned for a refill.

"No more, Sam," Ollie Sinclair said, sober for once. "The marshal's had enough."

"You my keeper?"

"You've been mine," Sinclair said. "I'd expect more from the man who stared down Jude Kincaid. That lawdog buddy of yours, Clagett, he's sorely disappointed in you, too."

"They can find a new marshal."

"Ol' Corb's doin' a fine job, I warrant, 'cept he's too busy frettin' over you. So is Holly."

Garrett slammed his empty glass on the bar. "I warned you about speaking her name in . . . ." He couldn't finish the thought, lost in his drunkenness.

"You've killed men before, Lin. I know that."

That was different. In the war, he had served as a gunner with Backoff's Missouri Artillery, likely taking many Confederate lives at Wilson's Creek and Pea Ridge, but he had never seen the faces of the men he had slain. And the others? Sure, while riding with old man Johnston along the Picketwire, they had hanged a couple of horse thieves. Summary justice, that skinflint of a rancher had called it. No trial. No jury. No appeal. Not even justice, Garrett understood, now that he looked back on those lynchings. But that had seem detached, as well. He hadn't slipped nooses over the condemned men's heads, hadn't slapped their horses out from under them, had just been there with the old man, Ollie, Ol' Corb, and a half dozen other riders for the brand.

Killing Castañeda had been different.

"You should have seen . . . ." Garrett shook away the image, tried to, at least, without much luck. "Damn, I'm almost forty years old. This shouldn't . . . but you should have seen his eyes, Ollie. It's like he . . . ."

" . . . like he wanted to die," Sinclair finished the statement for him.

"Yeah."

"Bully for the Yavapai Kid. That's how I'd like to go.

Thought about it myself, especially after . . . well, I can't mention her name in a saloon."

"You ain't funny, Ollie."

"Reckon not. And I'm over Holly, and, no, I really didn't think about killin' myself when I learned she was engaged to Mossman. Don't get riled, Lin, because I'm mentionin' her name in this bucket of blood. I'm sober, more or less, and talkin' about her with respect. But I do think the Kid had the right idea. He died game. Made his point. And if you had taken him to jail, then what? They would have hung him. Bullet's a whole lot more dignified than a rope."

Garrett tried to focus on the bar.

"Like you said, Lin, you're buckin' forty years. A man. A *law*man. You killed a man with a gun in his hand, and make no mistake, the Yavapai Kid was a man. A man who made his own choice. You remember this, pard. That gun was pointed at you. That gun had just killed one decent citizen already. You did what anyone would have done, Marshal Garrett. Now learn to live with it. It's better than dyin' with it."

Sinclair flicked the edge of the badge Garrett had forgotten to pull off.

"Else turn that thing in."

Chapter Nineteen

Evan Paine had grown impatient, threatening to leave Corbett and Garrett behind if they didn't hurry things along, screaming about all this dawdling, but Garrett knew that Paine would not leave Corbett and Garrett behind; Paine didn't trust them, fretted that once out of the posse's sight, the two old men would make a beeline for Ollie Sinclair. Something else bothered Paine. In his mind, pickings off the two men killed in Cedar Wash had been slim: a couple of pocket watches—not even good ones, but cheap numbers that cost less than $1—a lady's broach, and maybe $200 in cash and coin.

Of course, Garrett didn't understand that at all. In his day, $200 was better than six months' wages as a cowhand, and, as a lawman, he had never earned more than $125 a month, yet that cache must have been piddling for a bunch of hardcases lured by $80,000.

"We'll never catch Ollie before he reaches Lee's Ferry," Garrett said from Holly's porch. "You-all best know that. And once he crosses the border into Utah, you're out of your jurisdiction."

Chuckling in his saddle, Paine pushed back his hat, relaxed now that he understood they would soon hit the trail. "I reckon I'm a lot like Marshal Lin Garrett," Paine said. "I don't believe in boundaries."

Garrett caught Ol' Corb's glare, but ignored it, and stepped back inside to ask Holly if she needed anything. She didn't. By jacks, he had known that already. Holly never needed anything, not really. Stalling, he excused himself, and tried to give Benji a warming grin, although he imagined it resembled a scowl, then moved across toward the bedroom, cracking open the door and peering inside. Daric slept, softly snoring, his face looking relaxed, its pallor not as death-like. He pulled shut the door and walked outside without another word. Holly just stood by the sink, a cup of coffee in her hands, her face unreadable.

Outside, one of the deputies asked: "Are we ready?" Sarcasm laced the sentence.

Garrett unwrapped Scarlet Knight's reins, moved the horse so he could mount on higher ground, and, grunting, managed to pull his aching body into the saddle on the second attempt. A few deputies snickered at him, but he paid them no mind.

"Shouldn't you throw that saddle on a fresh horse?" another deputy asked.

He answered with a spit of contempt. The fool didn't recognize good horseflesh when he saw it, and Scarlet Knight was anything but winded. The horse would still be going, and going hard, long after even Holly Mossman's best horse had played out. Besides, Lin Garrett wasn't about to "borrow" one of Holly's horses the way these vermin had.

"Let's go," he said, and, taking the point, kicked the gelding into an easy lope.

At camp that night near Cedar Wash, Ol' Corb crouched beside Garrett's bedroll, holding a battered coffee cup in his gloved right hand. Garrett leaned against the old Gus

Ghormley saddle, staring at Paine and his Winslow posse as they laughed and drank while playing some new-fangled version of poker that needed wild cards and odd rules to hold the interests of drunken cads.

"You remember seeing poker for the first time?" Garrett asked.

Ol' Corb looked shocked, maybe from the question, maybe from the mere fact that Lin Garrett had initiated a conversation. Fact was, Garrett felt a little surprised himself.

"Uh . . . ." Settling his creaking frame down beside Garrett, Corbett glanced over his shoulder at the card game, and shook his head. "Can't rightly say that I do. Must've been during the war, maybe before. Just seems to have always been there, I guess, like a saddle and sack of Bull Durham."

"I remember," Garrett said. "Daddy had been downriver on a business trip, came home with a deck of cards he had picked up on the *Lady Larkspur*. Even remember the sternwheeler's name. And he proceeded to teach me how to play, till Mama came in and slapped the bitter hell out of us both. Wasn't at all like what them fools are trying to play. There were only twenty cards in the deck . . . aces, kings, queens, knaves and tens . . . and you bet after the deal, then showed what you had. No draw. They called it the bluffing game. That's the way I was taught it. Then, like you, I saw a lot of games during the war, only, by then, the deck had grown to fifty-two cards. I had to relearn the game."

"Well . . . ." Corbett slurped his coffee.

"I guess we have to relearn lots of things the older we get, the more things change."

"Reckon so."

"And you didn't come over here to talk about poker."

177

Ol' Corb fell silent.

"You came to start a fight. I saw that in your eyes. You've been madder than a hornet. Go ahead. Speak your piece. I've talked myself out."

His friend studied the battle-worn tin cup, turned it over in his big hands, stared at the bottom for several seconds, tapped it on his thigh, and finally set it on the ground.

"All them boys talk about is that money," Corbett finally said. "Not any reward from the railroad, but the money."

Garrett nodded.

"Iffen we catch Ollie, they'll kill him for sure. And us, too."

At first, Garrett didn't move. Then he stretched his arms and said: "I'm betting that Evan Paine can keep his posse in check. He'd rather be sheriff of Coconino County than wanted and rich."

"Maybe so, but he ain't got no intention of a-bringin' Ollie in alive."

"That troubles you?"

He could see the rage behind Randolph Corbett's eyes, boiling over, fuming. "Ollie Sinclair's a better man than anyone a-ridin' with us, Lin. I don't know why we don't just ride out, leave them jayhawkers to their own desires, fetch Ollie back our ownselves. We'd give him a chance."

Garrett jutted his chin toward the card game. "I'd rather keep them boys close. And not behind me."

Ol' Corb must have understood the wisdom in that, because he relaxed a little. Without another word, he pulled himself to his feet and muttered a good night.

"Why are you riding with me, Randolph?" Garrett asked suddenly. He figured he knew part of the reason. Back at the poor farm, Garrett's nonsense had sounded like a game, a little bit of fun, a chance to escape the Coconino County

Hospital for the Indigent. Lin Garrett and Randolph Corbett, reliving the old days, chasing down Ollie Sinclair. Now that everything was different, that the nonsense had turned ugly, dangerous, it would have been easy for Ol' Corb to have stayed behind once they brought Daric Mossman back to the trading post.

Ol' Corb stared down at him.

"You and Holly think I'm wrong," Garrett said. "I think I'm right. By jacks, I know I'm doing what's right."

His friend nodded. "I know you're wrong, Lin."

"Ollie's a liar . . . ," Garrett started, feeling his ears redden.

"So are you, Lin," Corbett bit back. "Oh, you don't tell no corkers like me and Ollie and more'n half the men we ever worked with. Just little ol' white lies, they call 'em, but then you convince yourself that you're a-tellin' the truth. You tol' that professor that you was a hack for a taxicab company when you got off the train. You . . . ."

"I didn't tell him that. He just . . . ."

"It's still a damned fib. Criminy, Lin, you've been a-lyin' to yourself for years."

He no longer felt angry, just sad, maybe even a bit ashamed. "Then why ride with me?"

Corbett snorted out a laugh and shook his head. "Because we're pards. Right or wrong, I'll back you right up to hell's back door." As he walked back to his bedroll, Ol' Corb added: "And so would Ollie."

His sleep, if he had indeed ever really slept, had been fitful, and he woke that morning, aching and irritable. At Paine's orders, they skipped breakfast. The deputy even refused to allow coffee to be boiled, fearing it would cost them too much time. Garrett didn't care one way or the other and, as his stomach felt a mite delicate that morning, skipping breakfast seemed right to him.

Saddling Scarlet Knight, he spotted the vultures, circling overhead.

"Corb." He spoke softly, jutting his chin skyward.

His friend studied the carrion briefly. "It's . . . ."

Evan Paine, who had overheard them, cut him off. "It's my dead horse, boys. That's all."

"Get a map," Ol' Corb snapped. "Your hoss got shot that way." His arm pointed northeast, down the wash, while the turkey vultures and ravens had found something more northward, out of Cedar Wash.

Paine considered that momentarily, realized the geography, and wet his lips.

"Probably a dead ewe, a coyot' or something," Paine finally said.

"Probably," Garrett said.

"Or it could be a trick." He turned angry. "One of your old pal's tricks!"

"That's likely, too," Garrett said.

Paine swore, snatched his hat off his head, and slapped it so hard against his horse's rump, that the mount reared and kicked. Once he got the horse calm, and once he himself had calmed, he sent the six men from Winslow down Cedar Wash while he rode toward the circling birds with Corbett and Garrett.

Amid the desert landscape, they found the killing ground. It wasn't a sheep or coyote, and nor had it been one of Ollie Sinclair's tricks.

Ol' Corb fired a couple rounds from his Winchester to scare off the ravens, turkey vultures, and coyotes. The shots would also signal the six men from Winslow to ride back. Two horses, still saddled, lay dead, the flesh picked apart by hungry animals. Blood, blackened by the sun, stained the rocks and sand, while flies swarmed around the sickening air. Garrett hobbled the gelding upwind of the carnage, then walked around the bloody scene, cradling his Marlin, studying the ground for sign.

Brass cartridges littered the ground near the dead animals, which the besieged had used as a fort, firing at a couple of attackers hidden uphill among the juniper. Eventually the attackers had given up and ridden out, leaving the others behind with two dead horses, and, if Garrett could read the sign right, one horse that wouldn't be going far.

Overwhelmed by the stench, he pulled the bandanna over his mouth and nose. Three men had been bushwhacked. Two had survived. Those two had dragged a third man, dead or badly wounded, into the shade on the hillside after the attackers had fled. The men had returned, mounted the one surviving horse, which was wounded or lame, and ridden north, toward the national monument.

"Well?" Evan Paine lifted his bandanna and spit out the bile. "What do you figure?"

Garrett pointed his rifle barrel at the hill. "I think there's a dead man up yonder," he said. "I think they buried him, then rode out . . . north."

Seeing the tracks and drag marks for the first time, Paine slapped his thighs and sprinted up the hill. Garrett's stomach roiled.

The Sinclair brothers, Handsome Harry Prudhomme, the ruffian named Riggs, and the kid from the train robbery had ridden down Cedar Wash, just as Garrett had predicted they would, but then Ollie Sinclair had changed tactics. He had left the wash, turned north and west, probably doubling back to try to set up an ambush. Only here, Riggs and the kid had ambushed the others.

Why? That he couldn't figure, not until he found some other details, or talked to Ollie, Troy, and Prudhomme, whoever wasn't buried atop that hill. Maybe Riggs wanted all the money from the train robbery. But he hadn't gotten it. Maybe he didn't like Ollie's plans or methods. In any event, Riggs and the kid had killed two horses, probably wounded the third, and killed either Ollie, Troy, or Prudhomme. Afterward, they had fled, only to see Garrett and the posse, and set up another ambush. Their second ambush had failed, however, leaving Riggs and the kid deader than the two horses here, and the body up on the hill.

Paine was shouting something, gesturing wildly, and Garrett slowly began climbing away from the stink. He felt Ol' Corb's presence beside him, but neither spoke, dread taking deep root as they pulled themselves up the ridge.

The wind whipped his face, and he wet his cracking lips with his tongue. A few feet away, Evan Paine stood shaking his head over a grave. Well, a hole, anyway. Not much more than that. The two survivors had not been equipped with a shovel, forcing them to dig the grave with their own hands, and roll the body of their friend into it, cover it up, and hurry away. No psalms, no prayers, no eulogies, no tears, no time. Nor had they erected a marker, leaving only a few rocks on the mound to keep the animals at bay.

Ollie Sinclair's voice rang through his mind. He could see that old red-headed reprobate sitting down at some groggery in Trinidad, Colorado, the saloon's name long forgotten, telling Corbett and Garrett: *"I don't care what you do with my body once I'm dead and gone. Six feet under or bones bleaching the prairie, why should I care?"* And Ol' Corb quipping back: *"It's a good thing you won't care, Ollie, because Lin and me'll just do what's easy on us."*

Wolves and coyotes had dug up the body—easily, shallow as the grave was—and, when Lin Garrett peered into the pit, his heart sank.

Chapter Twenty

The face on the corpse had been clawed and eaten away, as had much of the body, and Evan Paine cursed his luck.

"What's the matter, deputy?" Ol' Corb belted out. "You sore somebody else dug up this corpse before you could?"

"We'll never be able to identify this one!" Paine snapped, ignoring the allusion to Cañon Diablo. "That's what galls me, you old fool! And there ain't no money here!"

"Shut up," Garrett said softly. "The both of you." *Show some respect for the dead.*

Horses thundered, but Garrett didn't bother looking up. He knew who they were, before the six riders from Winslow shouted out questions, which Paine tried to answer as he climbed down the hill, leaving Ol' Corb and Garrett alone with the mangled remains of what once had been a man.

Heart aching, Garrett knelt. Clumps of red hair had been strewn around the grotesque flesh. Behind him, Ol' Corb panted and grunted as he squatted at the edge of the shallow grave. Neither spoke, the only movement coming when they waved off buzzing insects.

"Hate to speak ill of the dead," Corbett said after a long while, "but I never could stomach him."

Garrett's head bobbed slightly in agreement.

Paine had been wrong. The face might be gone, the body

desecrated, but the dead man was easily identified, even by two men who hadn't seen him in more than twenty-five years. Bits of red hair, the black broadcloth coat and pants, the stovepipe boots with a sliver of a red moon inlaid in the brown tops—all easy clues.

"I love him," Ollie Sinclair had once said. *"He's my brother. Reckon I have to love him. But I can't say I like him very much."*

Troy Sinclair, twelve years Ollie's junior, had always been the luckier of the two brothers. Troy's hair had never thinned, never turned gray. Troy had never spent any time in prison, always eluding the law no matter how many indictments he had faced. Cards always came to Troy when he needed them, and, when they didn't, he made them come his way, and seldom got caught. His luck had finally played out.

Although he had little regard for Troy, Garrett felt for Ollie. Sure, Troy Sinclair had been no good—even his older brother had conceded such time and again—but Ollie had always sided with him. *"You stick with your blood,"* Ollie had once said down in Prescott after Ol' Corb had questioned the wisdom of a rustling operation, *"the same as you stick with your pards."* Sometimes, Garrett wondered if he had forgotten that creed, chasing Ollie across the Arizona desert, blocking out the times Ollie Sinclair had watched his back, had stood beside him. In the end, though, Lin Garrett concluded that he was in the right, Ollie in the wrong—*Ollie hadn't stuck with anyone once Bob Clagett's posse came riding up on them in the Prescott Valley.*—and even a cantankerous, belligerent Virgin River Mormon would understand why Garrett kept his pursuit.

He looked down again at Troy Sinclair.

They had rustled stock together a few times, and Garrett

had even punched cattle—honest work—a time or two with both Sinclair boys. It must have been agonizing for Ollie to have to bury his brother here, knowing wolves would dig up the body, knowing he could never return to pay his respects. He thought of Penny, Holly's dead daughter, thought of her grave, somewhere far off in Pittsburgh, thought of Ollie . . . ..

"Ain't Christian to leave him like this," Ol' Corb said, "even if Troy weren't no Christian."

"Maybe." Garrett pulled himself to his feet. He tried to think of something to counter Corbett's argument, but knew his friend was right. Neither Paine nor anyone from Winslow argued with Garrett, although they certainly made no effort to help cover the corpse. They sat in their saddles, puffing Old Judge cigarettes—ready-made smokes for men too lazy to roll their own—and waiting patiently while Garrett and Ol' Corb shoveled sand over Troy Sinclair with makeshift spades.

Paine had finally relaxed. One of his riders had cut the trail, which pointed north toward the Grand Cañon. Two men on a tiring, wounded horse would not be getting far. Paine, and the men from Winslow, could smell the end of the chase. Luck had sided with them, had turned against Ollie Sinclair and Handsome Harry Prudhomme.

Sweat damped Garrett's shirt and face, and his mouth begged for water as he stumbled toward Scarlet Knight after shoveling the last bit of dirt over the grave. Barely had he slaked his thirst when Evan Paine presented him with an affidavit.

"What's this?" he asked.

"Read it if you want. All it says is that you positively identified the body as that of Troy Sinclair. I'll have it notarized when we get back to Flagstaff." He winked. "Don't want any reward money or glory eluding us, Deputy Garrett. At least we got us one Sinclair brother."

"We'll get the other two," a wide-mustached man said. "If we quit jawing and spur our horses."

Paine produced an Eagle Automatic Pencil from his vest pocket, and Garrett placed the paper on the saddle and scratched his name without reading a word. Ol' Corb made his mark underneath, and two men from Winslow witnessed it.

"Used to be a man's word was good enough," Corbett complained as he saddled the sorrel.

"Used to be," Paine echoed with a smirk, slipping pencil and folded paper into his pocket.

They found the dead horse at mid-morning the next day. How it had managed to carry two men that far, Garrett couldn't guess, but Ollie had always been able to sweet talk horses, dogs, and ladies.

"Won't be long now," one of the deputies said as they camped that night, promptly producing a bottle of bad whiskey to celebrate. Corbett and Garrett did not imbibe. Instead, they cleaned their rifles and revolvers.

Garrett checked the action on the Colt, pulled it to half cock, pushed in a .44 cartridge, rotated the cylinder, and paused before filling the next empty chamber, breaking a fifty-year-old habit. During the war, not once had he ever capped the second nipple, and, even after he had converted the Colt to take brass cartridges, he continued practicing safety. Keep the second chamber clear, load the rest, pull the weapon to full cock, and, when you seated the hammer, it fell on the empty chamber. Kept many a man from blowing his foot off.

Gingerly he slid the fully loaded revolver into his holster.

"You carry that six-shooter like a petticoat!" Ollie Sinclair's voice echoed through Garrett's mind. *"Do you know how high the odds are that you would actually fall in a way to make that gun go off? You'll find yourself in a bind, Lin, and needing to reload."* Ol' Corb had commenced to chuckling—*Where had that been?* Garrett wondered. *Colorado? Arizona?*—and snorted out his commentary. *"Shucks, Ollie, as bad as Lin shoots, iffen even he did cause that gun to fire, he wouldn't shoot off his big toe, but yours."*

Leaning against the saddle, Garrett pulled down his hat, and tried to sleep.

The tracks veered off the main trail into the brush, and Garrett swung from his saddle, bringing the Marlin out of the scabbard. Sinclair and Prudhomme had made it farther on foot than anyone would have figured, but they were a long way from the rim of the great chasm, and, even then, they would have had to negotiate their way down to the Colorado River and fight their way upstream to Lee's Ferry. They never would have made it, would have vanished in the wilderness like those men who had left Major Powell's expedition in the 1870s.

It's better this way, Garrett thought. *For both of us. Ollie Sinclair never was one just to vanish.*

With the sun sinking behind him, he stepped into the brush, fighting his way through piñon, Ol' Corb, Paine, and the other six men right behind him. At the edge of the woods, he stopped, crouching.

Two men sat in a clearing, the crumbling ruins of an ancient Indian pueblo behind them, warming themselves by a small fire even though Garrett felt anything but chilled. A metallic *click* startled him, and he whirled.

"Put that thing down!" he snapped, and the wide-mustached man glared at him.

"Use your brain, Charley," Paine told his deputy. "What if they buried the money?"

Reluctantly, glaring, the deputy lowered the .30-40 Krag-Jorgensen rifle, and Garrett leaned his Marlin against a tree. "I'm going down there," he announced. "Alone."

He tested the Colt in the holster, took a deep breath, exhaled, and walked toward the ruins. Ol' Corb didn't hesitate, moved right beside him, and Garrett fumed in silence. He wouldn't stop his pace, wouldn't commence to bickering with a man like Randolph Corbett, because it would be a waste of time. Yet, when he heard more footsteps, he whirled, furious at the sight of Evan Paine.

"Doesn't anyone listen . . . ?" he started, but Paine went right past him, and Corbett never slowed, so Garrett had to spin around and catch up, pass them, resume command. He found himself short of breath, and that galled him, too.

Maybe having Paine along was a blessing, he decided. Might keep the posse from shooting everyone in the back.

The two men looked up from the fire, rising slowly, backing away a few paces, letting their arms drop by their weapons. Garrett stopped a few feet in front of them, separated by the fire, and stared at Ollie Sinclair.

He had grown old, as weathered and weary as the ruins behind him. The easy-to-spot red hair had vanished, thinning now, coarse gray, the mustache and beard rough and unkempt. His eyes looked dead, his face pockmarked and pasty with sweat and dust, and the great bulk that had been Ollie Sinclair was no more. He looked so thin, Garrett didn't see how he kept his pants up, but then Ollie Sinclair grinned.

At least some things ain't changed.

"Well," Sinclair said, and moved his hand closer to the

Colt automatic on his right hip. "It's high time you got here, Lin."

Garrett nodded. "Ollie," he said evenly. "Harry."

" 'Evenin', Marshal," Handsome Harry Prudhomme said, grimacing in dirty, bloody stocking feet. Prudhomme's boots had been cut open and peeled apart. Another reason Ollie had camped here. Harry Prudhomme wouldn't be walking anywhere, as blistered as his feet were. He didn't see how Prudhomme could even stand, but he did, his right hand resting on the butt of a Smith & Wesson.

"Where's the money?" Paine shouted.

Sinclair ignored him.

"You seen Holly?" he asked Garrett.

He answered with a nod.

"She all right?"

"She was," Garrett said, "till your boys shot up her son at Cedar Wash!"

Rage filled Sinclair's eyes, and he cursed Riggs and the kid, whose name must have been Walter. "Daric ain't dead, is he? If he is, I'll kill those swine myself. I'll rip their throats . . . ."

"Daric's alive. And Riggs and the boy are dead. Tried to ambush us."

"Well . . . ." Sinclair's smile returned, but only briefly, for moments later he erupted in a violent, hacking cough, doubling over from pain. Instantly Paine started for his revolver, realizing the advantage, but Garrett reached out with his left arm and grabbed the deputy's wrist.

"I'm calling the tune." He jerked Paine's hand away from the holster.

Sinclair finally straightened, his eyes tearing, his lips flaked with blood, yet somehow he managed to grin. "Thought I could make it to Lee's Ferry. Be like old times."

"Reckon this will have to do," Garrett said.

"Yeah."

Part of him wanted to talk, to start up a conversation, re-live the old times, the good memories, forget the bad, but that had never been Garrett's way. Never a patient man, he deemed it best to get this over with, act now, before the posse grew impatient, before Garrett lost his nerve. "You're wanted, Ollie. You, too, Harry. For robbery of the Grand Cañon Railway. You want to come along peaceably?"

Handsome Harry Prudhomme clucked softly. Ollie Sinclair just stood there, so weak the wind might blow him away.

"Then I guess this conversation's over."

The bullet surprised him, buzzing by his left ear, and he turned sideways, uncertain, confused, before a cold under-standing enveloped him. A grunt. A yelp. Then a can-nonade of gunfire from the woods. Garrett realized he held the Colt, and he fired a round without aiming, looked back to see Ollie Sinclair, the Colt automatic sweeping right to left as pockets of dust flew up all around him. Ollie stag-gered—for a second, Garrett thought he had been hit—then Garrett made his play.

He was running, gripping the Colt at his side, diving, burying his shoulder into Ollie Sinclair's stomach, knocking them both toward the walls of the old Indian pueblo. He saw the opening even before he pulled himself to his knees, fired again, then tossed the revolver into the hole, grabbed Sinclair's shoulders, and dragged him inside.

A bullet spanged off the rock, showering his eyes with dust, and, momentarily blinded, Garrett staggered around the dark room, hands frantically searching for the Colt. He felt its warm barrel, snatched it up, and rubbed his eyes with the backs of his wrists.

Bullets thudded into the walls. Others whined off rocks.
His ears rang.

Then . . . a calm quiet.

As the gunshots faded into oblivion, his vision returned.

Ollie Sinclair sat against the wall, Colt automatic aimed at Garrett's heart.

Chapter Twenty-One

"You *hijo de la puta!*" Sinclair spat. "Bushwhackin'! That ain't your style!"

Garrett kept blinking, then looked outside, ignoring Sinclair and the gun while fighting the pain wracking his lower back. A rifle boomed from the room next door, and Ol' Corb cursed the six men from Winslow as squat assassins and lousy shots.

Well, not as lousy as Garrett had first thought. Handsome Harry Prudhomme lay dead beside the fire. Garrett didn't see Paine. He couldn't see the men from Winslow, either, even when they fired a couple more rounds. Smokeless powder made it almost impossible to tell where the men had positioned themselves.

Rifles and revolvers used to belch more white smoke than a cow town café's cook stove, but those French chemists who invented smokeless gunpowder had sure made things easier for bushwhackers over the past two decades.

"You gonna answer me, Lin? Look at me, or you'll get it in the back!"

Slowly Garrett faced Sinclair. The pistol remained trained on his chest, and Garrett thought about pointing out that those bullets had been aimed at him, too, not just the Sinclairs. Instead—"Misjudgment of character."—was all he said.

He had misjudged himself, too, thought he was as savvy as he had been thirty years ago. Not hardly. He was nothing but an old fool, hadn't thought things through, had been so bound and determined to make Ollie Sinclair pay, he had overlooked the obvious—even when he knew better. Leaving those six men behind him, that had been pure stupidity. Only last night, he had told Ol' Corb that very thing. Evan Paine couldn't control that posse. No one could, not with $80,000 up for grabs, and they'd take their chances, hoping the loot wasn't hidden. Now, he had put himself into a fine mess, had gotten Harry Prudhomme killed, maybe Paine, and had left Corbett, Sinclair, and him trapped in a crumbling, cramped ruins miles from nowhere.

Suddenly Ollie Sinclair broke out laughing, lowered the pistol, and shook his head. "Reckon we've both been played for fools, Lin," he said. "Reckon we've both played the parts like bona-fide Thespians. You should have known better. I should have known better. Ain't like old times, pard, when men like you and me walked proud and stood tall."

Walk proud, stand tall! He felt his blood rushing. *When did you ever stand tall, Ollie? When did you ever think of someone other than yourself? Look what you did to Holly!* A volley from the six men kept him from voicing his anger, and he hugged the dusty, cool wall, forcing himself to stay calm, until the gunshots faded and the ringing again left his ears.

Ollie Sinclair had moved closer to him. "I'm sorry, Lin," he whispered. "Sorry I got you and Corb into this. Sorry for Holly, for her boy. Hell, I'm even sorry for Harry and Troy. It's all my fault."

Relief swept over Garrett, if only briefly, for he was glad he hadn't snapped at Sinclair a few moments ago, thankful, that, for once, Ollie Sinclair wasn't blaming everyone else for his predicament. Mostly Garrett felt relieved that it wouldn't end the way he had figured.

He thought, sometimes even hoped, that it would come down to a killing, Garrett and Sinclair shooting each other. At times, the idea had seemed right. Sinclair must have hoped for the same, but, no, there would have been no justice in that. He had been wrong, looking for a coward's exit, only one without the stigma of Jude Kincaid's suicide. Anything seemed better than dying from uremic poisoning, the verdict those doctors at the poor farm had given him.

"Corb?" Garrett called out softly. "You all right."

"My arse is a-bleedin'." His Winchester boomed.

"Don't fire, Corbett, till you see a target! Quit wasting lead!"

From the adjoining room came Corbett's chuckling, then he turned solemn. "Lin, Paine's shot to pieces. I drug him inside, but . . . ."

"I'm sorry for . . . ." A violent cough slammed Sinclair against the wall, and Garrett stared at him until the fit passed. Sinclair wiped his lips with the back of his hand, and shook his head.

Garrett's facial muscles relaxed, and he slumped against the wall, reading Ollie's face. Sinclair was a dying man. Maybe that's why he had robbed the train, had refused to spur his way to Utah.

"Them prison doctors give me no better than six months." Sinclair spoke in a weak whisper. "Cancer." He tapped his chest. "On top of the consumption I got in prison. Ain't how I want to die, Lin."

After a light nod, Garrett made his own confession. "Uremic poisoning," he said. "That's what they say I have."

Tears welled in Sinclair's eyes. "But they can treat that, right?"

"Not as long as I waited." Corbett's rifle boomed again. "Don't tell, Corb," Garrett said. "He doesn't know."

"Well . . . at least . . . ."

"I ain't giving up," Garrett said. "I ain't about to be killed by them vermin outside, not without taking the lot with me. And I ain't dying in some hole in the ground."

Crawling over mounds of guano, through rubble, he made his way across the darkness, through the small door, and into the next room, slightly larger, brighter, but reeking of gunpowder. Ol' Corb sat by the opening, blood seeping from his left buttock, jaw working furiously on tobacco.

Sinclair trailed Garrett, and moved quickly toward Corbett, taking up position on the opposite side of the entrance. Garrett found Paine in the corner, two chest wounds making a sickening sucking sound, blood frothing from his lips, eyes glazing over, the rattle of death in his labored breathing.

"Fools," Paine said. "I told 'em . . . ."

"My fault," Garrett said.

He had thought the men would have listened to Paine's argument—*Wait till we find out where the money is.*—but guessed they liked the odds when they found the two remaining robbers, Garrett, Corbett, and Paine all in their rifle sights. Would have worked out well, too, if they shot worth a damn.

After a brief coughing spell, Paine shook his head and spoke again, clearer now, though softer. "Reckon I won't be . . . sheriff . . . after . . . ."

"Don't talk . . . Evan." He had to struggle to remember the deputy's first name. "I had you misread. You . . . you're a good man."

196

The dying man coughed softly. This close to Paine, Garrett couldn't smell Rowland's Macassar Oil, though he wished he could. No, the stink of death permeated the air. "No, I ain't," Paine said. "And you . . . didn't mis . . . . That money . . . ."

A shout from the woods commanded Garrett's attention.

"All we want is the loot from the train, fellas! Throw out that payload, and we ride off! Let you be."

He doubted that. They weren't that far from the Grand Cañon, where they could reach the depot and telegraph the authorities in Flagstaff and Williams. They weren't close, either; it would be a long, hard walk, but the chances were pretty good that they would survive. That posse couldn't afford to leave anyone alive.

"Where is the money?" Ol' Corb asked.

"Split it up at Cataract Creek." Sinclair fished out a few bills from his coat pocket, holding them out in his trembling left hand.

Corbett blasted the wall with tobacco juice. "That's it? They said you took eighty thousand dollars!"

"What?" After a moment's pause, Sinclair laughed, coughed, then laughed some more. "More like eight hundred, if that."

They were staring at Garrett now, and he felt ashamed, searching his memory, picturing the man on the telephone back at the Flagstaff depot. Garrett knew the gent had said $80,000, but nobody else had mentioned such a figure, an outlandish amount. *There ain't that much money in this whole county*, Corbett had argued, but he hadn't listened, or done just a bit of detective work. Swearing underneath his breath, Garrett realized he had been played for a fool again. His stupidity, his gullibility had gotten them all in this jam.

Paine chuckled weakly, too. "It figures," he said.

"Them dogs won't believe us if we tell them there ain't no fortune," Ol' Corb said.

"They'd kill us . . . for eighty . . . cents," Paine said, barely audible.

"What's your answer?" the posse leader called out.

"Come an' get it!" Ol' Corb answered, and the rifles spoke again.

Garrett dived behind a rock, covering his head as bullets ricocheted around him, whining, splintering, pounded rocks and walls for half a minute. They wasted more powder and lead than Ol' Corb. When the musketry ended, he rose slowly, checking himself for wounds, surprised to come out unscathed. That luck wouldn't last, if the posse cut loose again. Luck was already turning. At the doorway, Ol' Corb fingered his right ear, where a bullet had ripped off the lobe and carved a furrow across his scalp. Sinclair had caught a round in the left calf, and sat wrapping the leg with his bandanna. He glanced at Evan Paine, and frowned.

"That change your mind?" the leader cried.

"Give us one minute!" Ol' Corb answered. He pointed the Winchester's barrel toward another doorway behind Garrett. Light filtered through the opening, revealing clouds of dust and smoke. "We're a-walkin' out of here," said Ol' Corb, taking command. "I ain't a-dyin' in this place. Ain't gonna have my bones mistaken for some Injun that's been dead five hunnert years. Can Paine walk?"

Garrett shook his head. "Evan Paine's walking toward Saint Peter." He reached down to close the young man's eyes. Two bullets had slammed into Paine's head and neck, killing him instantly. Garrett pulled the nickel-plated automatic from Paine's dead hand, and shoved the weapon in his waistband. He considered automatics with disdain, but he might need the Colt before the day was over. In the corner of his eye, he caught the tin star, paused, and looked back at Paine's body. He reached for the badge, planning on wearing it when he died, calling himself a lawman as he faced those killers from Winslow. His fingers touched the cold tin, and he stopped.

Just the same as stealing. He left the tin star pinned on the dead man's vest lapel. *You earned it, Paine,* he thought, and crawled away.

"Let's get out of here," Sinclair said.

Leading the way, Garrett struggled over shards of broken pottery and a reed sandal, over rat droppings and more guano, squeezing, contorting his body to fit through the narrow opening. In the cramped confines, he felt suffocated, but light beaconed a few yards away, and he moved over more rocks and débris, through the chamber, and suddenly he was out and in the open, where the roof had collapsed. Filling his lungs with fresh, crisp air, he rubbed his back while Sinclair and Corbett bellied their way outside. They moved around the old pueblo, keeping close to the wall, heads down.

"You're time's up!" came the shout from the woods, and the rifles spoke again, longer this time, sending round after round into the two abandoned rooms. They had gotten out just in time. Crouching, Garrett broke into a sprint, trying to make some distance while the posse kept shooting. He skirted around toppled walls and brush, leaped over the spines of dead cholla, and stopped at the corner of the pueblo, a few feet from a collapsed kiva. Behind him, he heard the wheezing of Ol' Corb and Sinclair.

The rifles stopped.

"Let me . . . catch my . . . breath . . . ," Sinclair said.

The posse leader had started shouting again. *Idiots,* Garrett thought. Apparently they hadn't posted anyone behind the pueblo, hadn't put gunmen on the flanks, hadn't even considered the possibility that there might be a way out of those ruins. On the other hand, Garrett didn't see much of a way out of here himself.

"Leave me with Corb's Winchester," Sinclair said. "I'll cover you-all."

"That ain't a-happenin'," Ol' Corb said.

Garrett stroked his mustache, thinking. The railroad depot had to be at least twenty miles away. Neither Sinclair nor Corbett was badly wounded, but Garrett couldn't see them walking that far, and, even if they tried it, the posse would ride them down. They had one Winchester, and no water. Two automatics, two Colt revolvers. He should have brought the Marlin with him. Hopeless. They could neither wait them out nor hold them off.

"Why in blazes didn't you just run off to El Paso?" Corbett said before biting off a replacement for his chewing tobacco.

After stifling a cough, Sinclair shook his head.

"Troy and Harry met up with me in Globe," he said, "after I got out of prison. The doctors said I could stay there, die there, but I told them I wasn't interested. My sentence said twenty-five years, and that's all they was keepin' me for. Planned on going to Mexico, I did, but then one of the Tucson newspapers reprinted them lies about me. *I ain't welcome in Coconino County.*"

"And you had to show them up," Garrett said dryly.

"Well . . . it was Harry's idea, but . . . ."

"You're too predictable, Ollie," Garrett said.

"Maybe. But you know why I had to come back, Lin."

Garrett's anger flared. "You couldn't think about Holly, could you? Didn't once consider what your coming back would do to her . . . ."

"Boys . . . ," Ol' Corb cautioned.

The following silence lasted only briefly.

"I still can't see what Holly ever saw in Ben Mossman," Sinclair said, and coughed again.

"A good husband and a father," Garrett answered. "Something neither of us could ever be."

"I reckon so."

"I know so."

A puddle of tobacco juice suddenly appeared between them. "You boys might want to stop a-bickerin' over picayune history," Corbett said hoarsely, "and think about our present situation."

Fighting with Ollie Sinclair when six men were trying to kill them. Garrett almost laughed. Ollie had a way about him that would leave you wanting to kill him one moment, defending him the next. By jacks, even today Garrett had run the gauntlet, walking to the campfire bent on maiming or killing his old friend, and, once the shooting commenced, tackling Sinclair and pulling him into the ruins to save his life.

After replacing the empty cartridges in his Colt, Garrett peered around the corner. The posse leader was shouting something, but he couldn't quite make out the words. Then another voice chimed in, clear as the sky: "Maybe they're all dead."

He took a chance, moved beyond the corner, hugging the wall, stepping over cactus, inching toward the clearing, feet crunching on the remnants of icy snow. He could smell smoke from the campfire again. At the edge of the wall, he stopped, hearing new sounds. Footsteps. Slowly, carefully he peered around the corner. Four men were walking toward the pueblo ruins, rifles at the ready.

Getting smarter. Garrett jerked back. *Leaving two in the brush to cover them.* Garrett turned toward Corbett and Sinclair.

"Four are coming this way," he whispered. "Two, I reckon, are in the woods. You've got the only rifle, Corb. You'll have to find the two in the woods. Stay here. It's decent cover."

"Reckon I'll walk with you boys." Ol' Corb eared back the rifle's hammer.

Garrett's head bobbed slightly. He shoved the Colt into his gun belt and held out his hand. "I ain't always been the easiest man to ride with," he said, "but I want you both to know it's been a pleasure."

Corbett spit. "I'll shake your hand afterward."

Likewise, Sinclair ignored the gesture.

Just briefly Lin Garrett smiled. A second later, he stepped around the corner. Ollie Sinclair and Randolph Corbett walked right beside him.

Chapter Twenty-Two

They couldn't win.

He knew that as he strode toward the four killers. A Krag-Jorgensen, two Ballards, and a Marlin—*his Marlin!*—against automatic pistols, Colt six-shooters, and a .30-30 Winchester, providing Ol' Corb hadn't emptied his rifle. By all rights they'd be dead before they ever got into pistol range. But on they walked.

Proud.

Tall.

Determined.

Right.

At first, the four men didn't notice them, so focused were they on the holes into which the lawmen had crawled. Then, the wide-mustached man with the .30-40 Krag-Jorgensen must have caught movement in the corner of his eye, because he stopped, pivoting, almost staggering as he brought the heavy rifle to his shoulder, swinging the barrel toward the three walking men.

That's when Garrett heard the popping to his left, a series of shots coming from the road, sounding like Sheriff Oldridge's posse blasting away, riding to the rescue like the U.S. Cavalry in one of those flickers or penny dreadfuls . . . only . . . no, it didn't sound like gunfire.

"Son-of-a-gun!" Ol' Corb was saying, stopping, turning,

taking aim at something in the woods.

Another boom from the road, closer now. No, not gunshots. But . . . what?

It didn't matter.

Corbett's .30-30 roared, and the old lawman jacked in another round. Garrett didn't look, kept his eyes on the four men, who had all stopped and turned. Only the muffled explosions from the road also commanded their attention, and three looked away, glancing over their shoulders, wondering if these ambushers were being ambushed.

Garrett and Sinclair never slackened their pace.

Behind them, Corbett's Winchester roared.

"It's a damned automobile!" the wide-mustached man screamed at his companions, trying to rally them, and Garrett realized the noise came from some tourist fighting muddy roads and April weather to visit Grand Cañon National Monument. Backfires had frightened the six men from Winslow, and that bit of irony had allowed Garrett and Sinclair to move into pistol range.

He palmed his Colt.

The Krag-Jorgensen spoke first.

He saw the rifle's kick, if not a muzzle flash, and felt a buzzing off to his right. The man had rushed his shot, a mistake Garrett would not make.

He pointed the Colt, using his index finger as a natural sight, pulling the trigger with his middle finger—just the way he had been taught back in Missouri long before the War Between the States—seeing dust pop from the man's coat. A hit, low and to the left, not fatal, but a hit. The man slapped at the wound as he would a fly, brought his hand back up to the rifle, worked the bolt. Garrett relied on his instinct. He had years of experience. As far as the two men in the woods were concerned, he didn't give them a moment's thought.

They were Ol' Corb's problem, and, from the sound of the Winchester '94, he was solving that dilemma.

It wasn't hard, either.

The backfiring, which startled and confused the two sentries, came from a wood-bodied Sauer stake truck, a Plainfield, New Jersey contraption converted into a tourist car for Flagstaff's stagecoach company to compete with the Grand Cañon Railway. One of the Winslow men, well hidden, had been so spooked by the automobile that he had turned toward the pike, fired a quick round, then scrambled for the horses, fearing the Coconino County posse was charging the pueblo ruins. The other man had also been frightened, moved from his shelter, must have realized it was a truck, and took a knee, engaging in a marksmanship contest against Randolph Corbett.

Pitted against a veteran of the sack of Lawrence, the deputy lost.

"Got you, you snake in the grass!" Ol' Corb shouted, pitching the Winchester to the ground. Garrett heard the clattering, figured the .30-30 was empty, and then footsteps. Ol' Corb ran to catch up.

The second sentry ran like hell.

Garrett concentrated on the wide-mustached man with the .30-40.

Another bullet buzzed by his ear. He thumbed back the Colt and fired. Cocked the revolver again. Aimed. Squeezed the trigger.

He saw the wide-mustached man go down, unmoving, moved his arm to the left.

Beside him, Ollie Sinclair's automatic spit out round after round, and another man from Winslow turned and fled for the scattering horses. The two remaining assassins worked their rifles.

Garrett kept walking. His ears rang. He couldn't hear a thing, just fired the .44 once more, thumbed back the hammer, pointed, started to pull the trigger.

Instantly he was down, sitting on his hindquarters, legs stretched out in front of him, but the Colt remained firmly in his grip. He didn't feel any pain, not then, not even a numbness, but understood that a round had taken him squarely in the left shoulder. Maybe he felt the warm, sticky blood. Maybe that was just his imagination. To his left, Ollie Sinclair remained on his feet, firing the automatic, stopping to shove in another clip, shooting again.

Garrett swung his right arm, still co-operating, tried to sight the Winslow lawman with his Marlin, pulled the trigger. The Colt roared. Smoke stung his eyes. Another round from the Marlin tore off his hat. A second later, Ollie turned sideways, loosening the automatic's remaining rounds in the dirt by his feet, kicking up mud and bits of dust.

"Troy!" Ollie shouted as another bullet hit his chest, and he toppled forward, crashing against an uprooted, long dead juniper.

Garrett swung the Colt just a bit, raised the barrel an inch, squeezed the trigger, cocked the .44, waited. The head of the man with the Marlin exploded, and he fell backward, the heavy rifle toppling over a rock, crashing in a clump of brush.

The last man from Winslow had pitched his jammed Ballard and picked up the .30-40. Cursing, he drew a bead on Garrett a moment before Garrett pulled the trigger. Garrett heard the sickening *click*, immediately dropped the empty revolver, reached for Evan Paine's nickel-plated automatic shoved near his belt buckle. Behind him, Ol' Corb's Bisley belted out another round, which went wide, then *clicked* empty. Garrett hadn't even realized Ol' Corb had been shooting his pistol until then.

Garrett held the automatic. The thin man with the Krag-Jorgensen slammed in a fresh cartridge. The Sauer touring truck backfired again. Ol' Corb's reloaded Bisley and Garrett's gun belched simultaneously. So did Sinclair's automatic, surprising Garrett. Summoning the last of his strength, Ollie Sinclair had positioned himself so that he had a clear shot at the last man from Winslow. *Never count a Sinclair boy out of the game,* his glinting eyes seemed to say. Their three pistols sounded as one, driving the man from Winslow backward. The rifle slipped from his fingers, and he clutched his gut, fell to his knees.

Sinclair's automatic barked again, pushing the man from Winslow onto his back, his right arm pointing toward the sky, hanging there a moment, then falling across his head.

The Sauer truck belched one more time.

Then . . . .

Silence.

Slowly the din of battle faded, the ringing faded from Garrett's ears, replaced by the distant sounds of horses hoofs as the two surviving posse members fled. A few seconds later, there was nothing but the wind. The Sauer truck had stopped, the driver peering through the trees, followed by a handful of curious tourists, their mouths dropping open.

"Mother of God," one of them said.

It was over.

Blood turned to glue, sticking his shirt to his skin, but Garrett pitched the automatic to his side and climbed to his feet. He looked around, confused, uncertain, but it was true. He was still breathing. They had won, killing four men with rifles and sending two more lighting a shuck for parts unknown. Slowly Garrett looked behind him. Ol' Corb just stood there, about as puzzled as he was.

They hadn't a chance, not against those vermin, but they had won.

Well . . . almost . . . .

He staggered a few steps, fell to his knees, slowly rolled Ollie Sinclair on his back. The old Mormon's head rested against the dead juniper, and blood spilled from both corners of Sinclair's mouth and into his ragged beard.

Sinclair coughed, shuddered. Slowly a smile formed on his weather-beaten face.

Exhausted, Garrett slumped beside him, trying to catch his breath, longing to learn what had happened, why they had survived, how they had managed to win.

"Ollie . . . ," Garrett began. He sat up, unsteadily, and took Sinclair's right hand in his own. His shoulder now throbbed, and that was only the beginning. It would get worse, much worse.

"Showed . . . 'em . . . ." A rough coughing fit sent flakes of blood and phlegm everywhere. Sinclair shuddered.

A shadow darkened Garrett's face. Ol' Corb stood guard, Bisley in his right hand, jaw still working that chewing tobacco. His old friend spit, then sank to both knees, not wounded, just tuckered out. Toward the road, the driver from the Grand Cañon Stagecoach Company and somewhere between a half dozen and dozen tourists—odd birds, in leather caps, strange goggles, sheepskin coats, and what appeared to be plaid kilts—summoned up enough courage to creep ever so cautiously toward the survivors.

Their whispers rustled like the trees. "What happened?" . . . "Who are those blokes?" . . . "Land sakes! It looks like the Alamo!"

"We're the law!" Ol' Corb managed just enough breath

to shout. "Deputy sheriffs from Coconino County! Been after some train robbers!"

More whispers. "Train robbery, yeah, I bloody well heard about that." . . . "Goodness, they sure caught up with 'em." . . . "Mother will not like this."

"Well . . . ." Sinclair choked back blood. "You'll tell . . . Hol . . . ." Death began to fog over the thin man's eyes. Garrett squeezed his friend's hand.

Sinclair took a short gulp of air. Another spasm rocked him, then he relaxed. "You know," Sinclair said evenly. "It's funny . . . ."

Solemnly Lin Garrett reached down and closed Ollie Sinclair's eyes. Suddenly he felt weak, figuring he was a dead man, too. He caught a lungful of fresh air, turned to his side, and sank into the damp, cold ground beside his old friend, Ollie Sinclair, cowboy, cattle rustler, man killer, bank robber, train robber. Friend. Enemy. Friend. Always a man to ride the river with.

Hovering over him squatted Ol' Corb, his face a mask, jaws furiously working that rancid chewing tobacco, pressing his right hand against the pulsing wound in Garrett's left shoulder.

"You tell . . . ," Garrett began, knowing he lacked the strength to finish, "Holly . . . ."

A shroud covered the fading daylight.

Chapter Twenty-Three

He opened his eyes to the stark gray walls of hell.

Garrett's heart sank, recognizing the drabness, the coldness, the sounds of the Coconino County Hospital for the Indigent. Briefly he thought he had dreamed the whole thing only to wake to the nightmare of living out his days at the poor farm, yet his left shoulder began throbbing, his mouth and throat felt like sand, and he heard a woman's voice beside him. Slowly he craned his neck and stared into Holly Grant Mossman's lovely eyes.

He tried to speak, couldn't, and Holly rose from a rickety chair, filled a cup in the sink, and pressed the cold container into his trembling hands. She had to help him lift his arms, place the cup against his cracked lips. He drank, refreshed, and sank into the pillow.

"Where am I?" he asked, although he already knew.

"How did I get here?" he asked after hearing her answer.

Holly told him, waiting as a nurse he didn't recognize came in and gave him an injection that deadened the pain in his shoulder.

The Grand Cañon Stagecoach Company's truck, Holly went on, was bound for the south rim, carrying eight tourists from Edinburgh on an overnight camping trip. That, undoubtedly, had saved Garrett's life. Trapped twenty miles from the railroad, with darkness creeping in, if an automobile had not been nearby, Garrett would have bled to death or succumbed to lead poisoning or some other infection. Instead, Randolph Corbett deputized the driver, told him to leave the Scots with their tents at the ruins, and haul Garrett, *pronto*, somewhere to receive medical care.

"That turned out to be my place," Holly said.

The driver had suggested the railroad depot, but Corbett demanded Red Mountain, at gunpoint. They loaded Ollie Sinclair's body in the back of the truck, too, and Corbett rode along, urging the driver to make that Sauer roll, once even threatening to horsewhip the fool. After their arrival at the trading post, Holly telephoned the hospital, and a doctor drove up early the next morning. Before he got there, Holly had managed to stop the bleeding and clean the wound. The doctor dug out the bullet, which had flattened against his shoulder blade.

Afterward, they started the deathwatch, waiting for signs of infection, of shock, but Garrett refused to die.

"Figures," Holly said.

Once Garrett's condition appeared stable, they moved him into the back of the International Harvester and drove him to Flagstaff.

"But not the regular hospital," Garrett said.

"No, Curt Oldridge insisted that you stay here. You're on the county's dime, Lin, and, well, the sheriff and others are a bit confused about what happened. Evan Paine and four other deputies dead, and those witnesses from overseas say you, and Ollie, were shooting at the deputies."

"Deputies." Garrett spat, brought the cup again, without Holly's help this time, and slaked his thirst. "Cut-throats. Blackhearts, the lot of them. Planned on killing us and riding away with the money from the robbery."

"That's what Randolph says, and most folks here believe

211

it, but there's an inquest scheduled tomorrow morning. They keep delaying it. Kept hoping you'd come around, give them another witness besides Randolph. His idea of the truth, well . . . ."

He changed the subject. "How's your boy?"

"Daric? He's back in town, though that certainly wasn't his mother's idea. Working the desk. They might promote him to sergeant. Seems every man in my life is suddenly a hero."

He shook his head. "Not me. And your boy shouldn't be working. Too soon."

Smiling, Holly took the empty cup and refilled it. "Lin," she said softly, "it's been two weeks."

He sank deeper into the uncomfortable bed. Two weeks! He couldn't believe he had been here that long, but when he rubbed his hand across his cheek, the whiskers stabbed at him.

"You'd come to now and again," Holly said. "Talk . . . mostly out of your head. Do you remember any of that?"

He didn't remember a thing. Even the gun battle seemed murky.

"You told me about Ollie."

He closed his eyes, clenched his fists.

"I got him killed, Holly."

"Lin." She reached over and pressed her lips against his forehead. "Lin, Lin, Lin." Holly sighed. "You did what you thought was right, Lincoln Garrett. Maybe it was right. I don't hold it against you. I saw him, Lin, saw him when he came to the trading post during the blizzard, saw what he had become. Remember, I spent three years feeding Ben his breakfast, dinner, and supper with a spoon, changing his clothes, shaving him, trying to love the man I married when he didn't know who I was. Ben didn't get a chance to die with dignity. At least Ollie did." She brushed away a tear, then forced a smile. "Some traveler at the depot said they saw a write-up about him . . . and you and Randolph, too . . . in a Saint Louis newspaper." Her voice rose, sounding happy. "And there's been a moving picture man roaming Flagstaff, wants to make a flicker about this. I don't know, Lincoln Garrett, you might be a celebrity after all."

He didn't feel like one. He felt like a cad. Jingling spurs sounded down the hallway, and Ol' Corb filled the doorway.

"Howdy, ol' man." Ol' Corb sent a river of tobacco juice into the nearest spittoon.

"Corb." Just the sight of his old friend lifted his spirits, even more than seeing Holly had. "Guess I owe you my life, hauling me back here like you done."

"More'n your life, pard. Them European tourists was a-drinkin' some mighty fine Scotch whiskey, and I surely would have loved to have partook of that, 'stead of a-holdin' your hand on a holy terror of a ride back to Red Mount'n."

"Well, I'll buy you a round."

"Good thing. I'll be at Weatherford's place first thing in the morn. You can pick me up there on our way to the courthouse. We got to testify, let Sheriff Oldridge an' them others know what really happened. You feel up to it, Lin, or you want 'em to send over a court reporter and get your thoughts on the matter."

"I'll be there," he said.

He walked with a cane, ashamed that Holly had to guide him as he inched up the steps and into the Weatherford Hotel lobby. The cane had been a concession; Doc

Steinberg had argued for a wheelchair, but Garrett had said he'd kill himself before he'd be seen in public in one of those things.

Voices fell to hushed whispers, and men and women stared at him, respectfully, almost worshipfully. He shouldn't be here, should have asked for a stenographer to record his statement, but he couldn't stand being trapped inside the poor farm another minute.

One voice had not lowered, and, at a corner table, Ol' Corb slammed down a bottle after sweetening his coffee.

"I was just a-swappin' shots with that fiend," Corbett said, illustrating his story with his hands and arms as he held an imaginary rifle, working the lever, popping off rounds. "Marshal Garrett and Ollie Sinclair kept on a-walkin', ready to face them four vile men. That's the way it was done in the old days, boys. That's the way we showed them cowards from Winslow."

"Were you scared?" a teen-aged girl asked.

"No, ma'am. No time to be scared. I had to get them two men a-hidin' in the trees, and I did. Killed one with the last round from my Winchester. Tossed it to the ground. Watched the other snake in the grass a-hightailin' it for the horses, he was took so with fright. Then I run along to catch up with the marshal and our pard Ollie."

"But you were chasing Sinclair," a silver-haired merchant said. "I mean, he robbed the train."

"Sure. Ollie Sinclair done some vile things in his life, but he wasn't as low-down as them Winslow crooks. Criminy, they tried to shoot us all in the back. Ollie, he always faced a body when he went a-killin'. Good thing I caught up with them boys, too, my pards, because they was in a fix, sure enough. But I drawed my old Colt, and went a-blastin'. Dropped three desperadoes before the fourth one showed yeller and skedaddled. We lost ol' Ollie, but he died game. Died a hero."

"And you didn't get shot?" the girl inquired.

Smirking, Ol' Corb showed her his missing index finger. "Lady," he said, "they shot off my finger." He roared with laughter, and raked his fingers over the girl's hair. "I'm a-joshin' you, hon. You want to know how I lost this digit? From a-pointin' out all the sights there is to see in Northern Arizona. Shucks, I dug the Grand Cañon."

"What did you do with all that dirt?" Holly rang out.

Randolph Corbett winked. "Lady, have you ever heard of the San Francisco Peaks?"

After slurping down the rest of the coffee, he shot out of his chair. "If you-all will excuse me, I have to set the record straight for the court." He grabbed his hat, pulled it on tight, and walked to Garrett.

"You ready?" Ol' Corb asked.

Garrett nodded.

"Can you walk to the courthouse?"

"I'll make it," he insisted, although he wasn't sure.

"We'll drive," Holly said. "My truck's across the street."

They had driven from the poor farm, parking on Aspen Avenue near the hotel.

They moved outside toward Holly's International Harvester, and Ol' Corb fished a plug of tobacco from his trouser pocket, stepped off the boardwalk. He whirled around, straightening and turning, pressing his hand against the hood of a 1908 Oldsmobile. Garrett could only stare.

Ol' Corb's face had turned ashen.

"Something's wrong . . . ." He gasped for air, and dropped like a piece of timber.

"Randolph!" Holly screamed.

★ ★ ★ ★ ★

The entire town of Flagstaff, Arizona must have turned out for Randolph Corbett's funeral. Even the governor came up from Phoenix to pay his respects. Daric Mossman led a riderless horse behind the handsome hearse down Leroux Street, and women, children, and even some adult men sobbed at the passing of the hero of the last great gunfight in Arizona history.

Garrett didn't cry. He just rode along in the back of a black jerky, numb, wondering if it would ever sink in. In a couple of weeks, he had watched his two best friends die. When they reached the cemetery, Holly and Daric Mossman helped him down, guided him underneath the canopy erected by the funeral parlor and to a front-row seat beside Doc Steinberg, who scooted over on the pew to make room for Holly and her son, too.

"I killed Corb, too," he told Holly.

Holly gripped his hand. "Nonsense."

"Killed him," Garrett mumbled as a band struck up "Nearer My God to Thee". "Sure as I had put a bullet in his brain."

"Lin." Holly turned his face toward hers, and leaned forward. "Randolph's heart burst. That's all. It was fast, and he went without pain, and I'm telling you, this is how he wanted it."

He tried to shake his head, but Holly held him firmly, put pressure underneath his chin, and lifted his head. His eyes found hers, and locked.

"He was dying, Lin, the same as Ollie. He told me that months ago, long before you rode back into our lives. That's why they sent him to the poor farm. And that's why he rode out with you. You let him live again, Lin." He released her hold. "Look at this! Look at all these people.

216

God in heaven above, Lin, they'll be talking about this funeral, about Randolph Sebastian Corbett for the next fifty years. You *know* that's what Randolph wanted. You know he's looking down at this, chewing tobacco and telling lies, eyes bright, just beaming."

The eulogies began, first from Sheriff Curt Oldridge, then others. Even Percival Lowell was there, coming out of his mansion on Mars Hill, although he offered no remembrance. The manager of the Aztec Cattle Company did, as did Doc Steinberg. The governor spoke for ten minutes, pretty good seeing how he had never even met Corbett, and Mayor Fox read a telegram from Theodore Roosevelt.

When they had all left, Garrett walked to the grave. He knelt, fingering the fresh earth, feeling Holly standing behind him. Suddenly he found himself chuckling, shaking his head, cursing Randolph Sebastian Corbett for the scoundrel he was. In the front-page obituary, the Coconino *Sun* had printed an account of the shoot-out at the pueblo ruins south of Grand Cañon National Monument, an account virtually word-for-word the fanciful stretchers Ol' Corb had created at the Weatherford Hotel, poor farm, and David Tate's liquor store.

No headstone had been erected, but Fox and Oldridge vowed that Coconino County would spare no expense in dedicating an everlasting monument to a hero of law and order. Beside him rested Evan Paine, a simple wooden cross with only his name, nothing mentioning that he had been a deputy sheriff killed in the line of duty, and the year 1913. Far in the back, Garrett spotted a towering marble monument, beaten by the rain and snow. He knew that grave too well. Senator Owen Dunlap. 1821–1887.

The smile vanished.

"Where's Ollie?" Garrett asked.

"I'll take you," Holly said.

Wind swept down off Red Mountain, bringing with it the promise of spring. Garrett rubbed his shoulder, and opened the gate about fifty yards behind Holly's home.

He saw Ben Mossman's headstone, nothing fancy, just his name and dates of birth and death, and then a larger marker behind it.

Penelope Lois Mossman Carter
Our Beloved Daughter
Born February 20, 1883
Called Away May 3, 1906

Penny wasn't there. Garrett knew that. She and her husband were buried up somewhere in Pittsburgh, but it seemed right that she would have a marker here. And it felt right when he saw Ollie's simple cross next to Penny's tombstone.

Ollie Sinclair
A Good Hand With A Rope

No year of birth or death, and Garrett grinned at the epitaph. Good hand with a rope. How true, especially when throwing a wide loop over another man's steer.

The gate closed behind him, and he knew Holly had joined him. Shoving his hands in his pockets, he walked around Ben Mossman's grave and stood in front of the final resting place for Ollie Sinclair. Garrett closed his eyes, and remembered.

Chapter Twenty-Four

Arizona Territory
February 1883

Jed Dunlap was belligerent and drunk.

That's not why Garrett clubbed him with the barrel of his .44 in front of the Babbitt Brothers store, though.

The senator's son fell against the sandstone wall and slid onto the boardwalk, the blocks bruising and bloodying Dunlap's head more than Garrett's Colt had. Instead of slipping into unconsciousness, Dunlap jerked up, rubbing the back of his head and leveling a malevolent glare.

"You had no right to buffalo me, Garrett," he snapped. "My pa will have your badge, you son-of- . . . ."

Still holding the Colt, Garrett spun the revolver, thumbed back the hammer, and aimed at Dunlap's face. "Finish that statement, Jed, and you'll never finish another."

Dunlap paled.

If he pulled the trigger, Senator Owen Dunlap would wind up hanging Garrett. By jacks, he had probably already lost his job as town marshal by trying to crack the reprobate's skull. Garrett felt the stares, from John Weatherford, lumber magnate E. E. Ayer, and George Babbitt, pillars of Flagstaff, knew they stood behind him, literally if not figu-

ratively, waiting nervously, wondering if they would witness a murder.

"You talk too much." Garrett slipped down the hammer and shoved the Colt into his holster. "Come on. You're under arrest."

"For what?" Dunlap screamed.

"Drunk and disorderly. Carrying a side arm across the deadline. Expectorating on the streets. And being a jackass."

He grabbed Dunlap's coat, yanked him to his feet, shoved him against the red wall, then grabbed Dunlap's Bowie knife and .31 Manhattan, and pitched them into the mud.

"Hold those for Jed or his pappy, George," Garrett told Babbitt. "Let's go."

Just a matter of time before it all boiled over, Garrett thought.

Before Holly Grant had accepted Lieutenant Ben Mossman's proposal, she had filed on a quarter section near Red Mountain. Senator Owen Dunlap had taken exception, wanting that patch of piñon and water for his ranching ventures, but Holly had held firm. Now she was married, building a home at Red Mountain while waiting for her husband to retire from the Army to go into the horse-raising business. Hadn't been much of an engagement. By the time Garrett had heard the news, by the time he had sobered up after killing the Yavapai Kid, Holly Grant had become Holly Mossman.

A few months after the wedding, word came that Holly was with child, which certainly raised eyebrows. Garrett could tolerate the Presbyterian and Catholic blue bloods gossiping about it all, but he wouldn't stand to hear such slander out of Jed Dunlap's mouth. Dunlap had said something to E. E. Ayer in front of the Babbitts' store, a comment Garrett had overheard, detonating his wrath.

He sat in the office, staring across the room at the slowly sobering senator's son, cleaning his revolver while a visiting Ollie Sinclair rattled off nonsense about the price of beef and the ongoing drought.

"Ollie." Garrett lowered the Colt and cleaning rod. "If you toss a loop over anyone's beef . . . ."

"Calm down, old man. I ain't started a fight in town in three months, ain't cheated at cards, have behaved myself better than your mother, God rest her soul. I'm just sharin' what I learned from the ranchers and cowhands you're supposed to be protectin'."

Actually Garrett wondered why Sinclair really kept hanging around Flagstaff. Holly was out of his reach, although Sinclair rode up to Red Mountain every now and then to help her and her Mexican laborers, which also gave the sanctimonious ladies fodder to discuss over quilting bees and tea.

The front door slammed open, and Ol' Corb raced inside, almost knocking over a spittoon, and muttering something no one could understand. He tried to catch his breath, tried to calm down.

"Close that door, Corb!" Sinclair shouted. "It must be ten below out there!"

After pushing the door shut, Ol' Corb shook his head, and got his breathing in check. "It's Holly," he said.

Garrett had almost smiled, but hearing her name, he shot out of his chair, leaned forward, pressed his hands on the desk, steeling himself for bad news. Sinclair had pushed back his chair and sat there, coiled like a rattler ready to strike.

"She had her baby!"

Unsteadily Garrett sank into his seat while Sinclair leaped forward and cut loose with a war yell, pumping his fist with hat in his hand.

"Three months early," Ol' Corb reported. "Fermín Rojo's mama was there, and Fermín tol' me the news over at Pratt's just a couple of minutes ago. His mama was the midwife, you know, and he had been up there a-buildin' some corrals and barn."

I don't need the history lesson, Garrett thought, *just tell me how she is!* Yet he couldn't speak.

"Sent a rider down to Fort Verde to let Ben Mossman know. Baby's blue as blue can be, but Fermín says his mama says the baby will live, and his mama knows. I think she ain't just a midwife, but also a *bruja.*"

All through Corbett's report, Sinclair had whooped and hollered, making it difficult to hear, and now he slammed on his hat, threw on his coat, and bolted outside, letting in a blast of chilling wind.

The frigid air felt good. Garrett took a deep breath, slowly exhaled, picked up the Colt and cleaning rod again. Ol' Corb just stood there a moment, struck dumb, before slowly closing the door Ollie Sinclair had left open.

"Mighty peculiar," Ol' Corb said. "Didn't even wait to hear if it was a boy or a girl." Hearing the rattling from the cell, Corbett stared intently, straightening upon recognition of the prisoner.

"What's he a-doin' here?"

"Sleeping off a headache," Garrett said. "Well, what was it? Boy or girl?"

"Girl," Ol' Corb announced.

From the cell, Jed Dunlap sniggered. "Wonder who the kid will look like," he said.

Later, when he had time to think about it, after he had calmed down, he understood that had the revolver been loaded, he would have murdered Jed Dunlap that night. Garrett sprang out of his chair, toppling it over, and made a beeline for Dunlap's cell, gripping the Colt, intent on smashing his prisoner's head.

The office door opened one more time, and a cold, piercing voice stopped him. Jed Dunlap's eyes widened in horror. He wasn't so much afraid of Lin Garrett, not understanding how close he was to death, but of his father.

Slowly Garrett turned around as the door closed and Senator Owen Dunlap stepped closer.

"You plan on beating up my boy some more, Garrett?" the old man asked.

Garrett looked at his right hand, the knuckles whitening as he clenched the .44. He pitched the weapon onto his desk. Ol' Corb stood in silence, uncertain, his mouth working a quid of tobacco.

"You'll release him," the senator said.

"Can't." Garrett stood firm. "Bail has to be set. That'll be some time in the morning."

"Let him out."

When Garrett didn't move, the senator stepped closer. "Let him out, or it shall be you in that cell tomorrow morning."

Finally realizing the futility of it all, Garrett motioned for Corbett to unlock the cell door, and he moved back to his desk, righted his chair, and sat down heavily.

As soon as Corbett pulled open the iron door, the younger Dunlap sprinted toward his father, shooting out bold statements and accusations that the senator silenced with a backhand. Jed Dunlap lay flat on his back, his lips trickling blood.

"You idiot," father told son. "Drunk. Disorderly. Carrying a revolver in New Town. I have enough problems, boy. I should let you rot."

"But Pa . . . ."

With an oath, the senator turned his back on his son, and walked outside without another word. Garrett stared at the revolver, calm now, suddenly feeling sorry for Jed Dunlap, glad he hadn't killed the poor kid. He didn't hate Jed so much, knowing that the boy just wanted his father's approval, love, support, things he would never get. Certainly Garrett despised the senator, flaunting his power, not by demanding Jed's release, but whipping the boy like that in front of Garrett and Ol' Corb.

Neither of the lawmen looked up until Jed had pulled himself to his feet and walked into the night.

A week passed, and he still had his job. The senator had shown his power, Garrett reckoned, or maybe he was too busy trying to find a way to get that land by Red Mountain. Garrett had forgotten all about Jed Dunlap until a buckboard from the A-1 Company, a cattle operation north of town, pulled up in front of his office. The stoved-up cowboy driving the wagon looked uncomfortable.

Garrett spotted the tarp in the back, saw the scuffed black boots, and leaped into the back, pulled down the canvas.

The driver spoke. "Found him near Red Mountain."

He covered Jed Dunlap's face.

"A bit south of that lady's claim," the driver added.

"See anything else?" Garrett asked after stepping onto the street. He looked around, pleased the streets were quiet this morning.

The cowhand swallowed. "I'm hoping you'll leave me

out of this, long as you can."

"You can give me your statement at the undertaker's," Garrett said. "Quicker we get off the street, the better."

"I don't want the senator thinking I had anything to do with this," the cowhand said.

"He won't," Garrett said. *I know who did it.*

From the look on the cowboy's face, the old-timer did, too. Fact was, Garrett would learn, he had witnessed the shooting, saw Ollie Sinclair shoot Jed Dunlap dead. Saw him empty his revolver into the man's body after his first shot had dropped him. Jed Dunlap never made a move for his own weapon. Murder. Plain and simple.

Over Ol' Corb's objections, Garrett left his partner with the horses and walked into the house at Red Mountain, still unfinished but suitable enough for mother and child. He swept off his hat, nodded at Fermín Rojo's mother and an army of other women, attendants, and two water-drinking laborers who didn't look happy to see Lin Garrett here. Briefly they blocked his path.

"Let him in!" a tired voice called out from the bedroom, and the Mexicans parted. Garrett walked through them, moving closer to Holly Mossman as she sat in her bed, holding a precious little thing wrapped in blankets. She pulled down the covers as Garrett neared her, revealing a tiny face, red, wrinkled, not the blue Ol' Corb had described.

"Want to hold her?" Holly asked.

Garrett almost jumped back. "No . . . ma'am."

She brought the baby closer to her breast. "I never knew I could love anything so much in my life," she said, and Garrett felt out of place, wanted to be anywhere but here. Holly didn't seem to notice what she had just said. She was a mother now. It hadn't really sunk in until now.

"I'm looking for Ollie," he said stiffly.

Holly's head shook lightly. "Is he rustling cattle again, Lincoln Garrett?"

"No," he said after a moment, deciding not to give her the particulars. "He been around?"

"Yesterday." Her eyes clouded. "Everyone's been here, Lin. Ollie. Some officers and wives from Fort Verde. Everyone but you and Randolph."

"Corb's outside," he said. "I . . . been meaning to." He fought the urge to leave. "Has Jed Dunlap been here?"

Holly didn't answer. Maybe she didn't have to. The baby started wailing, and she mentioned something about needing to nurse. Garrett spun, bolted back through the midwives and laborers, made it outside, and took the reins to his horse.

"We didn't need to stop here," Ol' Corb told him. "You knew that. You just give Ollie more time to reach the border."

He kicked the zebra dun into a lope.

Maybe intruding on Holly had not been necessary. On the other hand . . . .

Garrett and Ol' Corb drove north at a hard pace, toward Lee's Ferry, knowing Ollie Sinclair would be riding that way. Garrett couldn't tell anything from the baby girl's face, just that it had pure blue eyes, a bunch of hair, and one healthy set of lungs. Didn't look like anyone, really, but it wasn't some tiny infant born three months early. He knew better than believe that.

For the rest of the trail, they rode with little conversation, rare indeed for Randolph Corbett, running cold camps and riding well before dawn till well after dusk.

The country chilled him, the vermilion cañon walls, the roar of the rapids, the clear sky that went on forever. Garrett felt so empty, so lost, until he spotted a man carrying a saddle along the road that led to the Mormon ferryman's fortress. He recognized the gait before he noticed the color of the man's hair, and touched his spurs against the dun and bolted ahead, screaming Ollie Sinclair's name.

He never saw Sinclair's horse, hadn't realized the mount had played out on Ollie until he saw his old friend afoot. By all rights, with at least a day's head start, Ollie Sinclair should have made it across the Colorado into Utah. Would have, but his horse had gone lame, forcing him to walk the last fifteen miles.

Sinclair had spun, dropping the saddle, drawing his revolver. The big man had managed to fire off a round, too, but it went wild—Garrett wondered if Ollie had even tried hitting him—as Garrett leaped from the saddle, crashing into the big, red-headed murderer. For a moment, Garrett thought he might just run over the old fool, but, no, he didn't want his horse to kill Ollie Sinclair. He wanted to do it himself.

And he would have.

The wind knocked out of him, too exhausted from the arduous walk, Sinclair could offer little resistance. The only thing that could stop Garrett would be the army of Mormons running out of the house and from the ferry, Ollie Sinclair's kinfolk. They could have killed him, but they didn't.

Ol' Corb stopped them with a couple rounds from his Winchester, kicking up puffs of red dust at their feet. A second later, Corbett had leaped off his horse, jerked Garrett off Sinclair.

"You'll kill him!" Ol' Corb roared.

Garrett heard him, yet didn't. "That's my intention," he shot back, and sprang to his feet. Too late he saw Corbett swing the rifle like a club, and down Garrett went into a cold, black void.

He woke at dusk, along a bend in the Colorado a few hundred yards from Lee's Ferry. Ol' Corb stood guard with his rifle, Sinclair sat at the small campfire, sipping water from a canteen. Garrett rose, gingerly testing the knot on his forehead, and shot a menacing glare Corbett's way.

"I had to do it, Lin." But it was Sinclair who spoke.

Garrett looked across the flickering flames.

"Jed Dunlap was gonna blackmail her, Lin. He . . . ."

"I don't want to hear it, Ollie." His head throbbed. He looked at Ol' Corb again, then swore.

"If you bring me in," Sinclair said, "Lin, it'll . . . ."

"Get out," Garrett barked. "Go to your friends, get across that ferry, go on to Utah." Sinclair didn't give Garrett time to change his mind. He corked the canteen and bolted to his feet, gave Ol' Corb a nod, and headed toward the crossing.

"But if you come back to Arizona, Ollie," Garrett called after him, "*I'll* kill you!"

Chapter Twenty-Five

"Did Ben know?" Garrett asked, turning away from Sinclair's headstone to look at Holly.

"He never said anything." Her eyes never faltered. "He never asked. I never volunteered. He was Penny's father."

The wind picked up.

"I made a mistake," Holly confessed. "I was trying to make a living, trying to realize my dream, Ben was off at San Carlos, helping put things together after the Cibecue outbreak, and Ollie came courting, loaded with charm. We weren't married, Ben and I, not even engaged. You know that. But . . . I was weak, lonely. Whatever, it happened."

He turned away, jealous more than angry, all those years of emotions bottled up inside him. Holly moved beside him, reached over to take his hand in both of hers.

"Ollie should have married you," he said, more of a mumble than anything else. "If he had been decent . . . after . . . ." He couldn't bring himself to say more. He felt Holly squeeze his hand.

"He asked, Lin," she said. "Asked often, even before . . . . And he begged, got down on his knees and begged me to marry him when I told him I was pregnant. I turned him down."

Garrett stared at her quizzically, trying to find a question.

"Ollie never could have been a good father, Lin," Holly said. "You know that better than anyone, or a good husband, not the kind I wanted. I thought about going it alone, but when Ben proposed . . . ." She shrugged.

For the longest while, he remained silent, waiting for Holly to release his hand, but she never did.

"You never asked me, Lin."

With a curt nod, he looked up, staring off at Red Mountain. "I . . . ." His stomach ached, and he felt a strange numbness, felt something like tears welling in his eyes. "I never . . . I couldn't have been a good father or husband, either," he finally said, and, with his left hand, pointed at Ben Mossman's grave. "You made the right choice."

"I know," she said. "Come inside."

Still holding his hand, although in only one of hers now, their fingers interlocked, Holly led him inside, guiding him to the table where he sat while she filled two cups with coffee.

He could picture everything so clearly—Ollie bouncing Penny on his knee after he had captured him in 1887 at Lee's Ferry, remembered the way Ollie's eyes had shone so brightly. Ollie hadn't given up so easily because of his friendship with Lin Garrett, had not really come back to Arizona bound to right a wrong because of newspaper stories. No, Ollie Sinclair merely wanted to see his daughter. That's also why he robbed the Grand Cañon Railway after his release from prison. It gave him an excuse to see Penny's grave—after all, he had been in prison when she had died—even if it was just a piece of marble over empty earth, even if Penny was buried back East.

Garrett had hated Ollie Sinclair for coming back. He remembered berating Sinclair for showing his face in Arizona, fearing his return would fuel more gossip and speculation.

Maybe someone would figure out what really happened, why Ollie Sinclair had really shot Jed Dunlap.

Dunlap had known, or had made a good guess. Looking to get in his father's good graces, he had blackmailed Holly, telling her to sell her homestead to his father or he'd let everyone, including Ben Mossman, know that Ollie Sinclair was the girl's daddy, that Holly Grant Mossman was nothing but a strumpet.

Sinclair had tracked Dunlap down and killed him, a shooting witnessed by a cowhand riding for the A-1. Ollie Sinclair became a wanted man, the scourge of Arizona, leader of the vicious Sinclair gang, another Mormon butcher. The senator had hired professionals to track down Sinclair, but they had failed, and, finally, the senator had died himself a few years after burying his only son underneath the San Francisco Peaks. Meanwhile, Ollie Sinclair kept out of Arizona until 1887, waiting until Owen Dunlap had died, thinking things might be safer then. Of course, Ollie Sinclair couldn't do anything quietly. Instead of sneaking across the border, he had to rob the Atchison, Topeka & Santa Fe at Williams, had to make things difficult, had to blame the world one more time for all of his woes.

Had to put Holly Mossman on the spot.

After Garrett brought Sinclair back from Lee's Ferry to stand trial, Holly had lied. Some might say she lied to protect her reputation, but Garrett knew better. Her perjury kept Ollie Sinclair off the gallows.

She told the county solicitor that Jed Dunlap had tried to rape her, and that was why Ollie Sinclair killed him. The prosecutor didn't want anything like that to come out in a trial, if only to protect the late Senator Owen Dunlap's good name. Thus, Ollie Sinclair went to prison and, even-

231

tually, Lin Garrett rode away. Memories faded. Then Ollie came back, to die.

"What are your plans?" Holly asked.

He shrugged.

"I want you to stay with me."

He spilled the coffee, looked up suddenly, eyes narrowing. Realizing that she was serious, he sank down into his chair. "I won't be a burden," he said, and, when he looked at her again, he told her. "Doctors say I have uremic poisoning. I don't know how long . . . ."

Her worn fingers pressed against his lips.

"You're staying with me. And you've always been a burden, Lin. I want Benji and Daric to get to know you. I want to get to know you . . . again."

"No," he said through her fingers, which slipped away.

Her face turned hard. "You don't have much of a say in the matter, Lincoln Garrett. You can't ride away. You're facing indictment."

"If you mean that shooting scrape . . . ."

"That's not what I mean. You and Randolph stole . . . *stole!* . . . two horses, property of the county. This may be a new century, sir, but we still treat horse thieves seriously. You're staying." She must have seen he wasn't about to concede anything, so she softened her stance, the way only she could, gave him that young Holly Grant smile, and pleaded with him. "At least for tonight. No promises. We'll see what tomorrow brings."

His head bobbed only slightly, but Holly took that for a yes, which is probably what he had meant, and they sipped their coffee in silence, enjoying the gloaming, the silence, and their company.

After a quiet supper with Holly and Benji, he sat in the

spare bedroom, getting ready for bed. His back didn't hurt so much now, although he felt strange. *No promises*, Holly had told him. *We'll see what tomorrow brings.* For a seventy-year-old dying man, wasn't that the truth!

A light rapping sounded, and hinges squeaked as the door cracked open, revealing the wide eyes of Benji Carter, standing there in his nightshirt.

" 'Evening," Garrett said, pulling off his boots.

The boy took that as an invitation to come inside, and Garrett let him, looking behind him, waiting for Holly to emerge, but she didn't. Benji stopped by the wash basin.

Garrett started to tell the boy to come closer, that he wouldn't bite, but jerked off his socks instead. He suddenly felt uncomfortable.

"I was wondering . . . ," Benji began.

"Yeah," Garrett said after the boy stalled.

"Grandma says maybe you could tell me a story . . . about the olden times."

"Never was much good at stories." He found Holly then, standing in the doorway, waiting.

"Could you tell me about the gunfight? You know, the one where . . . ."

He shook his head. "That wasn't the olden times," Garrett explained. "Happened only a couple weeks back."

"Well . . . Grandma says you are a hero."

I don't feel like one, he thought, but pulled back the covers silently.

He peeled off his shirt and trousers, not caring that Holly watched, and slipped underneath the linens, not speaking. For a few seconds, Benji stared, then, head down, turned away.

Garrett cleared his throat. "Boy . . . uh . . . Benji."

The kid looked over his shoulder, uncertain.

Motioning to the chair by his bed, Garrett sat up, readjusting the pillows. The boy raced forward, eager, ready to hear about the olden times.

Now what? Garrett refused to look at Holly for help. He had no stories stored away, nothing interesting, at least, not to him. Ollie Sinclair and Ol' Corb, they were the ones full of stretchers. He ran his tongue over his teeth, finally shook his head. A frown formed on the boy's face.

Silence.

And then, Lin Garrett remembered, even grinned, if only slightly.

"Yeah, I got a story, and it's the bona-fide truth. This is about two of the bravest men I ever knew." He liked the way the words had formed. "Two men to ride the river with. That's a saying we had in the olden times. Lot of lies have been spread about this, but what I'm telling you is gospel. I want you to remember that." The boy agreed solemnly. "This is about Ollie Sinclair and Randolph Corbett . . . Ol' Corb, we called him . . . and this is how they, not me, stared down a desperado named Jude Kincaid at Cañon Diablo back in Eighteen and Eighty-One . . . ."

Once she closed the door, Holly Mossman leaned against it, flattening her hands on the wood, trying to stop the tears, but they came anyway. She listened, smiled, prayed, listened again to Lin Garrett. It was a strong voice, and it gave her strength.

Acknowledgements

Many thanks to the following Arizonans for their generous help in researching this novel: the staff of the Coconino County Public Library in Flagstaff; Mike Finney, AZ Communications Group; Joseph M. Meehan, Arizona Historical Society; Jeff Slade, Detours of Arizona; and Khamsone Sirimanivong, Flagstaff Convention and Visitors Bureau.

About the Author

Johnny D. Boggs has worked cattle, shot rapids in a canoe, hiked across mountains and deserts, traipsed around ghost towns, and spent hours poring over microfilm in library archives—all in the name of finding a good story. He's also one of the few Western writers to have won both the Spur Award from Western Writers of America (for his short story, "A Piano at Dead Man's Crossing", in 2002) and the Western Heritage Wrangler Award from the National Cowboy and Western Heritage Museum (for his novel, *Spark on the Prairie: The Trial of the Kiowa Chiefs*, in 2004). Another novel, *Ten and Me*, was a Spur finalist in 2000. A native of South Carolina, Boggs spent almost fifteen years in Texas as a journalist at the *Dallas Times Herald* and *Fort Worth Star-Telegram* before moving to New Mexico in 1998 to concentrate full time on his novels. Author of twenty-seven published short stories, he has also written for more than fifty newspapers and magazines, and is a frequent contributor to *Boys' Life*, *New Mexico Magazine*, *Persimmon Hill*, and *True West*. His Western novels cover a wide range. *The Lonesome Chisholm Trail* (Five Star Westerns, 2000) is an authentic cattle-drive story, while *Lonely Trumpet* (Five Star Westerns, 2002) is an historical novel about the first black graduate of West Point. *The Despoilers* (Five Star Westerns, 2002) and *Ghost Legion* (Five Star Westerns,

2005) are set in the Carolina backcountry during the Revolutionary War. *The Big Fifty* (Five Star Westerns, 2003) chronicles the slaughter of buffalo on the southern plains in the 1870s, while *East of the Border* (Five Star Westerns, 2004) is a comedy about the theatrical offerings of Buffalo Bill Cody, Wild Bill Hickok, and Texas Jack Omohundro, and *Camp Ford* (Five Star Westerns, 2005) tells about a Civil War baseball game between Union prisoners of war and Confederate guards. "Boggs's narrative voice captures the old-fashioned style of the past," *Publishers Weekly* said, and *Booklist* called him "among the best Western writers at work today." Boggs lives with his wife Lisa and son Jack in Santa Fe. His website is www.johnnydboggs.com. His next Five Star Western will be *The Hart Brand*.